Simon

SORT OF

Says

Simon SORT OF Says

ERIN BOW

Disney • HYPERION

LOS ANGELES   NEW YORK

Copyright © 2023 by Erin Bow

All rights reserved. Published by Disney • Hyperion, an imprint of Buena Vista Books, Inc. No part of this book may be reproduced or transmitted in any form or by any means, electronic or mechanical, including photocopying, recording, or by any information storage and retrieval system, without written permission from the publisher. For information address Disney • Hyperion, 77 West 66th Street, New York, New York 10023.

The author is supplying the websites at the end of this book for your informational purposes. These organizations are not affiliated with the publisher or its parent or affiliated companies and they make no representations concerning the information provided.

First Edition, January 2023
10 9 8 7 6 5 4 3 2 1
FAC-004510-22322
Printed in the United States of America

This book is set in Sabon LT Pro/Linotype
Designed by Phil Buchanan

Canada Council Conseil des arts
for the Arts du Canada

ONTARIO ARTS COUNCIL
CONSEIL DES ARTS DE L'ONTARIO
an Ontario government agency
un organisme du gouvernement de l'Ontario

The author acknowledges the support of the
Canada Council for the Arts and the Ontario Arts Council.

Library of Congress Cataloging-in-Publication Data
Names: Bow, Erin, author.
Title: Simon sort of says / by Erin Bow.
Description: First edition. • Los Angeles ; New York : Disney Hyperion, 2023. • Audience: Ages 8–12. • Audience: Grades 4–6. • Summary: Two years after a tragedy saddles him with viral fame, twelve-year-old Simon O'Keeffe and his family move to Grin And Bear It, Nebraska, where the internet and cell phones are banned so astrophysicists can scan the sky for signs of alien life, and where, with the help of two new friends, a puppy, and a giant radio telescope, Simon plans to restart the narrative of his life.
Identifiers: LCCN 2022012737 • ISBN 9781368082853 (hardcover) • ISBN 9781368089999 (ebook)
Subjects: CYAC: Psychic trauma—Fiction. • School shootings—Fiction. • Interstellar communication—Fiction. • LCGFT: Novels.
Classification: LCC PZ7.B67167 Si 2023 • DDC [Fic]—dc23
LC record available at https://lccn.loc.gov/2022012737

Reinforced binding
Visit www.DisneyBooks.com

for survivors

CONTENT NOTICE
Though this book does not depict violence, it
deals with the aftermath of violence, including
post-traumatic stress disorder. Resources for
anyone seeking mental health help can be
found at the end of this book.

one

in which we are driven out of Omaha by alpacas

People are always asking why my family came to the National Quiet Zone.

Like we need a reason. I mean, who wouldn't want to live in a place with no internet and no cell phones and no TV and no radio? Who wouldn't want to live surrounded by emu farms in a town that's half astrophysicists and half people who are afraid of their microwaves? I mean, isn't that the American Dream?

Hint: no.

Obviously, there's a story. So when people ask, I tell them we left Omaha because we were driven out by alpacas.

Back in Omaha, my dad, who's a Catholic deacon, was the liturgical director at one of the big churches in the suburbs. That means he planned the Masses and things—like a wedding planner, but for Jesus. One of the highlights of his year was the Feast of Saint Francis, where they bless the animals.

1

The animal blessing can be a little tricky, even when it's just cats and dogs plus the handful of four-year-olds who bring gerbils in cages and goldfish in bowls. People aren't always super smart about it. They don't think, "You know, there are going to be dogs so maybe Mr. Tuna should stay in his kitty carrier for the *hour-long* Mass." Usually at least one cat climbs on at least one head.

But the year we had to leave, my dad forgot to make a list of pets you can bring and—this is the important part—pets you *cannot* bring. So in addition to the cats and dogs, there was a potbellied pig, two alpacas, a giant tortoise, and a great horned owl named Sandy.

St. Francis could talk to wolves, but Father Kirk was not so blessed. Three years ago a freaked-out tomcat named Pinky got spooked by the bulldog in line behind him. He leaped from his owner's arms and took refuge under Father Kirk's vestments. Pinky clawed his way up Father Kirk's leg and—well, let's just say it's a good thing Father Kirk had already taken that vow of celibacy.

The Pinky incident marked a real turning point in the relationship between Father Kirk and my dad, who likes to embrace what he calls "a little holy chaos" when he plans church stuff. St. Francis would probably approve, but Father Kirk did not.

And, last year. The alpacas. The ones my dad forgot to ban.

There were two of them, and they were being led up the aisle for a blessing when one of them blinked its cartoon

2

eyelashes and stopped so abruptly that the tortoise, being pulled up the aisle behind them, slid off the back of its dolly and started to make a slow break for freedom.

The frozen alpaca stood looking at the altar, and some kind of ancestral memory kicked in about Things That Used to Happen on Altars. It stood there blinking its big Bambi eyes, looking cute and seeing blood and knives.

And then it made this noise.

The noise started low, like someone had sat on a whoopee cushion, but as her owner tugged on her halter, the alpaca, whose name was Beth, got louder. She unhinged her jaw and made a noise like a bagpipe gargling. Then the other alpaca started in, and it sounded like angry Scots with chest colds were coming to kill us all.

The acoustics were very good in our old church. Sometimes musical ensembles would come and record albums there. So the noise carried as the alpacas debuted their duet for panicky death visions. The dogs started howling, and the cats started making that noise like opera singers who've been kicked in the privates, and Sandy the Great Horned Owl tore away from his owner's glove, circled among the pillars for a long moment, then swooped down to eat Mr. Tuna.

Father Kirk came dashing down the aisle to help, and the alpaca spit all over his vestments. Sandy the Great Horned Owl landed on the altar with Mr. Tuna's body in tow.

The media was there.

My father got fired.

There aren't many jobs out there for liturgical directors—there wasn't another one in all of Omaha—but my mother is an undertaker, and undertakers can work anywhere. And that's why we came here.

Anyway, that's what I tell people.

a note about Grin And Bear It

So, we packed up our stuff and moved to a little town called—I swear this is true—Grin And Bear It, Nebraska.

Grin And Bear It is a one-stoplight kind of town—the kind of town where the funeral home is called "Slaughter and Sons" and has been for so long that no one thinks it's weird. The kind of town where people give directions with the words "up" or "down" or "over," and tell you that if you get to the river you've gone too far. The kind of town where the hardware store is also the drugstore, which also sells various kinds of feeds and animal supplies, so you have to be careful that you don't go in for cough syrup and come out with animal birthing lubricant. It is home to the Grin And Bear It Fighting Badgers, and it is famous for three things.

First, that name. It's worse than Truth Or Consequences, New Mexico, or Come By Chance, Newfoundland, or even Intercourse, Pennsylvania. They call it GNB sometimes, but that doesn't help.

Second, it's got this cathedral-size church, way too big for a dinky little town. As far as I can make out, a hundred years ago a local priest thought he was going to get to be bishop but didn't, and somehow convinced people to build him this enormous church as a consolation prize. It's named for Saint Barbara, the patron saint of architects, explosives, and people in danger of a sudden death.

Third, and most important by a long shot, Grin And Bear It is surrounded by radio telescopes.

We first saw the telescopes from the air. The town council flew us out from Omaha because they were courting my parents pretty hard. Slaughter and Sons, the funeral home, had been without an operator for way too long, and they were so eager to recruit Mom she started to worry that there was going to be a sketchy backlog in the basement freezers.

But it turned out there wasn't, and we were interested, because the big church meant there was work for Dad, too. And of course I would have moved to Mars if it got me away from what had happened in Omaha.

When our tiny plane landed, for a second I thought we had. Moved to Mars, I mean.

Grin And Bear It is on the Dismal River, and on the edge of the Dismal River National Forest. The land's kind of rolling and has more trees than you might expect from western Nebraska, though fewer than you might expect from a—you know—national forest. They're scruffy and piney and dark.

It was winter when the town council flew us out. We landed around dawn, and there was mist coming up from the snow, and the pine trees on the hills looked black, and sticking up out of the mist and black rolling hills were these . . . things. Bone white, lighthouse-tall, roller-coaster-complicated skeleton ghosts in the fog. Radio telescopes. They listen to faint radio signals from space. If you agree to live in Grin And Bear It, or anywhere within a thirty-mile radius, (hint: there is nothing within a thirty-mile radius), you cannot let out any radio signals that might mess that up.

When I first heard about that, I thought that meant: no radio. And it does. But it also means no television, no cell phones, no microwave ovens, and no internet. When I heard *that*, I thought: *Perfect*.

two

in which my new seventh-grade class learns that a sackbut is a kind of trombone

The hardest thing about moving to Grin And Bear It, Nebraska, is not leaving Omaha, or giving up the internet, or even moving into a house that we frequently share with dead people. (Funeral homes in cities are businesses; funeral homes in small towns are actually *homes*.) The hardest thing about moving to Grin And Bear It, Nebraska, is starting a new school. In February. Ask anybody: That's the stuff of seventh-grade *nightmares*.

GNB is so small that it only has two schools: a grade school called Johnny Carson, and a combined junior high and high school called GNB Upper. GNB Upper buses in kids from miles around and it still only has a hundred-odd students.

I imagine every single one of those hundred-odd students is going to take a good look at me when I show up for school. A new kid in a place this small? It's like my dad says: There's no blending into an empty field.

(In addition to being a deacon, my dad likes to make up his own wise sayings. So that's Dad.)

At least I talked him out of walking me to school like a second grader. Even *without* Dad holding my hand, I have enough self-consciousness to fuel the robot uprising. When I leave our house I feel good about my shoes—red Chucks, good and scuffed, February-cold feet totally worth it—and okay about my Minecraft sweatshirt and my jeans. I'm even reasonably optimistic about my hair, which I managed to get to stick up only in the front. I don't like my stiff and clearly brand-new backpack, but I never got the old one back, so I power through that like a champ.

The school is down on the river, about a block away from Main. I scouted the route over the weekend and learned the best way to get there isn't down Main but down one of the side streets and up to the back of the school. The side streets in GNB are different from the ones in the suburbs where we lived in Omaha. There's something about the way the houses here spill onto the front lawns that makes me think no one in this town has ever locked a door in their life. In the distance, radio telescopes haunt the hills.

As I get close to school my heart starts to pound in my throat, but there is basically no way to get lost, and I arrive with plenty of time before the bell rings. It's weirdly warm considering it's February—the kind of day where in

Phoenix they might have on parkas with their shorts, but in Nebraska a few kids are wearing shorts with their parkas. Outside the school it's the usual scene: clumps of kids standing around on the sidewalk in the slush-soggy grass. Some guys are straddling bikes by the bike racks, stepping them back and forth like nervous horses. Some girls have spread their scarves on the concrete and are sitting on the steps that go from the staff parking lot down to the sports fields. They have their knees clamped tight and are blowing on their hands, but there's no way they're going inside.

Everybody—the bike boys, the clump kids, the stair girls—all of them turn and watch me go by. I stick my hands in my pockets like that's fine, heading past the bike racks and along the side of the school. I turn the corner and find the front door and another batch of kids who stare at me. I make it up the steps without tripping or dropping anything or falling prey to any of the other disaster scenarios my brain is working overtime on. (My brain, if you haven't got this yet, specializes in disaster scenarios.)

My dad was worried about me finding the office, but I manage somehow—maybe because it's right inside the door and labeled *office*. I meet the school secretary, fill out a bunch of forms, totally blank on my new address, fidget with a pen, get stared at like a zoo animal through the office's glass walls as the bell rings and the morning rush comes in, and eventually get introduced to the principal.

The principal's name is Ms. Snodgrass, and she looks like she's spent her whole life trying to overcome being called Ms. Snodgrass. Like, she's got a razor-sharp haircut and a fuchsia motorcycle-style jacket. On her face she has that look owls always have, like she's bored but barely suppressing suspicion and rage. She flips open my file.

There's not much in it. I was homeschooled all last year, and I asked my parents not to include the records from before that. At a glance I probably look like a homeschooler. But Ms. Snodgrass takes more than a glance, and the look she gives me makes me wonder if she's thinking: *Juvie?*

Or maybe she thinks all seventh graders are potential criminals.

"Simon O'Keeffe. Did you sign the good conduct pledge?"

"I think?" I signed, like, seven things.

She flips through the file until she finds the correct form. It's the goldenrod one. I have signed it. She squints one more time at my name, like she might recognize it, but—

"Well, Simon," she says. "Welcome to Grin And Bear It. We're glad to have you."

She smiles, owlishly. Like she would totally eat Mr. Tuna.

• • •

What with all the forms and stuff, homeroom is almost over before I get there. I sneak a peek through the chicken-wire glass rectangle in the door of room nine. Apparently, whatever teaching happens in homeroom is also over; from what I can see through the glass, people are just talking or last-minute-homeworking or doing their hair or whatever.

My fingers are cold and my heart is fast and I think

11

about waiting it out, but that wouldn't help; I'd just have to go to the next class. So I open the door.

It creaks. Of course it does. The whole thing is exactly like my brain thought it would be: Everybody falling silent, everybody staring. Even the teacher is staring. Going in is like stepping out onto a stage, I swear.

So I stay in the doorway. "Miss Rose?" Definitely gotta make sure it's the right class. No way am I going to do this twice.

The teacher, a young one with long hair and a long skirt, nods, stands up, and comes over to me. She half-smiles—she has a kind of Disney-Princess-sings-with-the-animals look—and takes the slip with my name and schedule on it out of my hand. She glances at it, then back up at me, her eyes going wide with a familiar expression. The "oh-poor-baby" expression. I hate that expression.

And, oh man, here it comes. Miss Rose reaches out and draws me into the room, wrapping an arm around my shoulders. It's sort of like a hug, except she's also making sure I'm in exactly the right place for the spotlight to hit me. The shoulder she's holding goes stiff.

"Everyone?" she says. "Everyone? If I could have your attention?"

I don't know why she even asks. New kid in class is a big deal anywhere, and in Grin And Bear It, it's like the circus has come to town. I stand like the acrobat on the high wire—drumroll and all—trying hard to smile and even harder to

12

make it look casual. The general reaction I am going for is: *Seems okay I guess,* or *Yeah, didn't really notice him,* or *Simon who?* I want absolutely nothing more than to be overlooked.

But that is so not going to happen. For one thing, Miss Rose isn't having it. "I would like you all to welcome, ummm, Simon O'Keeffe. Who is— His family just moved here from Omaha."

The room is swept by a kind of sigh: *Omaha, shining land of dreams and promises.* Yeah, right. I'm resisting the urge to run out of the room.

"Dude," says a boy with green hair in the front row. "Why'd you come *here?*"

"There was an . . . incident," says the teacher.

I interrupt her. "We were driven out by alpacas. It's kind of a long story."

A dozen hands shoot into the air and the green-haired boy says: "Tell it, man!"

"Simon," says Miss Rose, sounding like she's about to melt into a puddle of sympathy.

"Also," I say, before Miss Rose can launch into whatever she's going to tell them, "my mom bought Slaughter and Sons—the old funeral home? Which, seriously, is called that." My words are coming out like there's pressure behind them, and I can't seem to stop talking. "Plus, my dad wanted to leave the big city to concentrate on his art. He's a famous sackbut player."

Laughter—the kind that can only be called snickering.

13

A football-player-looking boy turns to the green-haired one and mouths *sack butt*?

"It's a kind of trombone," I say. My dad actually plays one. He's good—he's, like, the tenth-best sackbut virtuoso in the entire world. I think for him the hardest part of leaving Omaha was leaving his medieval-music ensemble.

"Sack butt!" says another boy. Yeah, I might be getting a new nickname.

"Do you live in the funeral home?" asks someone at the back.

A girl, breathless with delighted horror, says, "I dunno. A funeral home sounds so creepy."

"Would your mom rent it out for school dances and stuff?" asks another girl. She has a three-ring binder in front of her and a general air of "class president."

"Uh," I say. "I could ask."

"Sweet!" exclaims the green-haired boy.

Right then the bell rings.

The bell is loud—it's a real bell, being hit by a real hammer, sounding like a real emergency—and my body slams backward into the chalkboard, the eraser tray jamming into my hip. But none of the other kids notice. For them it's just the bell. The room fills up with a burst of voices—a cry of *sack butt*—and the zippers of backpacks and the squeaks of chair legs and the thump of feet.

In the receding tide, Miss Rose looks over my schedule while I rub the bang on my hip with the heel of my hand. "Math is two doors down," she says. "Room seven."

14

GNB Upper—*Go Badgers!*—has two periods before lunch and three after. That means I do the whole thing five more times. Miss Rose, homeroom and English, and Mr. Dwyer, the eight-fingered shop teacher, are the only people who make any fuss, thank you, *God*. (And thank you, Saint Barbara, who I invoke because I really do think I'm going to die all five times.) Miss Rose makes her sad eyes and lets me know that her door is always open if I want to talk. Mr. Dwyer hits me on the shoulder and says, "Glad to have you with us now, my son," and it could be he just does that to everyone. It's no reason to panic, brain.

And honestly nothing goes wrong. All the other teachers and all the kids just roll with things. The kid with the green hair is Kevin, and he's just one of those nice guys everyone likes. He's into Minecraft, as much as you can in a town with no internet. The big football-looking guy is Brett, and he spends a couple of days trying to make the nickname Sack Butt happen, but it requires too much backstory and it doesn't stick. The three-ring-binder girl is Joyce, and she is "on the leadership team." For my first few days it's a full-time job learning names and finding all the school's hidden corners and cubbies and telling the alpaca story a lot.

I answer questions about funeral homes.

I answer questions about Omaha.

I say the word "sackbut" until it loses all meaning.

I don't make any friends, really—maybe Kevin—but on the bright side I don't attract much attention. And there isn't any internet. No one looks me up.

15

three

in which I meet a girl (not in a kissing-book way)

By week two I have memorized the school layout. It's pretty simple: a T-shaped building with some portables for loud or flammable classes out back. There's a basement, with emergency signs that tell us to go that way in case of tornadoes, but the classrooms are all on one level, and they all have big windows. It's an okay place, even if the floor wax somehow smells like a popcorn topping.

I've even found a lunch spot that I like—one of the perks of leaving grade school is that you can pick your own spot to eat lunch. The one I've found is in the hallway at the end of one of the arms of the T, in front of the emergency exit. The music department stores some portable risers there, probably violating the fire code in like seven different ways. The risers are covered in grungy gray carpet, plus dried wads of gum that are the same color as the grungy gray carpet. You can hear the band practicing most days, and because the corner is by the home ec room you can always smell whatever the ninth graders burned that morning. All in all, it's not a popular lunch spot. But the end of the hall is out of the way, and the exit gives me an escape route, so it suits me just fine.

I'm halfway through my cheese-and-jam sandwich when a girl plops down cross-legged in front of me. I noticed her in homeroom this morning. Honestly, she was hard to miss: She has bright red hair, she's fat in a "yeah-what-about-it" kinda way, and she's wearing a purple hoodie that says *Truth AND Dare.*

The girl wasn't around last week, so when she walked into homeroom this morning I thought for a second she was another new kid and the pressure would be off me. But no one treated her like that, so I guess it was a vacation or a flu or something. I didn't see her in my other classes, but out of nowhere here she is. She has her hood up like she's on a secret agent mission. It's edged with tiny red and yellow pom-poms.

She puts her lunch box on the next riser up from mine and folds her hands in front of her. "What," she says—declaims, really, like she's on a stage and starting her big number—"is the most disgusting thing you know?"

"Hi?" I say.

"You're Simon, you're new," she says. "I'm Agate. I'll start. There are spider mites that are adapted to live only on human eyelashes. You have some on you right now."

"Uh-huh . . ."

"Ninety percent of household dust is made of human skin."

"I actually knew that one."

"Fine," she says. "You go."

"Most disgusting thing?"

"Yeah."

It's not that I don't know disgusting things. It's just that with one thing and another, it's hard to narrow it down. "Corpses fart," I say. "A lot, actually."

"Oh," she says, grinning. "That's a good one! We can be friends!" She flips down her hood—releasing a poof of frizzy carrot-orange hair—and leans forward like it's time for the next part of the test. "Are you good at science?"

"Yeah . . . ?"

"Math?"

"Uh, not really."

She squinches her face. She has a stub nose and a lot of dimples, which, unlike most dimples, seem to show up only when she looks skeptical. "I can do the math. Access to transportation?"

"I've got a bike?"

"That's what I mean. Obviously. Will your parents let you ride around after school?"

I take a bite of my sandwich because I have no idea what to say. My parents would probably be delighted if I asked to go riding around our new town after school. I mean, they'd sit at the kitchen table clutching each other's hands and holding their breath with suppressed panic until I got back, but they'd *say* they were delighted. "Yeah," I say. "They'd let me."

"Great," she says. "Do you want to help me fake a message from space aliens?"

"Uh . . ." I say, like a genius.

"It's Agate. Like the rock." Sure, because *her name* is the part that tripped me up. I'm running out of sandwich, but Agate doesn't seem to be running out of steam. "Agate Van der Zwaan. My dad's a long-haul trucker and my mom raises angora goats. I live on the farm and have a lot of unsupervised time."

"Aren't you going to eat?"

Agate shrugs and unsnaps the catches on her tin lunch box and starts laying out an assortment of little foods in cupcake papers: bright little tulips on the gray carpet. One's got pieces of cheese. One's got green grapes. One's got baby pretzels. One's a cupcake. "So," she says, starting in on the cupcake first. "Message from space aliens. What do you say?"

"I think I say: *Why?*"

She looks at me super seriously, her eyes wide and kind of sad, like she's explaining why you should get your pets spayed or neutered. "Because the scientists have been listening for ages and they haven't heard anything. I don't want them to give up hope."

"I mean—why *me?*"

It's a question I've asked myself a zillion times. I'm not expecting Agate to have an answer. But she does: She

19

answers like she's prepped for it, like she's reading her reasons off an index card, and pops a grape into her mouth for each bullet point. "You're new," she says. Grape. "You haven't picked a side yet." Grape. "And you can keep secrets."

I want to ask her how she knows I can keep secrets, but I'm afraid to. If you think about it, there's just no safe way to ask that question. I settle for: "Look, I'm trying to kind of . . . fly under the radar here."

"That's okay," says Agate, and for a second I think she's going to leave. But she says: "This doesn't have anything to do with radar." She pops her last grape and grins at me. And I was wrong. When she smiles, she has as many dimples as the moon.

a note about the sides

Agate is right: The town of Grin And Bear It can be divided into two sides.

There's Team Science: astrophysicists and other tech-types who work at the radio telescopes. And there's Team Farm: homesteaders and other socks-with-sandals types, drawn to the National Quiet Zone by low land prices and the promise of "a gentler, more organic pace of life," which is how the GNB real estate agent tried to sell us.

So, like, the town has two places to get coffee: the Rise and Shine diner, which serves drip coffee with your hash browns (Team Farm), and the Hello Hello, which serves cappuccinos with your halo halo (Team Science). It has two places to get dog food: the Healthy Barker Canine Kitchen (Team Science) and the feed store (Team Farm). It has two places to get breaking news: a local newspaper called the *Plain Talk*, which features cattle prices and Little League scores (Team Farm), and the News Agency, a tiny magazine and newspaper shop that carries things like the *Atlantic,* even though we are a looooong way from any ocean (Team Science).

I mean, there is some overlap. There are farmers who like an espresso and are willing to put up with the junior scientists huddled in the corner of the Hello Hello mainlining Filipino snack food and panicking about their funding applications. There are scientists who like farmers' market kinds of things and will venture into the Chèvre Shoppè or the Pick and Pack Produce Stand. And for sure the school's not divided into warring factions or anything. Schools aren't like that except in books, and it's not like the Team Science kids are building death rays while the Team Farm kids are flinging manure bombs.

Agate, for instance, lives on a farm but is definitely the seventh grader most likely to build a doomsday device. Kevin's mom is a radio astronomer, but Kevin's most notable obsession is with all things Cornhusker football. But still, sometimes the school seems like it speaks two languages: astrophysics and 4-H. Kids get sorted into Team Farm or Team Science the way they get sorted into boys and girls. Like—anyone can do anything, but that doesn't stop people from giving you whatever label they think you ought to have, whether you wanted it or not.

I'm not sure where that leaves me. I'm the funeral director's kid. I'm new in town. I don't know if I should pick a side, or if I'm going to get assigned a side, or what. On the plus side, having a team makes you less of a target, which is a real thing in junior high. On the other hand, sometimes it's smarter to sit with your back to the wall and your eyes on the exit.

To be honest, I was ready to flip a coin when Agate turned up like a penny landing on its edge.

four

in which our peacock meets a girl (in a kissing-book way)

I don't tell Agate I'll help her fake a message from aliens, but I don't tell her no, either, and so a few days later she just shows up at my house after school.

It's the early part of March and the weather has been having mood swings, but today it's definitely feeling like spring. I can smell the *gentler, more organic pace of life* being spread on the surrounding fields.

(It's manure. Organic farming is truly the way of the future.)

Anyway, I am sitting at the kitchen table with my dad, enduring the afternoon questioning: Any homework? What are you learning? Are you making friends? How's the new school?

As a tweenager I am only legally required to say, *It was fine, Dad.*

It's fine.

I'm fine.

It's like Dad thinks that if he asks me every day, one day I will crack and tell him everything.

"Dad, look," I say, halfway through today's interrogation. "I'm the new kid in a small town where everybody knows everybody. All I'm trying to do is blend in."

My dad rocks back, looking hurt. "Simon," he says softly, "I know this is hard—but we've talked about this. You really need to tell your friends—"

At that point we both hear the gate screech open. Dad leaps to his feet.

The funeral home we live in has two entrances, front and back. The front is the funeral part of the funeral home. The back is the home part. The front side, the funeral side, has an elaborate garden—I'm talking crunching gravel paths, little nooks with benches, a fountain, and an actual peacock. It wraps around the side of the house, and it's called the Garden of Peace and Memory.

The back side of the house has two garages—a hearse garage and a regular garage—and between them a scruffy little private yard, just big enough for some recycling bins and a saggy gray picnic table Mom wants to replace. It's fenced off with the same elaborate wrought iron as the Garden of Peace and Memory, but around the Garden of Recycling and Crabgrass the fence is peeling and rusted, and the gate screeches.

That would be fine, except the peacock—who has a tail the size of a golf umbrella and a brain the size of a shriveled lima bean—always thinks the sound is another male peacock. Like, *every day* he thinks this. And every day he comes bursting out from behind the hearse garage or down from the porch roof or up from the pits of hell to challenge that other peacock to a duel.

He yodels and sticks his neck out like a goose. He snaps and spits and attempts to rake you with his spurs. He is not the sharpest knife in the drawer, but he does have some very sharp parts. We call him Pretty Stabby.

Today, who should Pretty Stabby have in his sights but Agate. When Dad comes crashing out the back door, shouting and waving the wrecked umbrella we keep there for this purpose, Agate has her back turned and is dumping her bike against the inside of our fence. At the shouts, Agate spins around. Her windbreaker is sparkly green. She is wearing brown leopard-print leggings. The peacock is almost on top of her.

Then Pretty Stabby spots Agate's color scheme and pulls up short, the single circuit firing in his lima-bean brain. The circuit is labeled *girl peacock*.

Pretty Stabby looks at Agate, and Agate looks at Pretty Stabby. My dad waves his umbrella in a confused way.

Pretty Stabby snaps open the fan of his tail.

Agate tries to step around him.

The bird sidesteps to stay in front of her. He gives his tail the old *bump bump shaky*.

"Sorry," calls my dad, from one side of the tail fan. "Sorry. Peacock. Did you need—"

"I'm Agate Van der Zwaan," calls Agate from the other

25

side of the fan. "I'm a friend of Simon's from school!"

"Oh!" my dad shouts back. "Hi! I'm Simon's dad."

Agate tries stepping in the other direction. Pretty Stabby slides to intercept her, then prances in a circle until his back is to her. He arches and shakes his fully fanned tail. Even from the doorway I can hear his stiff butt feathers rattling like maracas.

Agate frowns. "I think your peacock is sexually harassing me, Mr. O'Keeffe," she says.

My dad snaps out of his trance and uses the umbrella handle to snatch Pretty Stabby around his elegant neck and wrestle him out of the way. Pretty Stabby thrashes and hisses like a cobra. Dad hangs tough. "Sorry," he tells Agate. "He came with the house."

"I understand. I live with goats." Agate strides right past the peacock drama and up to our back door. "Hi Simon."

"Hi, Agate," I say. "Uh . . . come in."

She does, then stops dead in the cluttered hallway. "This is a funeral home?"

"No, this is just the back part," I say. "Did you want . . . ?" I have a wild thought that maybe she wants the funeral part, maybe someone has died.

"No, I came to see you. I just thought it would be fancier." She takes off her backpack. I can tell from the way she holds it that it's super heavy, but she doesn't put it down.

My dad turns up, looking like he's just had a fight with a peacock. "Sorry about that. I'm Martin O'Keeffe. It's nice to meet you . . . Agate? Is that right? Come in."

Agate nods at her name and trails my dad into the kitchen. Not that she has a lot of options. There are only two downstairs rooms on the home-side: a kitchen and the den that Dad is turning into a music studio. The den has egg-crate foam stapled to the walls, and so many brass instruments in various states of assembly that it looks like something steampunk exploded in there.

My dad beams at Agate. You can totally tell that it's been a while since I had friends over and he's delighted. He needs to chill a little. "Can I get you kids juice boxes or something?"

"We don't have juice boxes." In our year of home-schooling, my parents completely got out of the habit of juice boxes. They haven't picked it up again yet.

"The packaging on juice boxes is very wasteful," says Agate.

"Well," Dad tries, "I know we have punch mix."

"Dad, no punch!" The reason we have punch mix—always—is that it's a funeral thing. I can't even stand the smell of it.

My dad ruffles a hand through my hair. "Sorry, Sy. Should I just let you—"

"We have a project," says Agate.

"We do?" I'm trying to smooth my hair down, but once it's tasted the sweet freedom of being ruffled, it's gone for the day.

Agate doesn't look like she cares. Her hair is frizzy, bright red, and everywhere. She's taken off her peacock-green

27

jacket. Underneath it is another homemade-looking T-shirt. This one says *Otter Space* and features otters zipping around in flying saucers. She's wearing it over a turtleneck like it's 1982.

I know for a fact we don't have a school project. But it's around then, maybe because of the shirt, that I remember about the space aliens.

Agate's heavy backpack dangles from her hand and bumps into her ankle. She does not put it on the table. She looks at me and raises her eyebrows like great big secret messages.

"Uh, we can work on it in my room. Okay, Dad?"

My dad looks flummoxed. The last time I had friends from school over I was in fifth grade and it didn't matter if they were girls. Now I'm in seventh, so maybe it does. I mean, not to *me,* obviously. But maybe Dad thinks it should.

Or maybe flummoxed is just his default state these days. Being the only sackbut player in Grin And Bear It, Nebraska, can do that to a man. "Sure," he says. "I'll bring you some crackers and cheese—no allergies, Agate? I promise the packaging is very eco-friendly."

"That's fine Mr. O'Keeffe thank you," says Agate. She talks to him like she's memorized a phrase book on how to be polite in English. It's a parent-pleaser for sure. To me, it kind of sounds like she doesn't know what to do with commas.

"My room's upstairs." I lead her up the creaky back staircase to the maze of rooms upstairs, where we mostly live. We wind our way to my room.

"Oh cool," she says. "You're in the turret."

"Like I told my parents: If I'm gonna live in a creepy huge house with dead people in the basement, I get the bedroom in the turret."

"There are dead people in the basement?" asks Agate, wide-eyed.

"Um? Sometimes?"

She covers her mouth with one hand. She has little spots of purple and turquoise ink like rainbow freckles on the backs of her hands. "Do you go listen to them fart?"

"Hardly ever."

Agate bursts, just *bursts*, with laughter. If she was all phrase book before, it's like laughter is her native language. She turns pink with it, and I'm smiling before I know why.

"Are there— Is there someone there right now?"

"I don't think so . . . ?"

It's not like I never go in the basement. Sometimes I have to help my mom carry down the embalming chemicals, or go get the weed whacker or the bike pump from the storage closet. But it's also not like I hang out in what my mom calls the wet room. In fact, I try not to know too much about what's happening on Mom's side of the building, just on general principle.

My dad comes through the doorway with a plate of Triscuits and cheddar, plus some carrot sticks with hummus. "Oh, Sy," he says. "It looks like a bomb went off in here."

It kind of does. My room is big and white and round, with blue curtains on the tall windows, and that part is nice. But the only thing I've unpacked are my Lego models, and half of them got damaged in the move and are spread around the room, waiting for me to fix them. My books are still in boxes—though the boxes are at least on the bookshelves—and my clothes are divided into clean (in the laundry basket) and dirty (everywhere else). I kick some of the more embarrassing laundry under the bed.

There's a proper desk by one window. The desk is drowning in piles, though, so Dad puts the snacks on the folding table in the middle of the room, beside the lightly damaged Lego Death Star. And then, thankfully, he leaves.

The room smells like superglue and solvent and just a little bit like dirty socks.

Agate sits at the Lego table and starts laying out little flower-colored cupcake liners, which apparently she takes with her everywhere. "I am an autistic person," she says, cheerfully, as she sorts the cheese and crackers and carrots into separate cupcake piles. "Separating food textures is one of my things."

"That's cool," I say, trying to sound as cheerful as she does. I mean, it is cool—I'm not an expert or anything, but Emma J. in my old class was on the autism spectrum and she was interesting and nice. But also: Agate being cool about her brain stuff makes me feel a little safer about my brain stuff. Not safe enough to get into it or anything—but safer.

I take the stuff off my desk chair and wheel it over. The chair is lime green, mesh-backed, and hydraulic. It looks like something that should be on the bridge of a starship.

"It's a crazy-expensive chair," I say, for something to say. "My mom bought it for the year I was homeschooled. She said I wasn't going to be one of those people with widows' humps who had to have their spines broken so they can lay flat in a coffin."

"Okay, wow." Agate looks at me with wide blue eyes. "You are super good at the disgusting things."

"Uh. Sorry."

"No, it's good. Disgusting things are also one of my things."

"Well, good news: I have basically a bottomless supply."

She beams. "I also like your Lego."

"You like Lego?" If there is one thing in the universe I can safely share with other people, it's Lego.

"It shows that you have technical skills. We'll need it for the build." She unzips her bag. Like I thought, there are some serious books in there. There's one about radio astronomy and one on SETI—the Search for Extraterrestrial Intelligence. One of things the astronomers around here do is a SETI project where they listen for radio signals from space aliens.

Agate finishes piling up books and starts in on her cheese slices. "Are you ready? I want to tell you about pulsars."

"Should I even try to say no, here?"

"SETI is really important, Simon. It's proof that we're not alone."

I catch myself thinking about being alone.

I don't want to make waves in my new town, and faking a message from space seems kind of . . . wavy. But Agate is looking at me with galaxy-blue eyes and her tongue pushing on her teeth like words are going to burst out of her, and to be honest, saying no to that seems like the more immediate threat. Not that she'd be angry—I mean S, maybe—but she'd be sad and she'd leave, and I kind of don't want her to leave. "Okay, fine," I say. "Tell me about pulsars."

Agate lights up and grabs a book out of her stack. "So! In the 1960s there was a student scientist named Jocelyn Bell. She was Scottish and she was very smart and she could swing a sledgehammer. She was in charge of building this homemade radio telescope." Agate apparently knows this story well enough to fill me in while simultaneously flipping through the book. "It took her two years—here she is!" Agate stabs her finger into the book where there's a picture of a young woman with a Beatles haircut and black cat's-eye glasses. "This is her. Jocelyn Bell. They were looking for quasars." She trails a finger under a line of text. "They were using interplanetary scintillation."

"What's interplanetary—"

"A not-important part."

"I don't want to tell you how to run your alien conspiracy, Agate. But maybe just skip the not-important parts?"

Agate shakes her head, like she thinks I'm joking. She's going to do this her way. "Jocelyn Bell found this different thing instead. A tiny little signal, but it kept repeating. The good part is here somewhere. . . ."

Outside, Pretty Stabby must have spotted, like, a shady-looking pebble or something. He makes his alarm call.

Actual peacock scientists—scientists who study peacocks, not peacocks who are scientists—officially call this sound a *bu-girk*. And it does sound a little like *bu-girk*—it sounds like someone shouting *bu-girk* while also being stabbed in the chest.

I always jump when Pretty Stabby starts in, but Agate is unbothered. She's bent over the book, munching her carefully separated crackers and cheese slices, scanning columns of text like a bloodhound on a trail, like she's forgotten I'm even there. I start working the Death Star apart along its crack. Several mini-fig stormtroopers go spinning out to their deaths. Agate reads about outer space. The peacock screams bloody murder.

Down in the kitchen my dad is probably standing at the sink thinking: *Simon is having a normal human interaction with a fellow student! Sound the trumpets!*

If only he knew.

"Look!" Agate cries, loud enough to make me startle. "I knew it was in here somewhere. This is the best bit! When Jocelyn showed her supervisor the signal thing she found, he labeled it LGM-1."

"LGM-1?" I say.

Agate is absolutely beaming as she spins the book around, tapping the picture caption as if too excited to speak. I'm almost afraid to look.

I look.

Whelp.

LGM stands for "Little Green Men."

five

in which I meet a boy (not in a kissing-book way) and reconsider that message from space

I think Agate could be a friend, but I don't get to see much of her at school. She's in homeroom every morning and English every afternoon, but otherwise she's taking all these eighth-grade and high-school classes, which somehow does not surprise me. She's not even around at lunch much, because, she says, as an autistic person she needs some downtime during the day, and the school has something called a wellness room where she can get it. (I've been there. It's dim and cozy, which is nice, but it also has only one door, which isn't.)

Anyway. I don't get to see Agate, so mostly I hang out with Kevin.

Kevin and me first got together on day two, because we were both wearing Cornhusker jerseys. He was wearing his jersey because he's a fanatic—he'd have to be, because the red shirt with his green hair and his extreme skinniness makes him look like the Grinch Who Stole Football Tickets. I was wearing my jersey because it was clean.

"Omaha, man!" he says. "I've got a cousin in Omaha."

"Is it Tim?" I say. "I totally know him!"

Kevin laughs.

Omaha, FYI, is a city of almost a million, and I'm not even technically from there. Technically, I am from one of the little towns where people used to live when they had to work in Omaha but didn't want to live in Omaha. It's out at the end of West Dodge Road. You would know the name. Everybody knows it now. But I've arranged my entire life in Grin And Bear It so that I never have to say it.

Anyway, Kevin's cool. After a while I even give up my lunch spot on the music risers and start hanging out with him in what Ms. Snodgrass calls The Commons and the rest of us call The Pits. The Pits are made up of sunken places with carpeted stairs going down into them, bigger than most stairs but great for perching. There are also carpeted stairs piled up in half pyramids against the walls. Basically it looks like a bad Minecraft build, but it's good for just sitting around. It's right inside the front doors, so there are lots of ways in and out, and you can spy on what's going on in the principal's fishbowl. Also there are vending machines. The whole GNB *gentler, more organic pace of life* works better if you can get your hands on Cool Ranch Doritos once in a while.

Kevin started out disappointed that he couldn't geek out

about football with me, but he is super happy about being able to talk Minecraft.

Kevin's family is on Team Science—his dad runs the Hello Hello, where the scientists get coffee, and his mom is actually in charge of the SETI project at the biggest radio telescope in town, the Very Large Radio Telescope. (That's apparently how scientists roll when it comes to names. According to Kevin, there are plans for an Extremely Large Telescope and an Overwhelmingly Large Telescope, but for now, the Very Large Telescope is where it's at.)

Kevin's family, he tells me, has computers they can use at home. His older sister, Zeny, is learning computer programming, which his mom wants to encourage, so they set their electronics up especially.

My chest gets all clenched up. "Wait. I thought nobody had computers at home?"

As far as I am concerned, "no computers" is half the point of Grin And Bear It.

"Nah," says Kevin. "You've just got to have special shielding."

I try to breathe in. There's a way to count with your breath to calm down: in for five, hold for six, out for seven. It's kind of obvious, though, so I don't want to do it. But I am totally capable of having anxiety about coping with anxiety, so I try box breathing instead: in for four, hold for four, out for four, hold for four. That doesn't work as well for me, but most people don't notice it.

"I'm making it sound way too nice, though," Kev says.

We're perched on top of one of the block stacks in The Pits, and the cinderblock wall behind my head feels cold. "They're just desktops with their Wi-Fi bits taken out, inside a Faraday cage. I've got a microwave in there, too, if you ever want microwave popcorn."

I mumble something low-key about missing Hot Pockets. Then I add, like I don't really care: "So you get internet in there?"

"No way, man. That's the whole point. Even if we had Wi-Fi enabled, the cage would soak up all the signal. Coming in, going out, whatever."

I try out a little grin even though my mouth tastes like I've been chewing tin cans. I can feel how my smile flickers and jerks. But Kev doesn't notice. One of the nice things about Kev is that he never thinks I might be hiding anything.

"Getting Minecraft up and running without internet was a P-I-T-A," he says, slapping a hand against the side of his *A* for the punctuation. "We ended up hauling the computer to Kearney, carting it into the library, and plugging it into one of their ethernet cables so we could get online and it would stop telling us to register it." He stuffs the trash from his lunch into his brown bag, crumples it into a ball, and three-points it into the trash can by the foot of the pyramid. "You should come check out my build," he says.

I decide to go over the next Tuesday, which I figure is soon enough that I look friendly, but not so soon that I look pathetic. Just a nice, normal kid. I preclear it with my parents—who absolutely would call the FBI if they didn't know where I was after school—and I walk home with Kevin. We're both expecting it to be just his sister Zeny at Kevin's house, but a blue Prius pulls into the driveway just as we're getting there. Kevin sneaks in an eye roll for my benefit before the car door opens and his mom gets out. Kevin told me that his last name, Matapang, is Filipino, but his mom turns out to be the whitest of white ladies: blond, Karen haircut, mom jeans, the whole package.

"Hey, Mom," says Kevin.

"Kevin," she says brightly. Keys and ID hang on a lanyard around her neck. "I'm just home for a couple of hours—we have to check a signal later, so I wanted to come home to throw some dinner in the oven and look at your homework charts."

"And to scope out my new friend?" he asks.

"And see you," she says.

Kevin grabs onto the ornamental lamppost in front of his house and leans way out, letting his body weight swing. "This is Simon. Like I said, he's new."

Wherever Kev got his unsuspicious nature from, it wasn't his mom. "Simon . . . ?" she says, letting it hang like a fishing line all baited for my last name.

"That's right," I tell her. Let her do her own homework if she wants to. "My mom bought Slaughter and Sons. We moved here in February."

"Well, and you're very welcome." She comes up on the porch and unlocks what's got to be the only locked door in town. She has a grocery bag in her hand, and she turns and smiles and lifts it. "Kevin says you like Hot Pockets?"

Her smile is another fishhook but since it's baited with Hot Pockets, I'll bite. I try to think about nothing but microwaved snacks as I give her a smile. She takes it and turns. "Kevin, do you want to go over your homework charts before or after you show Simon your Minecraft?"

"You're going to like Simon, Mom," says Kev. "His toothpick bridge, like, totally exploded today."

"Really?!"

In design and tech class we have been building bridges out of toothpicks and glue. Today was the day we set them up and loaded them with weights until they cracked. Only, mine didn't crack—it shattered and sent shrapnel flying everywhere. It was actually kind of embarrassing: I squealed like a rabid possum and threw my hands over my face. But Kevin doesn't seem to be teeing up that story, and his mom is giving me a well-done-young-man nod, like I just went way up in her books.

I don't get it.

"They crack along their weak points," explains Kev. "If they explode it means they don't have any weak points."

"Technically it means they can store a lot of internal stress," says Dr. Matapang. "But that's roughly equivalent. Excellent job, Simon."

"Thanks?" It sounds like a question, but I do mean it. It didn't feel like a good job when I was doing the sick marsupial impression, but it feels better now that someone is telling me why.

39

"How much weight did your structure hold, Kevin?" his mom asks.

"Mooooooom," he whines. "At least let me get Simon into my Minecraft build first?"

"Of course." She passes me the Hot Pockets and vanishes into the kitchen. Kevin leads me the other way.

At the top of the steps leading down to the sunken living room, a teenage girl swings into view, spinning herself with one hand on the door frame and ending up right in Kev's face. "How much weight *did* your structure hold, Kevin?" she singsongs. This must be Zeny, because she looks just like Kevin: wild curls, brown skin, super skinny, gangly limbed.

"It sagged like cooked spaghetti," I tell her.

"I had a strategy going where I glued the toothpicks into sandwiches before I built with them. But I don't think the glue dried."

"The word to use when you tell Mom that is 'lamination.'" Zeny looks at me. "Kev's friend Simon?"

"Kev's friend Simon," I confirm.

"So the deal with Mom is that Dad used to be a radio astronomer, too," she says. "But when Mom took this job he couldn't get a post out here, and now she wants me and Kev to be the best at stuff so we 'have *choices*.'" She says the last bit like she's quoting her mom directly—she wrinkles her face with concern and puts a hand on her hip, and she's got her mom impression nailed. Then she half-swoons dramatically and takes a backward hop down two stairs onto the forest-green carpet in the sunken living room. Like Kevin, she's acrobat quick. "Fair warning, Mom's super invested in academic performance. If you come within range—"

Kevin also leaps down the steps, spins on his toe, and mimes firing a shotgun at me.

I raise my hands to surrender, play it off as casual, then take two stairs in two steps because I'm a normal person.

Now that I'm in the living room Kevin spins around again and throws open his arms like a carnival showman. "Behold," he says, "the Kennel of Science."

"We're not calling it that," says Zeny.

"We're totally calling it that," I say. Because now that I see it, the name is perfect.

Originally, Kevin said his computer was in a Faraday Cage. Then when I made some random joke about not wanting to get locked up in a cage, he explained that it was more like a screen porch, but inside. Then, because I couldn't picture that, he described it as a giant dog kennel.

It is exactly like a giant dog kennel, with a couple of desks with serious computers inside. There are gamer chairs and wires and gadgets around, plus the forbidden microwave, of course. The whole setup is what would happen if Fido ran mission control.

"Do you play Dragon Age? Assassin's Creed?" asks Zeny. She has the same look on her face that Kevin got when he thought he might be able to talk football with me.

"I could learn."

"Don't," Kevin warns. "You'll be trapped here forever."

Zeny flips him off casually, then gathers her hair into a ponytail like she's Black Widow heading into a fight scene, snapping the hair elastic off her wrist and setting her jaw. "Kev, I'll go talk to Mom about my chemistry test, but you're going to owe me."

"Yeah, yeah," says Kevin, opening the wire door to the kennel. The U of desks holds two giant monitor setups. There are wires and cables and sound bars and stuff everywhere. It's such a weird space that it doesn't seem like a cage at all—you can see right through the mesh on the walls—and stepping through the door doesn't panic me.

"Your sister seems okay," I say, once she's out of earshot.

"She's not, she's the worst," says Kevin, and then he steals what's clearly her chair, spinning it around and pulling it up beside his. He puts a Hot Pocket in the forbidden microwave and fires up the forbidden computers.

I take another step in. The swinging screen door closes behind me, and I gotta say my throat catches. But nothing happens. Kevin gives me the first Hot Pocket, starts another one, then boots up Minecraft and shows me his tower and his farm and his antizombie wall and stuff. He's got some rare items in his inventory and a sweet crafting table set up.

Kevin is decent—actually, Kevin is pretty great. He's not super popular, but he's not, like, an outcast—he hangs with the other kids on Team Science and runs the lights for the junior play, etc. He wouldn't have to make space for the new kid, but he did. Before everything that happened, I probably would have invited him onto my Minecraft server.

It's not an option now: no internet. And anyway, Castle Simon has been sitting empty since fifth grade.

The forbidden microwave forbidden beeps. Kevin grabs the other Hot Pocket and bites into it way too soon—he has to hold his mouth open and pant for ventilation.

"Amateur mistake, dude," I tell him.

"For my science fair project I'm gonna do: How can the inside of a Hot Pocket turn to lava while the outside stays frozen like the tundra's crack."

"There's a science fair?"

"No stress, it's optional." Carefully, he nibbles off the other corner of the Hot Pocket and lets the steam out for a bit. "I mean, optional for you. Not for anyone in *this* family."

"Yeah?"

"Mom says she wants us to 'have *choices*.'" Which is exactly what Zeny said, so Dr. Matapang must say it a lot. Kevin shrugs and hands me the keyboard.

I dig around in his mines a little and get blown up by a few creepers, but it's not as much fun when it's not your world.

And of course mine is gone.

• • •

The next Wednesday, I come home from school to find my mom slumped pathetically at the kitchen table. "Coffee," she greets me. "Emergency. Hello Hello. Go."

I drop my backpack and get myself a glass of juice. I've been back in school a month now, and my parents are getting better at having OJ in stock for that quick after-school fructose rush. "Hey, Mom."

She flaps a ten-dollar bill in the air at me like a flag of surrender.

I take it. We have an espresso machine at home—actually we have two—so things have to be pretty bad if Mom is asking me to go to the Hello Hello for Team Science–style fancy drinks. "What happened now?"

"Curtis," she says. "Curtis happened."

Mom's assistant, Curtis, is one of the complications of our life in Grin And Bear It. He's supposed to be her callout guy, the person who picks up bodies from the hospital or the nursing home or whatever. He's worked for Slaughter and Sons forever—like the peacock, he came with the house. He also happens to be the great-nephew of Hershel Grubsic, who runs the local crematorium.

The thing is, though, Curtis is terrible at his job. Like, epically terrible. After her first week working with Curtis, Mom banned him from picking up people who had died in their homes—she didn't want him dealing with families. By the end of February she was so fed up that she fired him. When Hershel Grubsic got wind of that, though, all the Slaughter and Sons bodies mysteriously got moved to the back of the cremation line. It only took one disrupted funeral before Curtis got his job back. In most parts of her life, Mom doesn't back down for anything short of an oncoming semi, but she'll swallow a lot to make sure things go smoothly for grieving people.

44

"I need a proper mocha," says Mom. "Seventy-two percent dark Madagascar chocolate, microfoamed almond milk, and two shots of espresso, Yirgicheff bean, lightly washed." She lowers her head and rests it on top of the paperwork she has spread out on the table. "I have lost the strength to go myself, and you, my only son, must save me."

". . . Okay?"

She raises her head and looks at me, wild-eyed. "Curtis tried to take the wrong body."

"He—"

"At the nursing home in Bessey. From one of the double rooms."

I'm starting to get a bad feeling about this. In the other room a medieval brass instrument starts playing "Swing Low, Sweet Chariot."

"I sent him to pick up a new client and he tried to bag up the roommate."

"Who was also dead?" I ask, without much hope.

"Who was *napping*," Mom says.

I'm horrified. Mom's horrified. The silence is horrified.

"Why can't Dad go?" I say.

Dad's head pops out of the door. "Because this morning only Mrs. Delores Pellnor showed up for Mass." Mrs. Delores Pellnor is Dad's Ms. Snodgrass. She keeps giving him this look like he's come from the big city specifically to tempt her into heresy. "I had a sermon on the gift of sexuality planned and I gave it, just to her."

45

"Tell Doc I want it extra hot," Mom says. She slides her special thermos cup across the table toward me. It's double-walled steel and could probably be used to smuggle uranium. Her coffee order is on a Post-it Note on the side.

I take the cup and cast Dad one last "come-on-please"sort of look. "The sermon was ten minutes long, but my mouth just kept talking," he says in response. "If coffee was my comfort drug, you'd be buying two."

"All right, all right," I say. "I'm going."

It takes about ten minutes to walk clear across mighty Grin And Bear It, through the downtown, over the bridge. The Hello Hello is in an old ice-cream shop beside the public library. I push through the door, triggering a jangle of bells, and find Kevin's sister, Zeny, stationed behind the register

"Hey, Simon," she says. "Kevin's in the back."

"He is?"

"Yeah. Wednesdays is when we get stock in. Me and Kev help Dad load up the freezers and stuff."

"Isn't that a child labor law violation?" I say, which is also what I say when Mom makes me carry milk crates full of Cavity King embalming fluid jugs down to the basement.

"Family business exception!" Zeny makes the jazz hands ta-da gesture, then lowers her voice. "If you need his help with homework, you can get him out of it."

"I don't have any homework."

"But no adult has heard you say that!"

I glance behind me. There are in fact a bunch of adults who heard me say that. A half dozen junior scientists are huddled around the big group table that sits in the window, cups and dishes all around them, papers scattered everywhere.

"Postdocs," says Zeny. "They don't count."

"They don't?"

"Trust me, they're not listening. That's Mom's team, and they are in full funding panic mode." The junior scientists do all look awfully stressed. Zeny calls over her shoulder. "Kevin! Simon's here!"

Kev comes bursting through the curtain over the doorway that leads to the back of the shop. "Sy, my man!" He puts his hands on the top of the curved glass of the ice cream case like he's going to vault over it.

A man comes out of the back room behind him. I assume he's Kevin and Zeny's dad, because he's got their coloring and he moves like them, like he could dance in a ballet. He'd be an unlikely ballerina, because he's built like a linebacker and he's wearing a *Great British Bake Off* T-shirt that's a little too small for him, but still, he comes into the room as if he could float or leap. The postdocs all look up and cry "Doc!" in unison, like they're in a sitcom.

"Be right there, children!" he replies, then turns to Kevin. "Go bus their stuff. I'll make you and your friend some halo halo."

Kevin creases up his face, but he goes to work. His dad reaches across the counter and shakes my hand. "John Paul Matapang," he says. "Around here they call me Doc."

"Doc!" cry the postdocs again, like kids calling for their camp counselor.

47

Doc Matapang waves to them, then slides open the back of the cold counter and starts adding things to a pair of glass sundae goblets. He doesn't ask me what I want, which is okay because I don't know what to get. He puts red beans and clear strings of something in the bottom, a scoop of shaved ice in the middle, adds a ball of bright purple ice cream and some red jelly things to the top, and pours sweetened condensed milk over the whole concoction.

He passes one to me and one to Kevin, who's back from bussing duty.

"I'm actually here because my mom is having a next-level coffee emergency."

"'Tis the season," says Doc. "Zeny will fix you up."

I give Zeny my mom's Post-it Note and poke at my dessert with beans in it. Kevin is digging into his with the joy of someone who otherwise would have to stock shelves, so I try the top thing, the purple ice cream. It tastes kind of like vanilla, if vanilla were also a potato.

"Give me that." Kevin sets his sundae goblet down, takes mine, and uses the spoon to mix it up. He passes it back to me.

Kevin and me lean back against the cold glass curve of the counter and watch his dad hovering over the junior scientists like a teacher reassuring some weeping kindergarteners.

The postdocs look like they are having the kind of day my mom is having, and my mom is having a *capital* D Day. I try my halo halo again. Now that it's mixed it's cold and

48

chewy and sweet and complicated and kind of amazing. I point at the postdocs with my spoon. "What's up with them?"

Kevin makes a face around a spoonful of mixed-up stuff. "They're working on their part of the funding application for Mom's SETI project," he says. "She probably told them how if they don't do it right, their operating grant will get cancelled, the whole project will shutter, and their academic lives will be ruined."

The shaved ice I just ate is making my stomach cold. "Could that happen?"

Kevin half-shrugs. "Maybe? SETI scientists have been listening for space aliens for forty years, and they haven't heard anything. It's starting to be a tough sell."

He doesn't sound super worried. In fact, he sounds like he's hardly thought about what it would mean: His mom's project would fail—his family would probably have to move—the telescope would shut down—and the National Quiet Zone that protects it would get flooded with noise.

Maybe Kevin's not worried, but me? I start to get this horror-movie feeling, the one where you realize you did *not* leave that door open. My fingertips get cold, and hot pulses start behind my eyes.

If the SETI scientists don't get their funding fixed, then the internet will come to town, and that radar I'm flying under will lock on to me like it's a bombing run, like it's the end of the world.

six

in which I see the Large Radio Telescope, learn to pronounce "sidereal," and meet more of the Van der Zwaan family plus their dog, Todd

Okay. So maybe I was mostly playing along with the whole fake-a-mission-from-aliens mission. My mom calls this my Simon Says mode, where I do what I'm told and don't ask questions, because, hey, that's what keeps you alive in the game.

Maybe it's even simpler than that: Maybe I like Agate, and I want a friend.

But maybe, just maybe, her idea about keeping the SETI scientists employed is—like my therapist always used to say—"worth exploring."

Back at school, English continues to be the worst. Miss Rose hasn't stopped looking at me like I'm the shivering puppy in an animal cruelty commercial—and to top that off, we've just launched a journalism unit. We're studying the basic questions, Who What When Where Why and How. Miss Rose tells us to pair up and interview each other using the 5W1H method so that we can write stories based on what we find out.

Yeah, no.

I dodge this incoming disaster by whipping my chair across the classroom so fast that the rubber foot thingies squeal against the hard tiles, and I latch on to Agate like I'm Pretty Stabby spotting a green umbrella. Her face does a weird thing: Her eyes get wide and her mouth kind of opens, and I wonder if this is the first time she's been someone's first pick.

"So," I say, without any lead-up because Agate is the kind of person who starts a conversation with eyebrow mites, "*what* should our LGM message say, and *how* are we going to send it?" I hit the magic assigned words hard, so that anyone listening in will think we're doing our work.

"I don't know *what* we should say, but I think—" Agate drops her voice, pokes her own hand with her pen. "I think I know *how* to make the message look like it came from"— Agate looks around to see who's watching—"deep space."

Her whisper is the kind of whisper you use on a stage when you want the audience to hear you in the back row. Some of the other kids actually turn and look. Miss Rose starts swishing toward us. Whoops. Time for a different spin on the assignment. "My story," I say to Agate, and everybody else who's listening, "is called *Curtis Kidnaps the Living*. Your interview can now commence."

So Agate gamely starts asking questions, and I explain *who* Curtis is and *why* we can't fire him and *what* he's done now. Miss Rose backs off. I think some of the other kids are listening in. Can't blame them. It is a pretty good story, especially because it does not star me. The whole time Agate is doing her interview she's also writing and doodling on another piece of paper and slowly blushing hot pink like the world's worst redhead spy. By the time the bell rings, she has this second piece of paper tucked and folded into a little triangle. She slides it over to me in an over-the-top nonchalant way, practically waggling her eyebrows.

I stick the note in my front jeans pocket, and I make sure I'm tucked up behind my locker door before I unfold it. Like Agate said once, I can keep a secret.

The note reads: *The HOW/WHEN is called SIDEREAL TIME. Come to the farm. I will explain.*

Below that there's a map and a drawing of a clock.

At lunch I go to the library and look up sidereal time: "The timekeeping system that astronomers use to locate celestial objects," which, you know, clears that right up.

The sketched clock reads 4:00. That gives me enough time to go home after school, dump my bag, get my bike out of the hearse garage, and tell my parents. I mean, ask my parents.

Like I told Agate they would, they let me go, even though

it's outside of town. They look both terrified and overjoyed, as if they have been visited by angels. I see them actually take each other's hands as I ride away.

• • •

Following a paper map while riding a bike down gravel roads through the Dismal River National Forest is harder than it sounds. The gravel roads are muddy with the spring thaw, and the trees are still bare. I'm mud-spattered and cold, and it's closer to four thirty before I find the right place.

I can tell it's the right place because it has a big painted wooden sign suspended above the farm gate: *Van der Zwaan Angora Et Cetera,* it says in curlicue writing.

Looming on the other side of the road, behind a fence and across an open field, is the biggest radio telescope in town: the Very Large Radio Telescope. You can see it from everywhere, but I have never been close to it before. From town, it looks like it's made out of toothpicks. Up close, it's jaw-droppingly enormous.

I know from generally existing in GNB that the Very Large Radio Telescope—which the locals call the Big Ear— has a hundred-foot disk. When I heard that, a hundred feet didn't sound so big. After all, that's smaller than a football field, which is our standard way of measuring things in Nebraska. But in person it's huge. The disk is a dusty white saucer, tipped up to catch the sky, like something God's cat could drink out of. The scaffold that holds it up is as tall as a twenty-story building. It's probably the tallest thing between Lincoln and Laramie. It's surrounded by a cluster of ticky-tacky buildings, like a trailer park of science.

It feels weird to turn my back on the telescope, but I do. Inside the Van der Zwaan gate my bike goes bump bump bump across the cattle grate. I walk it up the gravel drive toward the house.

Goats are spread like a flock of floor mops in a field behind a peeling white farmhouse. There's a barn and some barn cats and some scruffy-looking white ducks and, in the middle of all of it, Agate. She's sitting on one of those submarine-shaped propane tanks, drumming her heels on the metal. Agate's always drumming or bouncing. "You're late!" she says.

"Give me a break." I toe the kickstand down and park the bike. "I haven't used a map in literally ever."

"It's okay. I was sure you'd come." She slides down the side of the tank and lands with a big thump. Today she is wearing a shirt with the Loch Ness monster on it. Its speech bubble says *I believe in myself.* "You've gotta come in for a second and meet my mom and then I have to tell you about star time."

"Side-real time."

"Sigh-deer-ee-el," she corrects me. "Sidereal time is the reason Jocelyn Bell knew the Little Green Men signal was coming from deep space. Because it was four minutes different, every day." She's by the back door already, bouncing eagerly on her toes. "Come in here!"

I wipe my hands on my jeans. I can only see one door

and I don't like buildings with one door. But probably there is a front door around front. I mean, farms are like that, right? Agate has her hand on the doorknob, but she twists around. "Time is going to be key," she says. "Four minutes. That's the key."

I stumble, but she's gone in. I give myself a shake and then follow her.

• • •

When I'm getting ready to do a big Lego build, I take all the parts out of all the packaging and lay them out. I have special trays that I use for this: They are clear plastic and divided into compartments. I square up any large pieces and lay them out in a line beside the trays, until everything is completely under control.

Agate's home is pretty much the opposite of that.

The mudroom is full of shoes and boots and coats and raincoats and scooters and soccer balls and garden tools and dog toys and raggedy towels and, of course, mud. There is a step up into the kitchen, and at the top of the step, a bunch of golden retriever puppies are squirming around in a puppy playpen. Someone has spread newspaper in the corner of the pen, but frankly not enough of it; I smell puppy pee. I'm no expert in dog ages, but I can tell these are really young—so little that their ears don't even flop. They look kind of like baby seals.

Beyond the puppy pen, the kitchen is full of things like dry beans in mason jars and garlic in braids and little bottles of oils. An industrial-size vat of something electric red is cooking on the stove.

Agate scoots past the puppies and through the kitchen, sliding open a pocket door leading into the next room. She sticks her head through. "Hi, Mom," she calls.

In what is probably the dining room, a woman with Agate's red hair is feeding two babies—twins—each strapped into a high chair. She is standing on a drop cloth, and there is an easel behind her and books absolutely everywhere: on bookcases, sure, but also big piles on the windowsill and the chair and floor. "Agate, my middle miss, you're home. Can you please stir the rhubarb and then take the puppies out to get socialized?"

"I've got a friend over."

The woman turns. "Oh. Hello."

Behind her one of the babies bangs their spoon against the tray, which makes the other one squeal and toss their spoon onto the floor. Sweet potato puree scatters over the drop cloth.

"This is Simon," says Agate. "He's new."

Agate's mom looks maxed out, like she can't fit one more person in her head. "New to what?"

"Town?" I try.

Agate's mom bends and picks up the spoon from baby #2, which of course causes baby #1 to throw spoon #1. She looks at the spoon on the carpet, then back up at me, with a smile that looks superglued. "Do you want a snack, Simon? We've got duck eggs."

56

Behind her, I notice, a toddler is doing an art project at the big table. The project seems to involve ignoring the macaroni and eating the glue. The toddler and the babies all have red curls.

"It's okay, Mom, I've got it," says Agate. She slides the door closed and gives the vat of red stuff a stir. "Do you actually want duck eggs?"

"That's okay."

"They're fresh," she says, sounding as happy as if she'd laid them herself. "I gathered them this morning. We run a Muscovy duck rescue. I could scramble one."

"Pass, thanks." I peer in at the puppies. "Busy house."

"There's seven of us kids," says Agate. "The twins are Mica and Amber, they're nine months, and Onyx is almost three. And then there's a gap, and then me in the middle, and then there's another gap. And then Jasper and Coral, who are also twins and they're at band practice, and Jade who's in college."

An adult golden retriever comes banging through the dog flap and up the mudroom steps. It wags its tail, snuffles at me, collects an ear scritch from Agate at the stove, then turns to the fridge.

Which it opens.

Seriously. The dog rears up, balances one paw on the counter, takes a rope hanging from the fridge handle in its jaws, and tugs the fridge open.

The dog drops back on its paws and grabs a can of Pabst beer out of the pocket shelf in the door. It carries the can across the room to the dog bowl, bites down, and drops the can into the bowl with a clang. The beer fizzes and bubbles out the tooth holes.

"Agate," I say. "Your . . . dog?"

Agate turns. "Well, don't just leave the door like that." No response. Agate raises her voice and points to the fridge, which is still standing open. "Todd! Door!"

The dog—Todd?—looks up from its leaking beer, puffs a sigh, then crosses the room to head-butt the fridge door closed.

"Ummm," I manage. "Did you see that he got a . . . ?"

"It's okay," she says. "He only has one."

"One . . . beer?"

"Todd's got hip dysplasia. He drinks beer instead of taking painkillers. It's really okay."

A family whose kids are named Jade, Jasper, Coral, Agate, Onyx, Mica, and Amber has a dog named Todd. And that is the least weird part.

"He was supposed to be a service dog," Agate explains.

"What for, bartending?"

"No, mobility. Like, for someone who needs to reach stuff or grip stuff. So he learned skills like opening the fridge and turning on the lights and stuff. But then he flunked out."

"Because of the drinking?"

"No, because he doesn't have enough drive to please people. A service dog has to have special skills and good judgment, but also he's really got to care about his human."

58

The beer can has stopped fizzing and leaking. The dog picks it up in his jaws and takes it over to the recycling. Then he returns to his bowl to lap at the beer.

"So. You've got a genius dog that can open doors and turn on lights and operate heavy machinery or whatever, but he *doesn't* care about pleasing people?"

"I admire him," says Agate, and she smiles like the moon.

It turns out that Agate's family, in addition to keeping angora goats and running a duck rescue, breeds golden retrievers specifically for a service-dog program. They don't usually get stuck with the washouts, but they keep Todd for stud. Despite his bad hip and his attitude problem, he apparently has a track record of fathering excellent service puppies.

"Usually the problem with service puppies isn't that they don't care about pleasing people," Agate explains. "Usually the problem is they care so much they do things they're not supposed to do. Most of them don't make it." She tells me that with most litters only 30 or 40 percent of puppies make it all the way through training, but with Todd's puppies, it's more like half.

Todd finishes his beer. He flops down on his dog bed, sighing like he's just had Thanksgiving dinner and settling his jowls across his folded paws. Todd is living his best life.

Agate and me load the puppies into a laundry basket and haul them outside. Agate tells me they're almost seven weeks old, and they need frequent free-running and human socialization. It's too muddy and cold to chill on the lawn, so we walk over to the barn, the laundry basket swaying wildly between us. "Pretty soon we'll put the vests on them, for service dogs in training," says Agate. "And then I can start taking one to school."

"Just one?" There are five of them.

"We have foster homes for most of them—Jade even wants one if the dorms will let her. Do you want one? We could give you mine. I've done the socializing before, and Mom says we always need to expand our pool of foster families."

It's kind of tempting. The puppies are super-duper cute. They keep popping up over the edge of the basket as we walk, and we keep having to nudge them back in like Whac-A-Mole. Their noses and mouths are wet-looking and black, and they have warm brown eyes.

We put the basket on the floor of the barn and three of them immediately start climbing over the side. The basket topples over and the puppies tumble out like Tribbles. The littlest one gets his belly hung up on the rim of the basket, and I boost him over it with one hand. His tummy is round and warm.

The other puppies are making a puppy tornado. I set the little one down, and he gives the pack a long, shy look before he decides to sit up against my shoe instead.

"My trauma specialist tried to get me a dog," I say, rubbing the little guy's ears.

"You've got a trauma specialist?"

Oh, great job, Simon. Why did I tell her that? But I love

60

the way she says "You've got a trauma specialist?" just as if she were saying, "You've got a telescope?" Like it's cool and interesting.

"Back in Omaha." I shrug. "The alpaca incident was very traumatic."

She looks at me seriously. "Do you find our goats triggering?"

"No," I say.

"I've got a sensory processing specialist but she's in Kearney," Agate says. "And the school has some services but not many because we are so remote. It makes sense that your specialist is in Omaha."

"Yeah, well . . ." The runt puppy starts gnawing on the loop of my shoelace. "Tell me about your star time."

She lights up like that girl scientist with the sledgehammer, and she tells me.

a note on time

So there is a day that goes from noon to noon, and that's called a solar day. It's twenty-four hours exactly. Sometimes there is more light in a day and sometimes there is more dark, but the length of the day does not change.

Agate explains this, unaware that behind her four golden retriever puppies have knocked over a plastic duck-feed bucket and are trying to gnaw the handle to death. The runt, exhausted from its shoelace-chewing adventures, leans on my toes.

Stars have a noon, too, Agate says. But the next day, the next time they have the same noon, only twenty-three hours, fifty-six minutes, and four seconds will have passed. And that's a star day—a sidereal day.

The *when* thing, Agate says, is that if a signal is coming from the stars it should rise not once every twenty-four hours, but once every twenty-four hours minus four minutes plus four seconds.

That's how Agate's hero, Jocelyn Bell—the radio astronomer girl with the cat's-eye glasses and the sledgehammer—knew her *blip-blip-beep* was a signal from space: because every day it came four minutes sooner.

"So," says Agate. "That's the how. Or maybe it's the when? If we send a signal almost four minutes earlier every day then it will look like it's coming from the stars."

I think that's bananas. I think it will take a lot more than that. I think I'm still mostly playing along.

But also I think the big telescope looks like it's made of toothpicks, and I think about my toothpick bridge, and I wonder how much internal stress the telescope can store. I think about what might happen if it blows.

I think: *Four minutes is the difference between this and another world.*

seven

in which Agate gives me a surprise

You know, it's amazing how fast you get used to living in a funeral home.

I mean, it can be a little weird. For example, where most basements have, like, bowling trophies in old cardboard boxes and Christmas decorations in big plastic bins, our basement has freezer drawers and floor drains and other stuff you don't want to think too hard about. And then there's the attack peacock and the endless work in the fancy garden that I'm thinking we could pave for extra parking. But if I avoid the part of the house with the shining wood and the stained glass and the crying people, and if I don't have to run down to the basement storage closet to get my dad the big slow cooker or help my mom carry jugs of unmentionable stuff, it's a pretty normal place.

One thing that's different is that there are two phones in the kitchen. They are both landlines—thanks for that, radio astronomers—and one is white and fairly new. The other is avocado green and has been there since telephones were invented probably. It makes a distinctive double ring that my mom calls "the party line." Like, "The party line is ringing," or "Time to get a party started." If you haven't gathered this by now, Mom likes her humor like her coffee: black. Like, espresso black.

Anyway. It's amazing how fast I got used to the party-line ring. I don't even stop pouring my Frosted Flakes anymore, I just shout up the stairs: "Mom! Somebody died!"

But one day it rings when Mom is out shopping at the Big Lots in Kearney and Dad is locked in his homemade soundproof den tuning his sackbuts. This is the part I'm *not* used to. I stare at the phone like I can see the noise and try to decide if I will be in trouble if I don't answer. But the answer to that is yes.

"Slaughter and Sons," I say, wedging the phone against my shoulder and fishing a notepad out of the rooster-shaped mail-and-keys holder on the wall. "I am afraid the director is out at the moment; can I take a message?" I sound like a robot but it's on purpose. If you sound enough like a robot, people don't tell you details about why they're calling a funeral home.

"Simon, you didn't give me your number."

I look around, but Agate is not actually standing behind me. It's just the super-her voice that makes me think she might be right there.

"Simon?" she says again.

"Because no one calls anybody on the phone, Agate. It's not 1980."

But tell that to the people who still print yellow pages, because Agate says: "You're not even in the phone book. I checked. Only the funeral home."

"Because—" Because after it all happened, the phone would not stop ringing. Literally, every time you put it back on its base, it rang right away. It rang in your hand. And when we stopped answering it, people just showed up at our door. They showed up at our *windows.*

The notepad that Mom keeps stashed in the rooster is headed "Fresh Undertakings." I doodle in a couple of extra gravestones, add a cross to a coffin lid. I can't find any words. Agate and I have been talking through the What When Where Why How of our message for a couple of weeks without getting anywhere really, but suddenly I'm stuck in that four-minute world and I don't even have a question for her.

"Simon," says Agate, "I'm bringing you a puppy."

I find words. "Agate, you can't. I totally need to check with my parents, and they're gonna say *no pets.*"

"It's not for a pet," she says. "It's for socialization. You keep it and take care of it and take it everywhere and teach it manners."

"How's that not a pet?"

"Because then you give it up for the service-dog program.

It's a good deed!" She sounds super pleased with herself. "You remember, I asked you before."

I remember that I didn't actually say no. I try to get a no out now. I mean, a dog, a puppy, yes, maybe. But giving it up, losing it—there's just no way.

"I'll be right over," says Agate, and hangs up before I can say anything at all.

• • •

I was going to try to intercept Agate in the yard and tell her *actually no*. But what happens is that she shows up pedaling a weird black bike with one wheel in the back and two in the front and a wedge-shaped cargo compartment between the front wheels. Slaughter and Sons is at the top of the hill that comes up from the river, and Agate is practically fuchsia from pedaling. She gets off the cargo bike and picks up a box from the trunk-in-front thing. She looks so pink that I grab the box from her and sit her right down at the picnic table. Later I figure out that Agate is actually in pretty good shape, she just has that kind of flush that makes redheads look like they are developing heatstroke— but just then I don't know that and I think Agate might die.

She doesn't die. She smiles at me, then opens the lid of the box.

I can't help it—I look.

My breath catches.

The puppy inside is reddish gold, flop-eared and wide-eyed

and tiny. "It's the runt, isn't it?" I say. "Oh, man, he's my favorite."

"I know that," says Agate, which is weird because I never said so. She slips her hands under the puppy's rib cage and lifts him gently from the box. Then she fishes around in her fanny pack—because, like I said, no one told Agate it wasn't 1980—and brings out a green bit of padded canvas. She slips the collar part over the bewildered little fellow's head and then clips a plastic buckle under his front legs. "There you go," she says. "He's official."

I don't want to bond with the puppy, but I touch his head anyway and run a finger up the crease in his skull between his ears. "Wow, he's soft," I say.

Agate has gone from fully pink to just splotchy, and the curls that got plastered down from under her helmet are starting to spring back up. It occurs to me that I should get her some water, but before I can, my dad comes out the back door with a pitcher of dead-people punch and a weird expression on his face. Like a cross between *oh wow* and *no way*. It makes a crooked wrinkle between his eyebrows.

"Hello, Agate," he says. "What have we here?"

"Hello, Mr. O'Keeffe," she says, bouncing on her toes. "I brought Simon a puppy."

My dad looks at her, looks at the puppy, and turns his gaze on me.

"It's not a pet," says Agate. "My family breeds puppies for a service-dog program. They have to be socialized before they can start training. The puppy is male and he will be good for Simon's trauma and anxiety."

My dad shoots me a look. I try sending him a message with my face: *No, she doesn't know, and don't you dare tell her.*

But it's like how Agate knows the runt is my favorite. She gets it and I don't have to tell her.

Dad pulls himself together. "Well, you know, Agate. That's still a big commitment. Simon's mom and I will need to discuss it."

And speak of the devil, my mom is pulling up by the gate with groceries and embalming chemicals and some new patio furniture loaded in the back of the hearse.

"Look, Isobel," says Dad, flapping his hands. "Agate has brought Simon a very surprising puppy."

"Oh really?" says my mom. She opens the gate.

Over the edge of the hearse garage comes a furious hiss and then the questing head of our attack peacock.

Mom turns and throws her arms open, a kind of "come-at-me-bro" gesture that has been known to give pause even to Pretty Stabby. "Don't you dare," she says. "I will roast you like a Roman dinner."

"Hi, Mrs. O'Keeffe," says Agate.

"A puppy, Agate . . ." Mom answers. "That's . . ." She leans over the table, her hand on my shoulder. I look at the puppy, who is trying to chew off the strap that fastens his vest around his ribs. He has managed to work his whole lower jaw under it and is chomping busily. The puppy sees me looking and tries to look back, but his head is pinned against his chest now and he just topples over.

"Hey, don't do that," I say, and scoop up the little fuzz brain. I cradle his soft butt in the crook of one elbow and gently ease his jaw out of the strap. His needle teeth prick at my hand, and he slobbers on me. Aww, man. I wasn't going to get attached, but the truth is I am in love even before the puppy, belly up in my arm, lets loose a little fountain of pee to claim me.

"Oh boy," says Mom. And that's how I get a puppy.

I name him Hercules, son of Todd.

eight

a puppy side-quest

My first night with Hercules is awful. We think about training him to sleep in a dog crate, but a) we don't have a dog crate, and b) the thought of putting him in a tiny space where he's scared and can't get out is just way more than I can handle.

Mom drops a kiss on my head and tells me she gets that and she will find Hercules a couch. She does not mean "couch" the way a normal human would mean "couch": It's also what funeral directors call the padded inside lining of a casket. They are removable. (It's best not to ask why.) A few minutes later she comes back up with one that's baby blue and child-size.

It's not a terrible dog bed if you stop yourself from thinking about it too hard, and I have a lot of practice with that. Herc seems happy with it—or at least, he immediately starts destroying it with his needle-sharp puppy teeth. But when night falls . . . it's Hercules's first night away from his home and he is freaked out. He wakes up whimpering what feels like every half hour. I lean over the side of the bed—trying not to fall out—and pet him and whisper to him until he settles . . . and wakes up again in another half hour.

By morning I am a mess. Mom's in the living room making coffee at the upstairs espresso maker.

I throw myself down on the couch (the regular living human kind).

"Oh my God, Mom—what did we *do*?"

"*We* let *you* get a puppy, Simon. He'll grow out of it."

I throw my arm over my eyes. I feel different, like the world is different, like my body is different, like I'm on a secret annoying side-quest in a video game called *Comfort Your Puppy* and the art is different and the rules about motion and stuff are a little off. "I think my actual brain is throbbing."

"You're just tired."

I am. For sure I am. But also, it's my job to take care of Hercules and what if I can't? He's so little. What if I can't take care of him?

My mother can read my mind, I swear. "You're doing fine, Simon. He'll grow out of it." She sits down on the couch by my head. I feel myself tip backward toward her weight and open my eyes for the upside-down view of her. She's bent over a huge mug of coffee like a hungover vulture. Curtis got stoned on Wednesday, and Mom has had call-outs every night since. She looks worse than I feel—and I'm so tired I can taste color.

"Nine-thirty a.m. is a perfectly respectable time for a

72

nap, Simon," she says. "Let your dad look after Hercules for a few hours."

So I sleep until one. And when I wake up, I discover that puppy ears are like the silky edges on baby blankets, and—well, there's just no looking back after that.

It takes about a week for Herc to start to settle in. Of course, by the end of that week I'm an absolute zombie, but both my parents are happy to recount tales of Screamy, Colicky Baby Simon and tell me that it will all be worth it as a sacrifice for love.

My sleep's not the only thing getting sacrificed for (puppy) love. Herc chews on everything. In his first week he destroys seven socks and three pairs of boxers, two sections of the Slaughter and Sons turn-of-the-century woodwork baseboards, and his coffin-liner dog bed. The bed is the first to go. Mom says it wasn't meant for such an active user.

And then there is the pee.

Herc has no idea what to do with pee. I mean, besides let it out, obviously. He's got that down. Like, a couple times an hour he's got that down. But he has no idea where. I learn to watch him till he gets this Certain Little Look in his eye, at which point I have to stuff him under one arm like a football and rush him to the backyard. If he manages to "do his business" outside I go dancey-happy for him, saying, "Good business!" over and over. I get the impression he has no idea what he's done right, but he's happy I'm happy. One time he picks up a stick that's bigger than he is, and half-prances, half-staggers across the yard.

73

We get into a habit where first thing in the morning I scoop him up and carry him outside to prevent accidents. And then we sit for a while on the back step of a funeral home in Grin And Bear It, Nebraska, watching the world wake up together. Sometimes it's still chilly enough in the morning that I wrap a blanket around my shoulders, and Herc snuggles in.

It's like . . . you know how you feel about the puppies in the Super Bowl commercials? It's like that. Even more.

nine

attack of the Jesus Squirrel

One Wednesday, just before Easter and a couple of weeks into my puppy-centric life, my dad is talking on the phone when I come downstairs before school. My dad is not a morning person—many sackbut players aren't—but as deacon, he has a crack-of-dawn service on Wednesdays. He's already been to that and come back. Mom is sitting at the table, too, clutching her coffee, her chin in her hand.

Dad gives me a quarter-wave to say he sees me but can't talk. I wave back and grab the cereal.

"Mrs. Pellnor, truly," he says into the phone, "I don't think a squirrel *can* commit blasphemy."

I stop, standing by the kitchen table with the Cheerios in one hand.

"For a start," Dad says, "blasphemy is a mortal sin, and one cannot commit a mortal sin before the age of reason, which is seven. And squirrels don't live that long."

Behold, the confidence of a man who lives in a town with

no Google. Who knows how long squirrels live? No one. Who knows the technical definition of blasphemy? My dad.

"I *am* taking it seriously," Dad insists, and makes a mock sign of the cross at me. Dad *is* serious about this religious stuff, but he doesn't *take* it seriously. Hardly ever.

Whoever is on the other end of the phone is loud enough that I can hear her voice, though not what she's saying. She sounds like a principal telling us we should all just *think* about our behavior. Dad holds the phone a half-inch from his ear and waits it out. Finally he says: "I'm afraid you'll have to do that, then." Pause. "Yes. You have a good day, too."

He sets the phone back down.

"And best wishes to the door that hit you in the—" Mom starts.

"Yeah," Dad interrupts. "Mrs. P is calling the bishop. But she says that we should have a nice one."

"Oh, Martin. The old place is falling down. It's not your fault."

I can't hold it in anymore: "Dad, what happened?"

"A squirrel," says Dad. Mom gets up and heads for the coffee machine, and Dad takes her place at the table. "Some squirrels made a nest between the wall and the altarpiece, and one of them managed to chew into the tabernacle." He rakes his hands up through his hair, from his ears to the top of his head. "Which I know because when I opened the tabernacle this morning—"

"Oh no . . ." I swallow hard because I don't want to burst out laughing.

"When I opened the tabernacle, in front of Missus Dolores P. and the Blue Hairs, that fuzzy little bugger leaped out, landed on my chest, bit my hand, hit the ground, dove beneath the altar, and then kept going all the way up the nave."

My dad's hands are steepled right on the top of his head. One of them has Band-Aids on it. He tents and flattens his fingers a few times. Behind him the milk steamer is howling like a jet taking off. My mom has decided this is a full-on cappuccino morning.

I hesitate: "In the tabernacle, did he—"

"Eat the Host?" says Dad. "Yes, he did."

"Was it—"

"Consecrated?" says Dad. "Yes, it was."

This is important because Catholics believe that consecrated altar bread—the Host—is actually turned into the body of Christ. Which is why we keep it in a super holy gold-plated (but evidently not squirrel-proof) cabinet.

"What, uh, happened to the squirrel?"

"That squirrel is now thirty percent Jesus by volume," says Mom. "It's our new god."

"Isobel!" Dad goes through the motions of being offended. A squirrel might not be able to commit blasphemy, but Mom has it *down*.

"I made you a mocha," my mom says, sliding the concoction in front of Dad and dropping a kiss onto the mess he's made of his hair.

I think before everything that happened my mom was on

better terms with God. Once, a long time ago, I overheard my dad describe her to someone as a mix of holy mystery and embalming fluid. But she's sharper now than she used to be. A little rubbing alcohol in the mix.

"The squirrel," my dad answers me, "got away."

"And in related news," says Mom, "your dad is going to the hospital in North Platte to begin a series of rabies injections."

"Isobel, I can't," he says. "Tomorrow is Holy Thursday. It's so busy—"

"Rabies is a ticking time bomb," says Mom. "You're going."

My mom and dad always say that they have an agreement: They make life-and-death decisions together, but Mom gets to make the death decisions all on her own. Dad goes.

• • •

So here's the deal with my dad and his job at the church.

Dad's first big day at St. Barbara's was Ash Wednesday—the day when Catholics get holy ashes dabbed on their foreheads to remind everybody about death, and also as a town-wide spot check on who actually goes to church.

Dad helped the parish priest distribute the ashes. How it works is people get out of the pews on either side of the church and make two lines up the main aisle to walk up to receive their death schmear. Dad did one line and the priest did the other. When they were done, the right half of the church had dainty little smudges of ash between their eyes and the left half of the church—Dad's half—had big, wild crosses that spanned their whole foreheads, like the Xs on pirate maps.

A little holy chaos.

Kind of the first hint that he might not blend in to his empty field.

They kept him anyway, though. The parish priest, Father McGillicuddy, is, like, 105—plus St. Barbara's shares him with another parish in the next county over, so they are seriously understaffed. A deacon isn't as good as a priest but still a lot better than nothing. Soon the parish council had roped Dad into adding a brass section (featuring sackbut) to the choir, running a First Fridays thing, and supervising the classes for the kids who are going to take new sacraments.

Like I said, he even serves morning Mass on Wednesday, and regular Mass every other Sunday. Deacons can do that, pretty much, if a priest consecrates the Host ahead of time. Though, apparently, it helps if the tabernacle is squirrel-proof.

• • •

When I get home from school that afternoon, Mom is on the phone talking to my dad, who is calling from the hospital in North Platte.

I hear that and of course my brain goes straight to disaster and I have to do breathing exercises, but my mom has got an arm around me and is simulcasting the phone news to keep me from panicking and it's *just vaccine shortage* yada yada *spoiled refrigeration batch* something something, and the upshot is Dad has to go to Omaha or Denver.

Since, of course, no one in my family ever wants to go back to Omaha, Dad picks Denver, and he's totally fine, but he's going to be away for three days.

"Just like Jesus," Mom says.

I can hear the phone say, *"Isobel!"*

There's a little more conversation. Mom tells Dad that the squirrel that bit him has not been captured and tested for rabies, so he definitely still has to get shots. (Apparently the squirrel has black tips on its ears and tail, so they'll know it if they catch it, but they haven't. Mom has dubbed it the Jesus Squirrel.)

Dad tells Mom that it's a disaster that he's missing Holy Week. Tomorrow, Holy Thursday, is the most elaborate and involved Mass of the year, and Friday is the ever-popular think-about-suffering-and-feel-guilt service, and Saturday is the Great Vigil, which features fire and darkness and up to nine Scripture readings and the ceremony where we make the Ash Wednesday ashes and another one where we welcome converts, and the whole thing takes hours. Now is exactly when St. Barbara's needs its deacon, and if it were, like, a store or an office or something, they'd probably fire Dad for ditching them during peak season, even though his excuse involves rabies.

They might fire him anyway, but probably not, because who else wants to do his job?

Anyway, at that point Mom hands the phone to me. I need to hear Dad's voice because, you know, he's in a hospital and I can't get to him, and that makes me a little nervous. "I'm totally fine, Sy-o," he says. "It's just shots, but it's so far that it makes sense to stay in Denver. Want to come? I could pick you up from GNB on the way by."

School will be closed on Friday, and a trip out of Grin And Bear It is tempting. We only have the hearse and the body-moving van normally, so trips to the urban paradise of, say, Ogallala, are pretty rare. So I kind of want to say yes. But the city—even this not-Omaha city—will have things I'm not sure I'm ready to see again. There will be sirens, and I might have to go with Dad to the hospital, which will have that smell, and—

Mom puts a hand heavy on my shoulder, grounding me hard, and over the phone Dad gives me the perfect out. "Assuming Hercules is ready for the big city, of course."

He's not. No way is he ready.

"Good," I stutter. "You know what, good point. Herc and me are good here, Dad."

But when I hang up, I realize that I'm looking down the barrel of a extra-long weekend with no school and no YouTube and not really anything to do. I've read all the manga at the mighty GNB library. It's too late for my mom to call her sister and order up an Amazon package of DVDs or books or Lego. It's too rainy for outside stuff. And obviously I'm too big for the Easter Bunny. "Hey," I say, "can I have Kev over Friday? Like, to stay over?"

Mom brightens. *Simon does another normal thing!*

You know . . . I wonder if I'm ever just going to be normal, without anyone celebrating it, the way I hope someday my puppy will pee and I won't have to wiggle around saying, "Good business."

Good tweenager, Simon, Mom's face says as she beams at me. It's almost like nothing happened to me at all.

ten

in which there are snacks and space aliens

The school is closed on Good Friday, and right after lunch Kevin shows up with his backpack and a sleeping bag, a Tupperware thing of cookies his dad made, and a bag of Cool Ranch Doritos. His being there gets us both out of going to church to contemplate the suffering of Jesus. We do Lego instead. I have a new build that I've got laid out— it's this great reissue of the *Star Wars* Y-wing. I show Kev the basics and he's decent at it: patient with the fiddly bits. He says it's basically analog Minecraft. We talk creepers and complain about school—for instance, how much it sucks that Miss Rose has us doing an independent-reading book report over our long weekend.

I am reading *Holes*, because I read *Holes* last year and can recycle my report. Dad was in charge of that project in my homeschool period, and since he's off avoiding rabies, there is zero chance he will notice. Kev, on the other hand, is reading one of those books with both a dog and an award sticker on the cover. "Oooh, bad sign," I say. "When dog books get a sticker, it's because something awful happens to the dog."

Kevin pulls his book out of his pack and we evaluate the cover. The award sticker is gold and shiny. The dog has big, soulful eyes.

"Oh man, Sy," says Kev. "This hound is going *down*."

Right then, Hercules whuffles in his sleep, chasing dream rabbits. He gets his short little legs going so fast that he shimmies right off the edge of his dog bed, rolls twice, and ends up on his feet, blinking his big eyes at the world.

"Ladies and gentlemen," says Kev, like he's introducing a pro wrestler. "It's Herc-U-Lees!"

Herc focuses, spots Kevin, and comes bumbling right over, his ears up high and his tongue out. Kev feels the same way about Hercules that Herc feels about Kev, and by the time the puppy has crossed the room, Kev is down on the floor. Herc woofs with delight and wiggles in close to Kev's face, licking his cheeks and his hair.

"Why," Kevin asks him, baby-voiced, "why would any author want to hurt you and make us cry, huh? Herc, huh? Why would they be so mean to puppies, boy, why?"

"Do you want to trade books? Mine's about kids in prison."

"Bet that's got a sticker, too." Kev looks disgusted—or as disgusted as a person can be when being licked by an ultra cute puppy.

84

"Get up before he pees on you," I tell Kevin. "He's been asleep a couple hours so he needs to go out, like, right now." There are certain things about puppy training you learn the hard way.

Kev does a totally unnecessary kip-up, flipping to his feet just because he can. I clip a leash to Herc's harness. Outside it's gray and sort of halfway to sprinkle-mist, but pretty warm.

"Okay if we go up Main?" I ask. "Herc's still got umbrellas on the list."

Agate gave me this long list of things, like umbrellas, that I have to expose Herc to. I'm working my way through them.

I am not training Herc for his future service-dogging. I mean, it's all I can do just to teach him that he should do his business outside. But Agate has explained that he is in the middle of his "fear imprint stage." That's when puppies leave their den and their mother shows them what things in the world are safe and what things are scary. If they see something and get scared of it, they might be scared of it for life. But if they *don't* see it, later they might not be able to trust that it's safe. My job is just to be Herc's mom and stick close and keep him happy and show him as many of the safe things as I can. If he gets scared at all, my job is not to push it, just to whisk him away.

Anyhow, Hercules has had a nap and he seems chill and happy, so he should be ready for a drama-free glimpse of an umbrella, if anyone's got one up.

The funeral home is a block off Main Street, on the corner of Third and Willa Cather. We're about five blocks up from the river, and only about three from the center of town, from mighty landmarks like the *Plain Talk* office and the library and Grin And Top It Pizza. We walk along the edge of the Slaughter gardens and go down Cather. Daffodils are spilling through the wrought iron, little drips on the ends of their flower noses. Herc pees on them. Pretty Stabby paces beside us, looking stupid and murderous.

We get to Main and head down. Hercules's legs get tired after a couple of blocks, and I pick him up and he's snug and safe. We head down the street and we *do* see someone there with an umbrella, plus a pickup, some cars (of course), and some teens who are risking being out on their bicycles, even though it's halfway to rain. We see a flag flapping and another dog, and Hercules isn't scared of any of it.

We stop at the Hello Hello and get ube milkshakes—Herc is an old pro at the howl of espresso machines—and in the parking lot we run into Agate, who is wrapping her family's library haul in reusable plastic bags and piling it into her weird cargo bike.

I put Herc down so he can greet her, and he wiggles so hard he can hardly keep in a straight line as he runs over.

I've been going over to her family's farm on the regular—April on a farm is super busy, especially with her dad away on the road, so she can't come see me. It's an okay way to spend time. She coaches me through the Herc stuff, and we

86

talk about how to fake a message from space aliens. You know, like you do.

Honestly, we haven't made a lot of progress on Project Little Green Preteens. We know the thing about four minutes, but we don't know how to make a signal, or what to say that will make us sound like aliens, or any of that. When I see Agate in town, right here by the site of junior-scientist-SETI-funding panic, it gives me a little jolt—like hearing a clock strike when you're trying to sleep. Like time might be running out.

Hercules finishes rubbing his face on Agate's ankles and starts chewing on the tongue of her left sneaker. "Hello, Hercules," Agate says, peeling the canvas flap out of Herc's mouth and giving him a scruffle. She looks up at us. "Hello, Simon. Hi, Kevin Matapang."

Agate and Kevin know each other, of course they do. It's a small town and they've been in the same school who knows how long. They're in the same homeroom and English class right now. But just then I realize that even though I hang out with Kevin, and I hang out with Agate, I don't hang out with Kevin *and* Agate. I'm just myself with both of them, but I'm not sure it's the same self. I'm not sure how to be.

Agate doesn't seem sure, either. She is looking at Kevin like she's looking at a litter of puppies and deciding which one to pick. "What," she asks him, "is the most disgusting thing you know?"

"That's easy: Latham's going pro."

Agate tilts her head at him. "I don't understand that."

"The quarterback for the Huskers? Who took us to twelve and two last year? He's going pro as a junior. He'll be in the draft, like, next week."

"I still don't understand that." If Kevin were a puppy, I don't think he'd be getting a new home today. Agate pivots to me. "Simon, what's your new disgusting thing?"

"Some undertakers put bras on the body before they embalm women. 'Cause otherwise things kind of slide—" I put my hands in front of my chest and then slide them out toward my armpits. "But the smart undertaker has a different plan."

"No, see," says Kev, deep in the football groove and trying to drag us all into it with him, "the team's going to have to start all— Wait, what?"

"The smart undertaker," I say, "uses duct tape."

Kevin sputters, and Agate bounces on her toes and beams: "You win!"

"You don't have one?" I ask her.

"I was going to tell you about duck genitals, but you would still win so there's no point now."

"Random, much?" Kev is shaking his green curls. "Seriously: You guys are so random."

"I was going to go to the funeral home and tell Simon about prime numbers," Agate says. "But your mother works at the telescope. So I am not sure."

"Agate, Kev's okay. He's my friend."

"So you think I *should* tell him about prime numbers?"

88

That stops me. Should we tell Kev about the space message conspiracy?

I don't know.

No, I *do* know. I don't want to tell him. It's not that I think he'll blow it—it's that I don't want him to think I'm crazy. Or have any reason to check out anything that might have left me a little crazy. The space alien thing doesn't seem too weird when I'm with Agate, out between the emu meadow and the giant telescope. But here and now, it *is* weird.

"I want to hear the duck thing," Kevin says.

"Were you heading to Slaughter?" I ask Agate, interrupting on purpose because I know the duck thing is going to be weirder than Kevin is counting on, and I want my friends to be friends. Also: "Heading to Slaughter" sounds wrong. It's so ridiculous that we live in such a teeny town that we're not allowed to change the extremely inappropriate name of our funeral home because people are used to it. On the other hand, *I'm* getting used to it.

My brain is working emergency overtime, and I feel like my teeth might start chattering.

"My mom's ordering pizza," I tell Agate. "You could come."

"I like pizza," says Agate factually. "Can I pick all the toppings off and eat them separately?"

"Sure." I pick Hercules back up and kind of lean and shuffle in a homeward direction, hoping Agate won't start talking about pulsars.

Kevin does a pirouette to follow me, and Agate pushes her weird bike along beside us as we walk up the sidewalk, under the awning and flags of Main Street. The rain or something has made Agate's hair even wilder than usual: It's so frizzed that it stands straight out from her head like a dandelion puff. She looks sidelong at Kevin and me. "Do you want to know the disgusting things I know about pepperoni?"

"Man, don't ruin pepperoni for us!" exclaims Kev.

I guess now we're an us.

We—all of us—head for Slaughter. That's good. I think that's good.

• • •

I don't know about Agate, but Kevin and me and Mom at least are supposed to be fasting for Good Friday—abstaining, technically, from what my dad calls sweets, treats, and meats.

We were already not doing a very good job on this—what with the milkshakes and the bag of Doritos and all—but Mom hits the letter of the law by leaving the pepperoni off the pizza order.

She lets us hang out by ourselves in the upstairs living room, sprawling on the old sofas with paper towels instead of plates. Since we can't have Netflix or anything like that, there's a DVD player (radio-astronomer-approved!) and a stack of movies and stuff. Kevin plops down and starts sifting through them. Agate kneels beside him. She's wearing another home-printed sweatshirt, this one of a badger blowing on a dandelion, captioned *The Hufflepuffiest*.

The two of them go through the piles of DVDs together. My parents have a lot of classic horror—stuff like *The Twilight Zone* and *The Outer Limits*—which Kevin's into but I veto. I have Lego movies that I'm into, which Agate vetoes, and all eight Harry Potters, which Agate's into but Kevin vetoes. It takes us so long to pick that the pizza grease starts to gather in little pools on top of the cheese.

Then, a breakthrough: "Here, look!" Agate exclaims, waving one of the DVD boxes in the air, practically bouncing on her toes even though she's kneeling on the rug. "Look!"

Kevin takes the box out of Agate's hands and cracks it open, plucking the DVD loose from its peg thing and popping it into the DVD tray. Only then does he pass the box to me. The movie they've picked is called *Contact*. The cover features a man and woman gazing seriously at nothing, in front of a line of radio telescopes.

Uh-oh.

Kevin zips through the start-up menu and launches in, and neither one of them notices that I haven't actually said yes to this.

"I'm going to take notes," says Agate, rapturous.

"And I'm going to make fun of the whole thing," says Kevin. "I have so much SETI pressure built up in my DNA—this is perfect."

The movie starts to play. It opens with a baby being born,

and the mom dying. Agate sits on the edge of the couch cushion and gets a mini notebook out of her fanny pack. Kevin throws himself down beside her. By the time they're settled, the baby with the dead mom has become a little girl and she's hanging with her sad-wise dad and their ham radio.

"Traumatic backstory time!" Kevin grabs another pizza slice and uses it to point at the screen. Movie dad has the same eyes as the dog on the book cover with the sticker. "I give pops there, like, five minutes max."

Herc is out cold on the rug, doing that full splay thing that only puppies can do, with his hips all the way out and his belly pressed to the floor. I ease myself down next to him and put my hand on his neck.

"The thing about prime numbers," says Agate, "is that they are very unlikely to be generated by natural sources."

"Hey!" Kevin objects. "Spoilers!"

"Kevin Matapang, mathematical facts are not spoilers."

"Yeah, okay, fair."

The movie is setting up sad-wise dad for a car crash. Kevin was right, it took about five minutes.

"But because they are not natural, they are one of the things SETI scientists are interested in," says Agate.

"What?" I say.

Sad-wise dad drives. My hands are going numb, which means bad stuff is sneaking up on me. I am not a huge fan of traumatic backstories. On-screen, a logging truck appears. Sad-wise dad swerves to miss a deer. The logging truck is coming around the corner.

92

"I can make popcorn," I say. "Popcorn, anybody?"

They say yes and I leave—okay, I bolt out of the room—and go downstairs to make popcorn in the radio-astronomy-approved stove-top fashion. I do that sensory grounding exercise where I name five things I can see, and four things I can touch, and by the time I get down to one thing I can taste it's popcorn, and I'm okay to go back upstairs.

It's been about ten minutes. Agate drops her head over the arm of the couch and beams at me when I come in with the bowl. "You missed the romantic subplot."

"Yeah, I have, like, zero interest in romantic subplots."

Kevin has moved onto the floor to hang with Herc, and as promised is yelling at the TV: "Man, you don't *listen* to radio telescopes. That's not what *radio* means." On-screen, the woman from the DVD cover is out in the desert, wearing a big sun hat and earmuff headphones. She is listening to her radio telescope. She has a look of dawning wonder.

"Is she the girl from before?" I ask.

"So far she's the only female character," says Agate. "Do you know what happened to Jocelyn Bell Burnell after she discovered pulsars?"

"To the who who discovered the what?" says Kevin.

"Jocelyn Bell is a scientist who built this radio telescope and found the Little Green Men number one signal," says Agate. "It turned out to be a new kind of star, called a pulsar."

I know who Agate means—her hero, the girl scientist with the sledgehammer—but Kevin probably doesn't.

93

Or maybe he does, because he asks: "So? What happened to her?"

"Nothing," says Agate, with smug outrage. "But her graduate supervisor got a Nobel Prize."

"Wow," says Kevin. "Jerk much?"

I put the popcorn down on the couch next to Agate and sit across the bowl from her. Kev sits on the floor between our legs with his back against the couch, Herc in his lap.

On the screen, the scientists are all getting super-duper excited. They have a row of big radio telescopes, and the disks are turning like sunflowers, slowly swiveling to catch a piece of sky. The telescopes are majestically slow, but the jargon is flying fast. "Hydrogen times pi," someone says. "Sidereal," says someone else, and the word makes my heart skip as it goes by.

The radio astronomer is cracking it now: "Seventy-nine . . . eighty-three . . . ninety-one . . . they're all primes, no way that's a natural phenomenon," she says. Her team is going wild around her.

Agate gets so excited that she stands up so she can toe-bounce. She taps the top of my head over and over like an excited woodpecker. "Told you."

This is the point she was trying to make about prime numbers. "What even is a prime number?" I ask. I know Mom taught me about them in sixth-grade homeschool, but somehow they've left my brain since.

Kevin rattles it off: "A number with no factors except one and itself. Like, you can't divide them by anything."

"I can explain later," says Agate, still standing, bouncing. Kevin grabs more popcorn.

On-screen they are saying a lot more stuff about the signal, a bunch of details that add up and make them sure the prime numbers are a message from aliens. Agate sits with her stubby pencil poised over her little notepad, but she's too engrossed to actually use it.

We watch. The smug bad guy scientist arrives right on cue, ready to steal the woman's Nobel Prize. "He cut her funding while you were making snacks," Agate explains.

Kev boos Bad-Guy Smug and chucks popcorn at the screen. "Who believes in SETI now, jerk-wad?"

Agate's loving this side of Kev, I can tell. Apparently they talked geek shop while I was making popcorn, because she leans over and taps Kev on top of his green spikes.

"Hey, tell Simon about your science fair project."

Kevin tips his head backward until his spikes brush the popcorn bowl. Upside down, he looks at me. "Hey, Simon, do you want to hear about my science fair project?"

"The 'why do Hot Pockets turn to lava inside?' project?"

Kevin's features crumple dramatically, and he rolls his eyes. "My mom is 'helping me refine it,'" he says, making the air quotes big. He tells me how his mom has him measuring the microwave radiation emitted both inside and outside the microwave. He's using rolls of cash register paper. If you spray them with water, they turn black when the microwaves hit them.

He tells me all this in a sort of stiff way, like he's already practicing for his science fair presentation. Based on the time I've spent with his mom, I can totally see how science fairs are high stakes for him.

Back in the movie, the message is definitely from aliens, everyone knows, and things have gotten political all of a sudden. Scientists and national security people are yelling at each other. The message involves Hitler, somehow.

Kevin flips his head back down. "Wait, where did Hitler come from?"

"Hitler is a not-important part," says Agate.

"Tell that to Poland," says Kev.

The movie has drummed up a second female character, who works for the president. New Character makes an Angry Military Guy back off a little and then Woman Radio Astronomer is in charge of the world. Agate glows in her direction for a minute, then scoops up more popcorn and issues a command to Kevin: "Tell Simon about the Australia thing."

"Oh," he says. "So this is a good one. There's a SETI project in Australia that spent *forever* trying to figure out the source of this one signal. It turned out to be the janitor in the maintenance shed fixing coffee in a defective microwave."

"They thought the signal was from space?"

"They were pretty sure it wasn't, because it never happened nights or weekends. But apparently the frequency of defective microwaves is bang-on alien. It took them seventeen years to figure it out."

Agate looks at me, big-eyed, and nods her head so fast that she vibrates, like a plump red-headed hummingbird. I know what she's thinking: *Behold, the signal maker for our fake alien message!*

My stomach drops hard, because Kevin is the only person I know with a microwave. When Agate finds that out, it's going to be—

On-screen, the desert compound with the radio telescopes is ringed with media trucks and emergency vehicles and crowds and crowds and crowds of people. Some of them are shouting about God or whatever.

I am suddenly not sure I want to do this.

I'm not even sure I want to see the rest of the movie.

Hercules wakes up, and it's like someone flipped a switch. He's up and zooming, tearing in circles around the couch and coffee table and tangling all our legs. Then he slows like someone dropped him into a lower gear and starts heading for the back of the couch again: a danger sign.

An escape hatch.

"Time to pee!" I say—sort of announce, really.

Kevin snorts at me: "Hey, man, thanks for sharing."

"I mean the puppy, doofus." I get up from the couch and Kevin levers himself up to steal my spot.

I click my tongue at Herc and leave my two friends sitting on the couch with the popcorn, watching Agate's SETI-gets-a-message plan turn into my personal nightmare on my family's flat-screen TV.

eleven

in which we need to talk about microwaves (but don't)

Okay. I don't know why it didn't occur to me that faking a message from space aliens would get all kinds of bad attention. Maybe I'm like an old-school computer and I only have one slot labeled *bad attention* in my brain, which was already filled.

But, whatever. Now that the switch is flipped, my brain is going six directions at once about Agate's fake message project. What if we fake a message and we get swarms of media and crowds of people talking about God in Grin And Bear It? What if we *don't* fake a message and Kevin's mom doesn't get her funding and all the junior scientists at the Hello Hello have nervous breakdowns and the town gets the internet back and all my classmates learn how to google? What if, what if, what if? My brain specializes in disaster spiraling, and oh boy is it circling the drain.

Meanwhile, Agate's just excited. She's doing all this

research. She gets her dad, when he's away on the road, or her sister, Jade, in college to send her printouts of articles and Wikipedia pages. She keeps saying things like "Math is the universal language!" and "Microwaves are perfect!" She dimples and she glows, and I don't want to crush that. I like having friends again.

I don't want these ones to get hurt.

So, I pull the Simon Says special. I don't decide—I hide. I dodge heading to Agate's farm. I twist conversations so that space aliens don't come up, which in Grin And Bear It is harder than you'd think.

I do have one secret weapon though: A week after Easter it's time to start bringing Herc to school.

I strap him in his future-service-dog vest. I stash liver treats and poop bags and a collapsible water dish in my backpack, and I brave the wild hordes of GNB Upper. Herc and me get coos and grins in the hallway, and when we get to homeroom we are instantly swarmed. Miss Rose with her Disney Princess attitude toward furry critters just lets that happen, and for a second it's scary—the whole class coming at me, like they're going to pile on.

But of course that doesn't happen. Everyone just wants to see Herc, who at twelve weeks old has reached a new peak of ball-of-fuzz cuteness. He even has his tongue blepping out. Everyone loves him. Even Football Brent is making goofy heart eyes.

On the other hand, people are standing awfully close.

"Okay, okay," I say, scooping my puppy into my lap.

99

The whole class falls quiet, like they did for the alpaca story back on day one. "This is Hercules. He's going to be a service dog."

"Usually you shouldn't interact with service dogs, because it distracts them from their work," says Agate, in her expert voice, with her heel-drum. "But Hercules is being socialized, not trained, so it is okay to pet him so he learns that people aren't scary."

Except that people *are* kind of scary. Or at least, Herc seems to think so. A squeal went through the class when Agate said people could interact with my dog, and his soft little shoulders got all hunched. I let a couple of people pet him—"One at a time, one at a time!" I scold—but after a moment we have to take a break. I go to the back of the classroom and sit on the floor with my puppy in my lap while the bell rings and everyone says the Pledge of Allegiance, and I look at the world from a brand-new angle.

And that's how it goes all day, all week. People love up my puppy, and if he gets scared—if they come swooping in from over his head, for instance, which happens a lot, because he's teeny—I get to tell those people to back off a little. I sit on the floor with Herc and massage the floppy part of his neck until he relaxes enough to bumble off to meet the next person and get petted. Then I give him a treat.

In a single week I go from being the new kid who lives with dead people to the new kid who brings a puppy to school. People still don't know what team to put me on, but they like puppies, so: major upgrade.

Maybe that's why school seems so different all of a sudden. I don't know. Hercules is growing fast, but he's still super small. When I try to imagine what his world looks like, it looks bigger.

• • •

But then suddenly it's May.

What's weird is that I got so busy with thinking about Agate's space message plan and socializing Herc that I forget to count down to the anniversary and brace myself and all that stuff. But it's like my body remembers even though my head forgets. 'Cause all of a sudden I'm not sleeping so good, and loud sounds are like needles heading for my eyes—they just totally freak me.

The week before the anniversary, Agate slips me another note at the end of English.

Like always, I unfold it behind my locker door. After all, it's from Agate. She still hasn't broken out her disgusting thing about duck genitals. A note from her could say *anything*.

What it says is: *Simon we need to talk about microwaves*.

At the word "microwave" my heart fires up at maximum power and starts to throw off sparks.

Okay. Okay. Agate is my friend, and there is no reason to panic. I do a little counted breathing. At the bottom of the note Agate has added some emojis—hand-drawn, because radio astronomy. Goat, Goat, Barn, Rocket Ship. There's a drawing of a clock again, and it says 10:00. It's Friday, so 10:00 must be tomorrow morning.

I have until tomorrow morning to figure out what to say to Agate.

It doesn't feel like it's going to be enough time.

I don't sleep—again—but I go to Agate's in the morning anyway, because I actually have learned some things in all my therapy, one of which is that putting stuff off just makes it bigger. This is big enough. My heart-brain system is on high alert, like a meerkat.

Thanks to my dad, my bike is fitted with one of those trailer-tent thing you use for little kids so that I can use it to take Herc places. We had to take it slow at first. This is the key with future service dogs: Once they pass the fear imprinting stage, they have to have "positive socialization experiences." So when something new is too much for Herc, we have to back off and take it super slow, like do the same thing but in a less intense way so that he can ease into it.

It took us a while to get to "positive experience" with the bike, but now we've been at it a couple of weeks and Herc is hanging his head out the side of the bicycle trailer, with his little ears flapping and his eyes squinting closed with puppy joy. I'm so proud of him.

I still haven't decided what to say to Agate. Agate being Agate, I'm probably not going to get to ease into it.

When I finally get down to Goat Goat Barn Rocket Ship, aka the Van der Zwaan farm, it's way busier than usual—which is saying a lot. Agate's mom is outside, and so are her older brother and sister. The babies are in a playpen under the crab apple tree. But most of all, the yard is full of goats.

"Close the gate!" at least two people shout at me when I open the gate. I get my bike through in a hurry and pull the gate shut behind me, fast.

Agate's family raises goats. I know that. It was one of the first things she told me, and it's on the sign over the driveway, and there have been goats around every time Agate and me were talking space aliens. Nevertheless, I can't say I've thought about goats much.

Now I think about goats.

They are Angora goats, which means (Agate explained once) that they are grown for their fur or wool or whatever, instead of for milk or meat. If that's true, the Van der Zwaans are going to be rich: The goats have so much curly dirty gray fur that they look like Muppets with horns and noses. Pink ears stick out from near the horns, and two buckteeth stick out from beneath the nose. They are milling around the farmyard while Agate's little brother Onyx rides through them on a tricycle, whacking them on their butts with a bit of rope and trying to yodel.

What's obviously happening is that the goats are getting sheared. Over by the barn Agate's mom—whose first name is Pearl—has one clamped between her knees and is going at it with huge electric clippers. It is bleating. Baa-ing? Anyway, it's making a noise like it's getting murdered and finds getting murdered kind of annoying. She finishes and lets it go. It wobbles up and then shoots off, weirdly skinny and totally outraged, like a cat that's just been dunked in a water bucket.

Agate un-headlocks the goat she is holding, passes it to her mother, and comes trotting over to me.

"Simon!" Something makes her stop short and look at me. "What is it? Is Hercules having a negative socialization experience?"

I glance back. "He's asleep, actually."

"Are you finding the goats triggering?"

"Nah, I'm good."

I'm not—my brain is going a million miles an hour. If my brain was a microwave, I would always smell like scorched popcorn.

Microwaves. Prime numbers. The fake message, the real funding, the media, the what if. I don't know what to say.

But I told Agate I was good and she trusts me, so she grins: "Mom, I have to go talk to Simon about a science project, okay?"

"No way," says Jasper. At least I think it's Jasper. Everyone in Agate's family has the same head of red curls, except her teenage twin sibs, Jasper and Coral. They are identical twins and have identical shaggy emo haircuts, dyed identical raven black. They make their own T-shirts (it's where Agate gets the screen-printing equipment), and they both play tubas in the marching band. Sometimes it's hard to tell them apart. Jasper is the boy. He's shearing a goat. He's a lot slower at it than his mother, and it looks more traumatic for the goat. It's thrashing. If I were Jasper I'd be regretting wearing black. And maybe every other

104

twist of fate that had brought me to this moment where I had to keep a goat locked between my knees.

The other twin, Coral, pauses from gathering up the fleeces and stuffing them into a burlap sack. She's also wearing black—a T-shirt on which a silhouette of Hogwarts is flying a Trans Pride flag—and even more covered with wool bits. "Mom, tell her no way." She puts her hand on her hip like Agate yelling at Todd. "You said this was an all-hands-on-deck job."

"We can spare Agate for half an hour," says Pearl.

"But that's not fair," says Coral.

"Fair exists only in baseball," says Pearl. She turns back to her shearing, and Agate takes the opportunity to flick out her tongue at Coral, like a lizard.

"Mom!" Coral whines. "Agate—"

"Coral, just you do your bit. Let me worry about your sister." Mrs. VZ lets go her latest goat and pauses to stretch for a moment, her hands on the small of her back. "Agate, half an hour. Check your watch, okay?"

Agate waves her wrist in the air. The watch is a serious-looking black digital number, huge on her dimpled wrist. She looks ready to start her four-minute Sidereal Subtraction right this second. I pick up Hercules, who is half asleep, and we strike out across the goat meadow. Coral shouts after us: "You better be on time, you weirdo."

"Yeah, well! Coral's not even a real stone!" Agate shouts back.

Herc yawns hugely and wiggles deeper into my arms.

"Where are we going?" I ask Agate. The goat meadow is sunny and everything, but it's also covered with goat droppings that I'm hoping to avoid having a socialization experience with, plus my brain is beeping and sending out sparks.

"We've got an old tree house on the property line there," says Agate, pointing to a windbreak full of trees. Then, like she can't contain it anymore, she spins around and grabs one of my arms, which makes me jump a little.

"Sorry!" she says, then bursts like when you accidentally open a Coke that's been shaken: "But, but, but: I have the best news! Vega rises right behind it."

I feel so overloaded that Kevin could use me for a science project. Also, I feel confused. In *Contact*, Vega is the place the message comes from. "From the movie? Vega's real?"

Agate blinks at me like she thinks I might be kidding. "Vega is the fifth-brightest star in the sky. It's been described since antiquity and its name is Arabic for 'falling vulture.' And it's perfect, Simon! I am trying to find the exact date, but in a month the tree house will be right on the line between Vega and the Very Large Radio Telescope."

"Okay," I say, because I don't know what else to say. This sounds like the *when* of the big plan. It's all coming together. What if it all comes together?

Hercules is awake. I set him down, get his leash out of my fanny pack—I take back what I said about Agate; fanny packs are cool—and clip him in. He is instantly drawn to the little pebbly piles of goat poop. "Leave it," I tell him, giving him a teeny tug. But "leave it" is a new skill for him and he doesn't have it down yet, and the goat droppings are totally puppy-fascinating. He's in deep snuffle mode. "Herc, leave it," I say, and give him another tug.

I do it a little too hard and he almost loses his balance, but he does look up at me. I slip him a liver treat. Agate's looking at me, too, like she saw that jerky tug. But she doesn't say anything. We cross the field, clamber over the fencing, and head into the trees.

And there's the tree house. No matter what else my brain is doing, it's gotta take a beat and admit that the tree house is awesome. It's a real teeny house complete with a cedar shingle roof and crazy mismatched windows, plus it has a big porch part with a railing. It's high up but there's a solid ladder. I tuck Hercules tight under one arm and climb it one-handed. Agate comes up behind me. The tree house is even sweeter on the inside. There's a crate full of books and a couple of beanbag chairs. I lower myself into one. I would have loved this when I was little.

I still kind of love it.

Hercules doesn't seem quite as sure. He didn't like the ladder, definitely. I spend some time massaging the back of his neck, which always calms him down. Meanwhile, Agate's done climbing. She flops into the other beanbag so hard that puffs of Angora goat wool (and to be honest a puff of Angora goat smell) fly into the sunbeams. Today she is wearing jeans and a mustard-yellow T-shirt that has a sloth drifting through space in a bubble helmet. It says

Slothed in Space. "Fun fact," she says, tapping her heels on the floor. "Vega. It said in the movie that Vega is twenty-six light-years away, but it's actually twenty-five."

"That's not a fun fact," I say. "Fun facts are things like 'possums have two penises.' Or 'rabbits have to eat their own poop to survive.'"

She lights up: "You've been finding me new disgusting things!"

I have, and they're not even all about corpses. My dad, expert in both Catholic liturgy and medieval brass instruments, says it's important to be well-rounded, so he brought me a complete set of old *Ripley's Believe It or Not* annuals from Denver.

But I don't want to talk about Denver. It's too much like Omaha.

I say: "What even is a light-year?"

"Just the distance light travels in a year," she says. "When we see Vega, we're seeing light that left the star twenty-five years ago."

Herc climbs out of my lap and goes snuffling around the tree house while I try to make twenty-five light-years fit inside my brain. "If we send a message that's supposed to be from Vega," I say, "how do we make it look like it's been traveling for twenty-five years?"

I am not quite sure why I say this—maybe I'm just looking for a reason this won't work, so I don't have to make a decision. Agate pauses like I've made a good point, though, and scrunches up her face. "I think we don't have to," she says slowly, like she's working it out as she goes. "I think— It's like when you see a photo, it doesn't look different because someone took it a while back and a long way away. You see it and it's the same. A photo is now."

She says that, *a photo is now*, and all my muscles tense up, as if someone's about to hit me. I find myself squeezing the back of my own neck, but it doesn't help me like it helps Herc. My puppy has bumbled out onto the porch part so I get up and follow him. Who knows how safe the railing is, right?

Agate follows me out.

"That can't be right," I say. "That when you see a photo you're seeing now—that can't be right." But that's not what I mean, exactly. I mean: I don't want that to be right.

Agate comes up to me and I feel the porch floor wobble. I take a step away from her, just in case. The railing is made of tree branches, not boards, and there are places where a puppy might squirm through. I scoop Herc up. He yips, alarmed. I'm squeezing him.

"Simon?" says Agate.

She scoots closer to me again, and again I feel the floor sag and creak. "Stop!" I tell her. "You're too—"

I stop myself before I tell her she's too fat.

Anyway I think I might mean *close*. She's too close.

She stops an arm's length away. "Simon, is this about your trauma and anxiety?"

"No," I snap.

"Are you worried about the red-shift implications of general relativity?"

A laugh puffs out of me, and I look at Agate. She's serious about the red-shift whatever, because of course she is, but she also has a look on her face like she's afraid I'll break if she touches me. "I just—"

There are times when the worst thing a friend can be is right. This is about my trauma and anxiety, because I have suddenly remembered the date. And I'm suddenly thinking about the photo. There's more than one, I know that. They are still the first things that come up if you google "Simon O'Keeffe." But there's this one. When they finally kicked the door in and shouted at everyone to raise their hands. The police body cam captured the exact second I saw everything, the exact second that they shouted, *Raise your hands*, and I did, but it was only me.

"I just—" I stutter. "Agate, I just want to be normal. I want to live my normal life in Grin And Bear It, Nebraska, with my mom and her dead people and my dad and his sackbut obsession and my service puppy Hercules and my friend who wants to fake a space message. Okay? I want to be the kid who has that life and not be Simon O'Keeffe ever again."

"But you are Simon O'Keeffe." She sounds baffled.

"I just—" I say, "I just want to be the one from now."

110

another note on time

I think there's never going to be a now.
I think there's always going to be a before, and an after.

twelve

in which teenagers are given craft supplies and left unsupervised

The actual anniversary, May 15—5/15—is on a Friday.

The leadership team gets in early on Wednesday the thirteenth so that they can pass out lengths of orange ribbon to everyone going into the school. (Orange is the memorial color.) They probably didn't think this through beforehand, because it quickly becomes a schoolwide where-is-the-most-ridiculous-place-to-put-a-ribbon contest.

There are ribbons caught on pencils that are poked into the ceiling tiles. There are ribbons on the basketball hoops in the gym. A couple of boys on the volleyball team have tied their ribbons into a ball and are playing keep-away in The Pits. Joyce from the leadership team stands in the middle with her binder, nearly in tears, saying, "You guys, you guys, that's so disrespectful. . . . Come on, you guys."

I'm kind of late getting to school, so when Juniper Higgins from the cheer squad shoves the ribbon into my hands, what she says by way of explanation is "*Don't* do anything stupid with it."

My first instinct is to tie the ribbon to the first thing I see and get rid of it, which is clearly what some people have done: The handrails on the steps leading up to the front door are fluttering.

I tie the ribbon to Herc's future-service-dog vest instead.

When I get to homeroom, Kevin has his wrapped around his head and tied into a big bow, which flops around among his green spikes. "Herc," he says, "great look. Rocking."

"Sure," I say. And then I have to leave for a second to go count some breaths in the bathroom. There are ribbons around the pipes that lead down to the urinals.

They're the one thing I can see.

• • •

By the end of the day, the school has got ribbons flying from the tops of the flagpoles, ribbons around the trophies in the (locked) trophy case, and ribbons taped into crime-scene Xs over the doors to the main office. A weird smell, like scorched feathers or burned spices, hangs in the air.

We're all called into the gym. They've pulled down the bleachers for the high-school students. Us junior high kids have to sit on the floor. At the front of the room there's a microphone on its stand, which generally means that either we're going to have a speaker or we're going to get yelled at about the way we treated yesterday's speaker.

I'm betting today's a yelling day.

Kevin has come with me from design and tech, and before we get totally settled, Agate slides in on my other side. Hercules is excited to be sitting on the floor and so happy to see both of them that he can't decide which way he wants to wiggle. Like they've scripted it, Kevin and Agate both reach in to pet him at the same time and end up with an ear each, scrunching me in the middle.

I now have a friend leaning on each shoulder, which is great, obviously, but which is also too much like a pile on. I can feel my stiff body getting stiffer.

Agate pulls back so she can look at me. "Simon," she whispers. "Are you okay?"

Agate needs remedial whisper training. Her voice carries at least three rows, and a bunch of people turn and look at me.

"I'm fine," I tell her, tell everyone.

This is the point where the narrator voice-over would say "He was not fine." Instead we get our principal, Ms. Snodgrass, marching up to the mic in her high-heeled boots.

I bet right: This is a yelling assembly. Ms. Snodgrass lists some of the places the orange ribbons have ended up. She tells us we need to *think* about what we've done.

"Seriously, though, man," says Kevin. He actually can whisper. "Are you okay right now?"

"Hardly ever," I say. I actually meant to say "good as ever," but like the narrator voice mentioned. . . . I think I might throw up.

Ms. Snodgrass says she's not angry, just disappointed.

114

(Spoiler: She is totally angry.) She says it happened right here in Nebraska and it isn't funny.

Then Ms. Hafsaas gets up. Ms. Hafsaas is the junior high gym teacher and the grade nine health teacher and the vice principal in charge of yelling at us, so I guess there's going to be more yelling.

"Sy?" Kevin murmurs. Herc pushes his way onto my lap and tucks his nose into my armpit. This is not good guide-dog behavior, but when I'm freaked out Herc loses track of what he's supposed to do and I lose track of how to keep him on track.

"Simon?" Kevin sounds really worried, like he's about to raise his hand and get help. I want to tell him I'm okay but instead I finger the orange ribbon on Herc's harness. It's silky, slippery.

"Is this about Vega?" Agate stage-whispers.

"Is this about what?" says Kevin.

Agate launches in—"Simon and me have this plan . . ." And I absolutely cannot deal with that right now, I cannot deal with being outed to Kevin as a Space Message Crazy, cannot deal with the What Ifs of sending the message, of not sending the message, not right now, and meanwhile Ms. Hafsaas is telling us that some of the orange ribbons got tied around the tailpipe of the school van.

"Agate," I say helplessly, and can't say anything after that. Ms. Hafsaas tells us that the tailpipe ribbons caught fire. Kevin turns sideways and is staring at me and Agate, and Agate is still explaining the space message thing, though

115

she's started way back with pulsars and sledgehammers, and Kevin looks baffled.

Ms. Snodgrass, of all people, saves me. She's been cruising the aisle like a shark. "Agate Van der Zwaan!" she bites out.

Agate yelps like a kicked puppy and shuts up.

"What you may not have heard," Ms. Hafsaas thunders, "is that I had fifty-seven pounds of turkey feed in the van. Because I keep turkeys. Because teaching you doesn't pay the bills, kids. It doesn't pay the bills."

Agate, who is not the kind of kid who gets yelled at very often, has turned pale. Kevin is goggle-eyed. Ms. Hafsaas says: "What you may not have heard is that the turkey feed also caught fire."

For a beat, the gym is totally silent and like everyone is holding their breath. Then Kevin starts shaking like he's sobbing, and all through the audience there's a kind of rumbling pause—and then a hundred kids burst into laughter, like a fireworks factory going up.

Hercules gets up and turns around. I ruffle my hand through his fur, saying, "Leave it, boy. Leave it."

The wave sweeps us, and then all at once is gone. Ms. Hafsaas sits down to plot vengeance. Ms. Snodgrass comes back to the microphone and pushes the boundaries of the church-and-state thing and asks us to all send our thoughts and prayers.

thirteen

5/15

I spend two days walking around school on orange ribbons and eggshells, but the actual day, 5/15, I don't even bother to try. I don't go to school. My parents don't ask me to go to school. My dad makes me French toast for breakfast and everything in the kitchen seems both too quiet and too loud. Like there's a poison fog that's going to keep any words from carrying, but also there's no air at all to block the sound of the eggs cracking on the side of the bowl, the bang of the skillet onto the stove burner. Even the little hiss and puff of the gas burner lighting is a lot.

Everything seems just too loud and too bright. And the French toast, which is my favorite, tastes as metallic as if it just came out of a tuna-fish can.

I end up lying on my bed, and then under it. It's kind of hot for May, but being wrapped tight in a blanket is a proven panic killer, so I do that. It doesn't help. My lips are numb and my chest hurts because I'm not getting enough air, because my own panic is going to crush me like an anaconda.

My parents try. I mean, I know they're trying. They take turns under the bed with me, not complaining about the laundry or even when they step on a Lego. Dad brings me cookies with my grilled cheese and jam.

After Pretty Stabby throws one of his alarm fits that leaves me almost blacking out, Mom goes, "That's it," and storms out. From the garden come the sounds of brief and fierce peacock combat. Dad and I lie under the bed and listen. After a while, Mom comes back and slides in on my other side.

She rolls to face Dad. Dad rolls to face her.

There's a long pause where we very definitely don't hear the peacock anymore.

"Isobel, you didn't . . ."

"I locked it in the hearse."

"It's gonna s-h-i-t all over everything," says Dad.

I pull the blanket down under my chin. "Uh, Dad? You know I can spell now, right?"

"My little boy," says my dad, theatrically. "All grown up."

My parents, one on either side of me, take each other's hands and close them over my chest.

"If he does, I'm driving him straight to the taxidermist," says my mother. "I'm donating him to an avian flu research program. I'm plucking his feathers and using them to fletch arrows. I'm gonna set those arrows on fire and—"

She stops short and makes a little gulpy noise that

118

sometimes she makes instead of crying. My dad joggles her arm back and forth. We all breathe together. There's a faint and distant sound that somehow makes me think of a screaming peacock trapped inside a hearse.

Mom lets Dad go and puts a hand in my hair. "Doing better, hon? Oh, hello—" The "hello" is for Herc. My mom has her head propped up on her hand and Hercules is shoving his nose through the little triangle made by her bent arm. Mom lifts her ear off her palm to admit a whole puppy head—and then the whole puppy wiggles through.

Hercules sniffs and snuffs his way up the gap between me and Mom, and then starts, gently, to chew on my hair. "Good boy," Mom murmurs, scratching his ears.

He's not supposed to come under the bed. But then, I'm not supposed to be under the bed either. Herc sticks his nose in my ear. It's weird; I wiggle.

Dad leans his weight along my other side, pressing into me like my dog does when he wants to be petted. He reaches across me to also scratch Herc. "Such a good boy . . ."

The puppy licks my neck, and Mom reaches past him to pat *my* head instead. "Your hair's just soaked," she says, weaving her fingers through it, teasing it into little spikes. "There's cortisol and adrenaline in fear sweat. I wonder if dogs can taste—"

"Mom, no science . . ." I mutter.

"Do you want a bath, boy-o?" asks my dad. "Sometimes that helps."

119

He's right, sometimes it does. And I'm gross with sweat, I know that. But. "I think—I want to take a walk." That seems unlikely, so I wait for a second for my whole body to go *no way*. But it doesn't. "Yeah. I want to take a walk."

I move. Dad slides out and climbs up so I can get out, too. My legs feel somehow both extra stiff and also rubbery, the way legs feel if you've run forever.

Hercules knows the word "walk" because he's a hecking genius. He comes prancing out from under the bed, stretches—downward dog, then upward dog, like a baby-fat yoga buddy—and then sits at my feet and grins up at me, mouth open.

"You sure, Sy?" asks Mom gently.

"I think—yeah."

"Alone?" she asks.

It would just kill them to send me out alone. I mean, they'd let me. But it would just kill them. And anyway: "Can we all go?"

"Sure," says my dad.

With Hercules bouncing in the lead, we creep down the stairs. We're all walking, like, extra careful—like we're in a horror movie and we're taking a poker to the basement to check out that weird noise. This is a crazy idea. And yet, there's something good about the way my feet hit the ground. I'm walking.

Two years ago, I was locked in a third-floor classroom with only one door, and I couldn't get out. But now I'm walking. We're walking.

120

We emerge into our backyard, blinking in the sunlight like cave people. There is the muffled sound of a desperate peacock, a pickup rumbling down Main Street, the wind. The real world, the now. We walk out into it together.

a note on lockdowns

I said we couldn't get out, back then.

The worse truth is: We didn't try. We did what they told us to do. We did what we had practiced. We waited. We hid.

We sheltered in place.

fourteen

in which Kevin googles alpacas

"Do you think I could get the parish to celebrate Ordinary Time?" Dad asks.

It's the Sunday after the Friday that is 5/15, and we have survived. We are on our feet.

It feels like a turning point.

The diocese has authorized urgent repairs to St. Barbara's. The squirrel nest has been removed from the paneling behind the altar, but it was uninhabited. The squirrels have relocated; they can sometimes be heard scrambling around inside the steeple. The Jesus Squirrel himself has not been seen since Easter. Dad jokes he has probably ascended into squirrel heaven.

Dad told this joke during his homily at Mass today, and even though it's pretty normal for Catholic homilies to start with humorous anecdotes, this one did not go over well with Mrs. Pellnor and her squirrels-are-blasphemous crowd. Dad has already had a call from the bishop's office.

He's doing some liturgical planning now, thinking out loud as he assembles the layers of a baked ziti in a Crock-Pot for dinner. I can tell he's out of sorts.

Mom's at the table and she's completely focused on her coffee. I am polishing off as many of the Pillsbury cinnamon rolls as I can before someone stops me. The kitchen is crowded in a happy way. Spring is sliding toward summer—next week is the last week of school. I've almost done it: I've almost survived my first year back.

"Celebrating Ordinary Time seems like a hard sell," says Mom. "Can you call it something else?"

"Not without, like, a permission slip from the Pope," I say. (You don't get raised by a liturgical planner without learning this stuff.)

"Anyway, the ordinariness is the point," says Dad. "Day-to-day life, one week at a time, without counting down to the great solemnities . . ."

Ordinary Time is the liturgical season between the Easter season and the Christmas season, and it's just numbered. It used to bug me back when my parents made me go to Sunday school. Hey, kids, today we're celebrating the 753rd Sunday of Ordinary Time with some pipe-cleaner crafts! But right now: "That sounds good to me. Like summer vacations."

Mom gets it. She smiles up at me over her coffee, and her smile turns wicked as she plucks the last cinnamon roll right out of my fingers.

"Hey!"

124

"You stole the other ones," she says. "You're lucky I don't take the hand." She tears a strip off the outer coil and just pops it into her mouth, like threatening to dismember your only child is a normal thing to do.

"Can I go to Kevin's?" I usually go straight home with Kev after Mass, but he didn't show up at church today. "Since the cinnamon rolls are *gone now.*"

Both my parents say "Sure" at the same moment, and both of them glance at each other, like: *Hey, look. We're doing a normal thing.* The last week of school, and the Sunday after that is Pentecost—we're almost to Ordinary Time.

• • •

Kevin lives across the river, all the way at the edge of town, which in mighty Grin And Bear It is like eight blocks. Even at puppy speed it doesn't take all that long to walk over.

His mom answers the door. "Oh," she says. "Simon." She smiles at me, but kind of pushes her lips together when she does it. It's an intense look, and for a second I wonder if she found out about Agate's space message, if she's about to yell.

I think she's about to say *Come in* when Zeny shows up behind her, shoots me a look, and goes: "Hey, Mom—can you look? This subroutine won't compile."

Dr. Matapang half-turns and in that second Kevin comes crashing out past her, onto the porch. He has dyed his green hair purple since I saw him Thursday—it's dark and deep and instead of being spiky it tumbles into his eyes. He shoves

125

it back and looks sideways at me. "Sy, my man!" He puts up a hand for a high five, and I plant one, 'cause I don't leave a friend hanging, even if I don't know what we're giving fives about. "I was gonna—I was just going to go for a walk. Okay, Mom? Simon and me are going to take a walk."

"Oh, of course, Kevin." Another weird smile. "You boys take care."

Behind her head Zeny mouths, *Run*.

We hustle off, heading for the back of the house. There's a laneway back there, behind all the garages, and past that is the scruffy rim of town—a gas station, a motel, a place called Heaven's Lawn that sells yard gargoyles and statues of the Virgin Mary, a couple of fruit-and-veg stands.

"What was that about?" I ask, when we're out of earshot.

Kev doesn't answer right away. We walk down the laneway, which is thin and weedy gravel: bike ruts and car ruts and the dry crackle-dirt hollows of puddles. Herc is doing pretty good at not pulling ahead or stopping to look at things. Kevin kicks a stone ahead of him, scuffing the red leather of his new sneakers. "My dad told me he used to kick a stone all the way to school and then back home," he says. "The same stone, both ways, until it was round. Took me forever to figure out it wasn't true."

I know it's hard for Kev, caught between his mom, who wants him to kick that rock so he'll "have *choices*," and his dad, who is happy being an unrounded stone. I know it's hard, but he doesn't talk about it, and I'm not going to be the guy that pushes him.

126

Kevin's got something to say now, though. I can tell even though he doesn't say it right away. His laces are undone, the shoe tongues flop as he walks. The laneway peters out and turns into a dirt path that's great for bikes. There are those flowers that look like lace doilies and smell like carrots. Grasshoppers go flying all around us. Almost summer.

Kevin kicks his stone again but loses it off the narrow dirt path. "Look, Sy," he says, squinting down at his shoes. "I was just looking for a video of the alpaca thing."

Herc freezes: He's spotted a garter snake. For a second I'm just watching that—snake freeze, puppy freeze—and Kevin's words don't sink in.

Then they do.

"Oh, man," I say—it's what he would say. I echo him helplessly, bending forward so I can keep breathing. "Oh man, Kev, oh man."

The snake has whipped off. Herc springs after it and comes up short on the end of his leash, and I don't even tug him back or tell him leave it; it's too late for that.

"Kevin," I say. My face is blazing like a pulsar. "You googled me."

"We had to go to Kearney—research for my science project, you know. My dad needed coconut strings and Zeny had these books she was getting on interlibrary loan, and my mom found these papers on microwave radiation she wanted me to read and—Sy, I was just looking for the alpacas. Like, you said the media was there, with the alpacas in the church and—"

"They were," I say. "They *were* there."

None of it was a lie. There were alpacas; they were on the local news. There was a tortoise making the world's slowest break for freedom and the owl that ended up in the rafters with the back half of a cat, and they had to call the fire department to get them down. None of that was a lie. It's just not the only thing.

It's not the main thing.

Not *the* thing.

Kev digs a toe into the dirt. "I figured, what are the odds that's not on YouTube?"

"Is it?"

"Dude, of course it is. There's a remix that makes the alpacas look like they're dropping a trap single. It slaps."

But that's not the first thing that comes up if you google my name.

Hercules is kind of lost at the end of his leash. He whines once. I think he can tell I'm tense.

"It's okay, Herc," says Kev, and wanders forward to keep the puppy from getting too frustrated. "Come on, Sy, it's okay."

I try to walk after him and stumble a little, my knees are so locked up. Kevin steadies me for a sec, and then we walk along. He's so close that we keep bumping shoulders. I sort of want to apologize to him, but he hasn't said the thing I thought he'd say. He hasn't said *Why didn't you tell me.*

"I read how they reopened the school," he says. "That's so messed up. I don't blame you, man, getting out of there."

"It wasn't that," I say. "I didn't— I never had to go back there."

They reopened the school after just two weeks. The police investigation wrapped fast—because what was there to investigate, really—and they worked hard to get things scrubbed and painted.

Other kids went back. Other kids were hashtag Omaha Onward. But I didn't have a class to go back to. *My* friends—they're all dead, and when I think about it it's like having stones piled on me.

"I didn't go back," I say. "My parents homeschooled me."

But even that hadn't been enough, so we came here.

"Dude, I'm super sorry about the ribbon." Kevin touches his hair. It's purple now but I remember the orange bow in the green spikes.

"Don't be," I say, and knock my shoulder into his. "It looked cute on you."

He laughs a little.

We've walked the dirt trail into a dip that gets wet when it rains. The bike ruts are deep, and there are stones washed to the top of the dirt. That would be my science project if I were doing one. How come stones wash *up*? Kevin stoops and wiggles one free, tosses it from hand to hand, and then beans it at a nearby boulder. It hits with a crack and Kev pumps a fist like *all right*.

I pick up a stone, too, and throw it—and miss—and then we spend a while hurling stones as hard as we can, our hands and jeans getting dusty and our throwing muscles getting warm and loose. Herc helps dig the stones out.

When we run out of stones, we go sit on the boulder. I lift my puppy up onto my lap and try to brush some dust off him.

I still kind of want to say sorry, and I know Kevin does, too, but neither one of us needs to because neither one of us did anything wrong. Things are wrong because sometimes the world just sucks, but my last therapist worked hard to teach me not to apologize for that. I don't know where Kevin learned not to but it's cool that he doesn't.

Still, I know him well enough to know he's got something to say. And he manages, eventually: "The thing is, now my parents know. Like, my mom knows."

I swallow and bounce my heels off the stone. "Will she tell?"

"She won't take out an ad in the paper or anything. But she'll probably call your parents. And the team she works with— She says she wants to make sure you have support."

"You've got to tell her not to!"

Kevin has his fingers knotted together. I can see the knot is tight, too, his fingers pressing into each other. "Sy— I— You don't get my mom. You can't tell her anything."

"Kev, you've got to."

Fingers still laced, Kevin does a weird snaky spin with his wrists. "She was at work already last night. And, Team Science, you know— Some of her team have kids at our school. This is a small town, Simon."

130

He means, not like Omaha. But I'm not from Omaha, technically. I'm from a small town that got swallowed by Omaha.

I'm from Eagle Crest. As in Eagle Crest Elementary.

Our school colors were orange and white.

And at 9:56 in the morning on Wednesday, May 15, two years ago, a guy with some guns blew through the glass on the front door, killed the teachers in the hallway, and then, when the alarms started going off, dodged into the stairway and ran up to the top floor. Four minutes after the alarms started sounding, he kicked open the first classroom door on the left.

Mrs. Donaldson's fifth-grade class.

My class.

He wasn't a student. He didn't know anyone there. He could have stayed downstairs, where the first graders were all in the gym with the lights off, where the second graders were jamming themselves in the art supply cupboards, where the librarian was toppling a filing cabinet in front of the door. He could have run up just one flight of stairs, not two. When he got to the top, he could have turned right, not left.

He didn't, and there's no reason.

Sometimes things just happen.

The way this morning it was almost summer.

There's a stone at my foot. I pick it up and throw it as far as I can.

a note about explosives

I saw an episode of *Mythbusters* once where they put out a fire with explosives.

I mean, the Mythbusters use explosives for everything, including cleaning trucks and making steak. But the firefighting thing actually works, because the shock wave from the explosion blows all the oxygen away.

So, Sunday night. I haven't told my parents that Kevin's onto me—onto us—but I do get into this awful fight with them about absolutely nothing. I remember how my therapist taught me that's a symptom of not saying something you need to say. So I do.

The fight stops. All of its oxygen got blown away.

"That was always inevitable—" says my mother, glancing at my father.

Dad's turned white, as if I'd hit him in the stomach.

"Martin?" Mom says.

He rattles his head from side to side. "Of course. I just—there are so many people I'll need to tell—and they'll think I was . . . oh."

"We could put out a notice," says my mom, who professionally puts out notices. "*The O'Keeffe family is traumatized to announce* . . . This is Simon's crisis, remember?"

"Yeah," says my dad, scrubbing his hands over his face. "Or, you know what, no. This is us. We're in this together."

This is a thing we fight about, too: whether what happened is something that happened to me and then crashed into my family, or whether we all crashed together. (Hint: The right answer is the first one.)

But my dad is saying how things are already awkward because of the Jesus Squirrel, the bishop's office is even sending someone to spot-check his theology—and now it will look to people like their deacon wasn't honest with them. Some of the air is coming back into the fire. I know that Dad didn't tell people because I asked him not to, and I get that now it's kind of weird for him, but not compared to what it's like for *me*, I say. Flames start up.

Then Mom blows away all the air again: "Simon, have you told Agate?"

Oh, man. Agate.

I shake my head and drop my chin. My mom puts her hand on the back of my neck. My dad wraps his big musical hand around my arm.

The shock waves just keep rattling through me.

fifteen

in which there are emus

My parents have suggestions about how to tell Agate, but there is just absolutely no way to do it that makes sense. There's no way to lead up to it. "Hey, you know, I forgot to mention when I met you that I'm the famous survivor of a famous school shooting and FYI I hate loud noises and rooms with only one door, hello."

But then again, Agate is terrible with lead-up. Maybe we just play a game called What's the Most Traumatic Thing You Know? Maybe she's the last person I need to worry about.

But I do worry. What will I say? What will she say? Will she look at me with her hands in fists and a little scrunch in her eyebrows—look at me with pity? Then I imagine standing next to Miss Rose, because I'm going to have to do that. She'll touch my shoulder, and I'll watch the whole class just *stare*.

I'd rather go to school naked.

Yeah. I can't *imagine* why, but I don't sleep very well. When I wake up for like the fourth time, it's four a.m. I feel like my body is a kitchen sponge that had been soaked in stress and is now being wrung out. I'm, like, achy and dry and empty.

Also, I have to pee.

So I get up. Outside the window it's the gray time before dawn, when the world looks like a video game that hasn't finished rendering, like if you went outside they wouldn't have the end of the street created yet. It doesn't seem quite real, but it's peaceful. Even Pretty Stabby the peacock (his tail feathers bent and battered) is asleep.

I try getting back to sleep, but end up rereading Percy Jackson and wishing that I could just binge a YouTube channel instead. Say one of the mythology ones. YouTube has this way of pouring information over you so fast that you don't need to think; you just soak some of it up as it goes by. I totally want that, a stream to fill up the dry-sponge holes in me. But of course I can't have it, because, you know: radio telescopes.

I can't imagine anyone confusing Overly Sarcastic Productions with space aliens, but what do I know. Maybe that's exactly what a signal from aliens looks like: just a weird thing that drenches you as it goes by.

I'm reading about Medusa and the garden statues and kind of drifting off finally when the phone rings.

Double rings—the party line.

I'm used to it ringing at all hours, and it doesn't usually

make me jump out of my skin, but of course today's a little different. My heart jolts and I'm wide awake again.

Across the hall I hear my mom stir, mumble, answer. A moment later she's carrying the phone into the hallway, trailing its coiled cord and pulling the door closed behind her so that Dad can sleep. She sees me up and waves. She's wearing plaid pj pants and a T-shirt that says Got ~~Milk~~ Formaldehyde?

"What I don't quite see is why you're calling me," Mom says. Whoever it is can't be a bereaved relative, because she doesn't deploy her Soothing Professional Manner. She mostly sounds annoyed. "No, I can see why they wouldn't, but—" Whoever it is must cut her off. She stands there listening, twirling her fingers in and out of the coils of the phone cord. "You know what, fine," she says at last. "Give me the address."

There's a pen-and-paper caddy on the wall outside my parents' bedroom door, kept there for exactly this reason. Unlike the one in the kitchen, which people might possibly see and is therefore normal-shaped like a rooster, this one is shaped like a coffin. My mom, ladies and gentlemen.

She repeats the address as she writes it down.

It's Agate's address.

I shoot out of bed and an instant later am hanging onto the doorway, panting. Mom catches my eye. "But just to confirm. No one is dead." She puts her hand over the phone and mouths at me: It's okay.

I don't quite believe her. I mean, why would I? Behind me, Hercules is running away from something in his sleep. His feet pedal; he makes a whiffling noise.

My mom keeps eye contact with me. "Yes, Mr. Greenway," she says. "I'll be right there."

Mr. Greenway is the county district attorney, which for some only-in-Nebraska reason also makes him the county coroner, and therefore someone my mom talks to all the time, because it's his job to decide if dead bodies have to be autopsied or if they can just be buried or cremated or whatever. It's not weird that he called, and it's not even weird that he called at four-something-a.m. But it is weird that he called if no one is dead.

I have time to think about this while my mom ducks back into her room to hang up the phone. I have time to think: *The address is Agate's.* I'm trying but I can't let go of the door frame.

Mom comes out again. She's now wearing jeans with the formaldehyde T-shirt and is snapping a ponytail elastic off her wrist and around her hair. "Apparently," she says, "the Van der Zwaan farm has been overrun by emus. Breathe in for five, Simon."

I breathe in for a count of five, hold it for six, breathe out for seven. I let go of the door. Mom clasps my arm for a second and we pick back up. "Emus, not a death," she says. "Not even dead emus, as far as I know."

"Okay . . ." I say, because this is my life now.

"Greenway says that the sheriff called him because they can't get enough people to round them up. For some reason the state police won't come."

"For some reason."

"Can't think why," says my mom, glancing past me at my sleeping puppy, my clock. It's not quite five in the morning. "Sy, I'm— I know that spooked you. But your friend is fine. Probably chasing emus in her nightgown. But fine."

"Sure," I say. "Can I come anyway?"

• • •

In the hearse, Mom fills me in: According to the coroner, the sheriff called him (Mr. Greenway), because Pearl Van der Zwaan called her (the sheriff), because her dog (Todd, presumably) had left a gate open, which led to their neighbor's emu herd breaking out of that farm and onto the Van der Zwaan farm, which was bad because the goats are about to kid and the ducks were nervous, and the emu farmer wouldn't come help because he was both angry and afraid of electromagnetic radiation.

"I *think* that's right," Mom finishes. "It was a very Grin And Bear It phone call."

"The GNB-est," I agree.

The hearse rattles along the gravel road in the yellow dawn light.

"Mom . . ." I say, watching the road dust smoke in the headlights.

In Omaha, Mom was super successful, a pillar of the

community. Now she's taking her own removal calls in the middle of the night and gulping down emergency coffee while heading for an emu roundup. Also, despite the hours Dad put in over the weekend, the hearse she's driving still smells like peacock poop. There are several long claw slashes on the upholstery and tiny turquoise feathers stuck in the dashboard vent. I start plucking them out one by one.

"Mom. Are you sorry we came here?"

"Not a bit." After a sec I feel my mom's hand on the back of my bowed head. "It wasn't just for you, Simon, you know. I knew those kids, too. I knew their moms and dads, and then I . . . You're not the only one who wanted to get the h-e-l-l out of Eagle Crest."

"Again with the spelling . . ."

She ruffles her hand up through my hair in the way she *knows* causes maximum stick-up-age. "It was my decision, too. So you can ditch the guilt and help me catch some giant flightless— Is this the right place?"

But she doesn't need me to confirm it. It's dawn, and the Van der Zwaan circus is open for business. There are yard lights on, the entire volunteer fire department is out, and there are cars with roof lights parked every which way. There isn't even room left for the hearse inside the gate.

The shadow of the Van der Zwaan sign falls across the road, pointing right at the gigantic radio telescope and its trailer park of science. We park in the gravel pull-off where people sometimes stop and take a picture of Big Ear. Then we walk onto the farm.

There are emus everywhere.

I guess I was expecting, like, three emus. This is more emus. This is a lot of emus. This is maybe twenty emus.

If you're thinking twenty emus is not a lot, then you've never seen emus. I don't think I had, up until now. We don't get them much in Omaha. They are bigger than I'd thought they'd be: like five or six feet tall. They have bodies like huge gray-brown feather dusters, and long, long necks like they are actually Muppets and someone's entire arm is in there. Their legs are like dinosaur legs, bare and lean and strong. They use their legs to run at absolutely top speeds, and they use their necks to twist and flop around comically, and they don't use their brains at all. They are driven by a mix of curiosity and panic.

I read about them later in Agate's book and learn that one very bad strategy for herding emus is to run at them, shouting and waving your arms.

In the pasture behind the Van der Zwaan farmhouse, people are trying to herd emus by running at them while shouting and waving their arms.

Mom sighs, tugs her ponytail tighter, and wades in, leaving me hovering by the fire truck and wondering what to do.

"Hi, Simon," says Agate—and I jump right out of my skin. She completely snuck up on me. "You probably shouldn't go in there because emus have five-inch talons and can kick with the force of a sledgehammer."

I look at the other people running around the field. Emus

are dodging and weaving, bobbing like carousel horses, making tight turns like squirrels in a corner. They do not look like they are going to kick people with the force of a sledgehammer. They also do not look like they are about to be caught.

"Should we, uh, warn people?" I ask.

"I think it's okay," she says. "Emus don't usually attack humans. You just have to be wearing a jacket or something in case they get scratchy."

The sheriff's deputies and the firefighters are indeed wearing their uniform jackets, so that should be okay. Agate's mom, Pearl, has on overalls. My mom just has her morbid T-shirt, but as I watch she reaches out and grabs an emu by the neck and then clamps it between her knees, and I figure she's probably okay.

"Where are Coral and Jasper?" I ask.

"Feeding the babies." Agate's wearing fleecy pajama pants and a T-shirt featuring a feathered flying dinosaur thing and the slogan *Not an Early Bird*. She has serious bedhead. Despite this, she seems wide-awake.

I need to tell her.

"I am supposed to be opening and closing the gate, but I think everyone is here now. Do you want to go down to the tree house?"

"I guess." Because I need to tell her, and that's as good a place as any.

Agate leads the way around the outside of the goat pasture, along a little footpath in the tall, dewy grass. An emu careens into the wire fence right in front of us and rebounds with a cartoony *sproinggg* noise. Its long neck and long legs flail every which way for a second and then it rights itself and zips off. "How did the emus get out?"

"Todd," she says, as if that's all the explanation that's required. Which, fair. After a minute she adds: "Mr. Bagshott, our next-door neighbor, is an emu rancher. Our goat pasture connects to his emu pasture, for when he needs to get a truck in. There's a gate."

"And Todd . . ."

"Opened the gate. Mr. Bagshott's really mad, but I think Todd was just going for a stroll."

At the join between the two pastures, I spot someone who pretty much has to be Mr. Bagshott. He's not helping with the emus—he's not coming onto the Van der Zwaan land at all—but he is shouting a lot. The reason I'm sure he's Mr. Bagshott is that he's wearing an emu-decoy hat. It is broad brimmed and topped with a mop of gray feathers. A dummy emu head sticks up from the crown like a sock stuffed with newspaper. It's listing a little. I try not to actually stare but it's hard.

Agate is still talking: "Todd could climb through the gate usually, but his hip was probably hurting."

"Sure," I say. "Sure."

Over in the corner, the newly shorn Angora goats are gathered in a sleepy mass, bleating and chewing hay with placid sideways shifts of their jaws. They are being kept in the corner by an unrolled length of bright orange plastic

142

windbreak. Mom's phone call said the goats were upset, but it doesn't look to me like the goats have even noticed.

"Did you know that humans once fought a war with emus?" says Agate.

"Seriously?"

"It was in Australia. The emus were eating the crops, so the government sent in troops with machine guns."

The two volunteer firefighters, whose names are Andy and Doug, are trying to creep up on an emu that's in the corner of the pasture. They have, maybe without noticing, adopted an emulike gait to do this, swaying with their hips and bobbing as if tango music is playing in their heads. The emu watches them come, looking brainless and blinkless. Its head is black and bald except for a few comb-over wisps. Its eyes are a weird reddish color. It has alpaca eyelashes. The firefighters salsa closer. Doug reaches out, slowly—and the emu darts right between them, knocking them down like bowling pins.

"We got a book when Mr. Bagshott moved in, to help us be neighborly," Agate is saying. "It was called *Everything About Emus.* I read about the emu war there. It happened in 1932."

"Did the humans win?"

"No," says Agate. "It was a decisive emu victory."

An emu bolts along the fence opposite us, its beak open in a weird red scream, its neck flailing about like Kermit the Frog.

We are almost around the pasture now, near the gate.

One of the sheriff's deputies comes running past us and gets lucky on a flying tackle. An emu goes down and the deputy gets it in a scissor-hold. The emu starts shredding the man's pants with its five-inch talons.

"Stop!" Mr. Bagshott bobs up and down, holding on to the rim of his emu-decoy hat. "Stop, stop! Those are very valuable birds!"

"A breeding pair of emus can sell for up to twenty-five thousand dollars," says Agate. "Hello, Mr. Bagshott."

"Hello, uh, Rocky." His emu-decoy head is tilting down over one ear.

"It's Agate," says Agate. "This is my friend, Simon O'Keeffe, whose mom is here helping."

Mom, in fact, comes by that moment. She is sit-walking astride an emu as if it's a hobby horse, holding on to its neck and steering it with her knees. Her ponytail is coming out and she is flushed and glowing. Mr. Bagshott hurries to open the barn door for her; she shoves the emu in.

She pauses on the way back out. "You good, Sy? What are you up to?"

"Oh," I say. "The usual. Agate said I shouldn't tackle emus without a jacket."

"Smart girl." Mom flutters her finger through a rip in her shirt, then brushes away a small cloud of emu feathers. "Okay. Once more unto the breach." She dives back in.

I can't help but notice that Mr. Bagshott doesn't dive back in, and Agate notices me noticing. "Mr. Bagshott is very sensitive to electromagnetic fields," she explains.

144

"Your farmstead hasn't been screened." Mr. Bagshott is wild-eyed, and if those are really twenty-five thousand dollar birds being chased around like sugared-up toddlers at a Chuck E. Cheese, I don't blame him. There are feathers flying in the air, and the emus are making noises like truck engines trying to turn over. "They're doing it all wrong!"

"What's the right way to do it, Mr. Bagshott?" asks Agate.

"You have to," Bagshott sputters. "You have to *lure* them."

"Then why don't we do that?" says Agate. She puts two fingers to her mouth and whistles. It's so loud and piercing that I've got my hands halfway to my ears before I realize it's coming from her. "Everybody stop!" she shouts.

It's a miracle, because everybody does. The emu in the scissor-hold flips to its feet and head-butts the sheriff's deputy. He goes down, but before the roundup can deteriorate again, Agate presses on: "Mr. Bagshott says we have to lure them!" she shouts. She turns to the farmer: "How do we lure them, Mr. Bagshott?"

He stares at her like she's overloaded the fuse box in his brain. Which, to be fair, is a look a lot of people give Agate. Fortunately he rallies. "You have to—just, if you lie down on your back and bicycle your feet in the air . . ."

"Like this?" says Agate. She lies down in the grass and pedals her feet. Her pajama pants slide down her round calves and pool around her knees. Her yard boots sprinkle dirt into her face. I stare at her.

145

But the emus are staring, too.

A weird hush falls across the field of emus, goats, and government employees.

"Come on, Simon, you lure them, too," says Agate.

Which is how I end up beside Agate in the dew-damp, goat-poop-pebbled grass, propping my hips up on my hands and riding an invisible upside-down bicycle. The nearest emu comes walking toward me cautiously. I can just see its big three-toed feet, like T. rex feet, coming step pause, step-pause, step.

"I'll open the barn," whispers Mr. Bagshott, and he scurries off. There's a latch clunk, a hinge squeak, and then a rattle that's probably emu food being poured into a hopper. The emu that had been bending its black beak toward my face looks up at the last sound. It goes step-pausing off.

I pedal. Agate pedals. Emus walk up to us cautiously. Firemen and deputies gather at a distance and stare. Mr. Bagshott does not turn back up. We're alone.

I played out telling Agate a thousand times during the night, and not one time did I picture it like this.

But we're alone.

"Uh, Agate?" I say.

"Yes, Simon?"

"There's something—" I pedal. "There's something—" I stop pedaling and breathe in for five, hold for six, out for seven. I've closed my eyes and when I open them again, Agate has rolled her head to face me. She is pink with

146

pedaling and being upside down, and there is grass and emu feathers in her tangled red hair, but she looks at me the way people look at stars. There is nothing in her eyes but openness, and wonder.

"Do you remember—the—" I can't get the word out for a second. "Do you remember the shooting? Two years ago, at Eagle Crest Elementary?"

"Of course," says Agate. "That one's famous."

"It was me." My voice comes out in a croak. I'm not pedaling anymore. My arms are trembling under the weight of my upper body—locked in place but shaking like they're about to buckle.

"No," she says, her feet slowing down. "That one was an adult intruder. Also I think in that one he killed himself at the scene." Emus slide by us, majestically. They make weird booming noises, like my heart in my ears.

"There was a kid," I say. "In that class. All the kids were jammed in the supply cabinet at the back of the room and when the guy opened the cabinet door they all fell out and one kid ended up on the bottom of the pile of— And he played dead. There was a kid who lived."

Agate stops pedaling. She wiggles a second and shifts her hips higher into the air. I would say I can tell she's thinking hard, but I think she's always thinking hard. "And that was you," she says. "You were on the bottom of the pile."

I was on the bottom of the pile. I can't breathe. If I didn't already have my knees elevated, I'd probably pass out.

"You know, Simon, I don't think it's good that you

said that all in the third person," Agate says. "You should discuss that with your trauma specialist."

I boom like an emu. So much like an emu that the nearest one bends slowly down to look at me. I see its red-brown eyes and black brainless head framed between my ankles. I drop my feet and it hops backward like a startled cat.

I'm flat on my back in the grass now. "Agate . . . I . . . I just wanted to tell you."

"Why?" she says.

I hardly hear her. "You're going to hear soon. We left . . . the press was awful, and the way people looked at me, at us— There's this photo. . . ."

When you google "Simon O'Keeffe" you see a photo captured by a police body-cam. They came crashing into the room shouting for everyone to raise their hands. I struggled up and I raised my hands in the air. And that's the picture: the kid from the bottom of the pile, all smeared, with his hands up and his face shattered. He's a third-person kid. He's light-years away. But sometimes I'm still frozen inside him. He's a still image so his lungs don't work so good, and I have to tell him how to breathe.

"Kevin found it," I say, meaning the picture and just trusting her to keep up like she always does. "And his mom— You're going to hear, at school. So I wanted to tell you." I take this huge breath and it comes out kind of shuddering. "I wanted to tell you because you're my best friend."

Agate's eyes widen, and then she smiles like—not even like the moon. Like the sun coming up. She *shines*. "I am?!"

I hear a noise behind me and tilt my head. I get an upside-down view of Mr. Bagshott shaking emu feed at the bottom of an old plastic milk jug with a side cut out. The emu who was inspecting me—the last emu—goes striding over to check it out.

Bagshott kind of huffs, encouraging the emu, and then shoots us a glare.

"Okay, Rocky, you can stop that now."

"It's *Agate*," says Agate, as irritated as I've ever heard her. She drops her feet to the ground. "I'm *Agate* and this is *Simon*. And you should say 'thank you.'" She gets up. We retreat through the gate and Agate closes it, carefully, behind us. "I am very sorry our dog Todd let your emus free, Mr. Bagshott," she says, across the fence. "You can come screen our property for concerning electromagnetic radiation anytime."

We turn around. We're not holding hands but we're close: Our pinkies are brushing together. There are tears on my face and there are tears on Agate's face but no one can see that, and we are both smiling. Agate waves to her mom and to my mom, to the police, to Andy and Doug, the volunteer firefighters.

The people in the field break into applause.

sixteen

in which my plan is not to have a plan

The emus are all captured and the goats are released and the ducks are calmed down and it's still only 6:30 in the morning. The sheriff's deputies and the firefighters have all gone home, the teenagers have gone back to bed, and me and Agate and my mom and Pearl Van der Zwaan are sitting on the farmhouse porch eating pancakes.

Buckwheat pancakes made with duck eggs, of course. Agate eats hers plain, rolling them up like burritos.

Todd is lounging under the porch swing with his beer. Onyx is also under the porch swing, finger-painting Todd's rump with maple syrup. The twin babies, Mica and Amber, are crawling around on an old quilt at our feet.

And today's the day.

Agate knows. Kevin knows. Kevin's mom knows, and she wants to "make sure I have support" and so . . .

Today's got to be the day.

My mom is asking Pearl about buckwheat like there's

any chance she's going to cook with it. (Mom goes mostly for things with lots of preservatives, like Pop-Tarts. She says it's pre-embalming and saves her work later.) Mom's shirt is ripped and her pants are filthy but she's braided her hair and she looks happy as I've ever seen anyone look after an emu rodeo, even though Pearl is in the middle of telling her how kasha is just buckwheat that's been toasted, which I know for sure Mom doesn't care about.

I look at Agate.

Agate looks at me.

She nods like she's understood something.

"Mom," Agate says (interrupting a thing about how buckwheat isn't wheat at all), "today Simon told me something." There is a pause and I think Agate and I are both deciding if I should say it or if she should.

Mom has done that mom-magic thing where she's scooted closer without appearing to move. Pearl puts her syrupy plate down—it's already attracting bees because Agate's family also keeps bees because of course they do— and looks at us. She knows something is up, but she doesn't know enough to make up good questions. I guess the whole thing feels serious enough that she doesn't try.

Mom squeezes me in tighter for a sec. "I'll talk to Mrs. Van der Zwaan, baby. Why don't you two go . . ."

"Oh!" says Agate, bouncing off the edge of the porch steps. "I've got to go gather eggs! Gathering eggs is my morning job. Come on, Simon, I'll show you how to gather eggs."

I put my plate down and Agate stacks hers on top and we go. Behind me my mother starts talking. I can't make out words, but I can hear her funeral director voice, soft and calm and saying the unthinkable.

Who'd have thought that voice would come in so handy?

I almost can't stand it, how handy her voice is.

Agate walks me over to the duck rescue. There's a fenced yard that slopes down to a pondy bit. At the top of the slope there's a shed-hutch thing with a door and a duck hatch with a little ramp. Tall white ducks are coming down the ramp, waddling like drunk sailors. More are milling around the yard. Agate opens the gate and the ducks rush over in a honking wave. She scatters some dried peas for them. They fall on the peas with a crescendo of quacking, and Agate leads me into the shed.

It's warm and damp and dim in there. There's a smell, a little like peacocks locked in a hearse, a little like hay. I expected nests but eggs are just sort of lying everywhere. Agate picks up a scuffed plastic bucket and starts picking her way through the straw.

"Ducks usually lay eggs at night," she says. "So morning is the best time for eggs."

"Do they mind? You taking their eggs?"

"They don't seem to notice," says Agate, laying a couple of eggs gently on top of the others. They are bigger than chicken eggs, and they make a tongue-click sound when they settle against each other. "Honestly I don't think ducks are very smart."

152

"Do you get ducklings ever?"

"We don't keep any drakes right now," says Agate. "We sell them for meat."

"Fun."

"A fun fact about ducks is that their penises are eight inches long."

I do an unwise thing and try to picture that. "No way."

"Yes way," she says brightly. "They're sort of . . . spring loaded."

I push my hands over my eyes, as if I could block out the mental image. "Ugh, I am so glad you didn't tell that to Kevin." She'd been about to, on our movie night. I can't imagine how that would have gone. It would have been a heck of a first impression.

Of course, Kevin's first impression of me was the alpaca story, which was also pretty weird. Oh man. Kevin googled alpacas.

Out of nowhere, Agate says, "I think we should use a microwave."

"What?" I say.

"For the message," she says. "I was going to say that last week in the tree house when you freaked out. I think we should use a microwave as our *How* to make the signals, but I don't know where we can get one so we should talk to Kevin."

My head spins. In the two whole days since 5/15, Project Fake Space Message has been the last thing on my mind. "Agate, I can't think about that right now."

She puts the last of the duck eggs on the top of her scuffed-up white bucket—the Blue Bunny Ice Cream logo just barely shows through the dirt and scratches—and looks up at me with her round, open face. "Why not?"

"Because— This was why I wanted to fly under the radar, get it? Because of Eagle Crest."

"But our message is a separate thing."

For her. For her, it's separate. For me, it never has been. All the reasons I wanted to try it, all the reasons I was afraid to try it, they were all tangled up in keeping Eagle Crest secret. Now the secret is getting out, but they still seem tangled. Like a giant ball of string that's rolling fast.

"Simon?"

"Agate, I just—can't right now."

Kevin knows. Team Science— They know, too, or they'll find out soon.

So. I should just tell everybody. Get ahead of the story. (That's what the media advisors and lawyers and publicists who called us and tried to sell us their services used to say: "Get ahead of the story.") I should ask Miss Rose if I can stand up in front of the homeroom—or maybe even the whole school—and somehow make my mouth say words. When I think about doing that, my tongue gets stiff and my heart gets fast, until I can feel it like someone standing three inches behind me and tapping their fingers on the pulse point under my jaw.

I can't.

"I could talk to Kevin about the microwave by myself if you want me to," says Agate.

"Yeah," I say, knotting a hand in my hair. I notice I'm doing it and make myself drop it. I wish I'd brought Hercules, though probably the emu roundup wouldn't have been a positive socialization experience for him. He's kind of shy.

It's Monday. Really early Monday, but Monday. There's one more week of school. On Friday, I'll have made it through seventh grade and it will be summer. People could hear about Eagle Crest during summer and do their shocked thing on their own time, where I don't have to see it.

"Just," I start. "Just give me a week, okay?"

A week. In that moment, in the warm, dim, smelly duck coop, I decide.

I decide—this is not smart and I know this is not smart—but I decide to fake it. Shake off the emu feathers, get the goat poop out of my hair and the duck penises out of my brain, strap the service vest on my puppy, and head into GNB Upper like nothing has changed.

Maybe—you never know—there will be some other kind of miracle or catastrophe and everyone will have something else to talk about.

Maybe I'll never have to send any kind of message at all.

• • •

Step one in my terrible plan: actually go to school.

I hug Agate good-bye, and Mom takes me home. I hit the shower, put the vest on Herc—who, yes, peed in my closet

155

because I wasn't there to pick him up and haul him out first thing—and head on in.

I'm late getting there, so I miss Kevin in homeroom. My first chance to see him is in science, where we sit next to each other. It will be my first time seeing him since he told me he'd googled alpacas and found way more. We can't talk about that—not at school—but I want to tell him about the emus. I want to find a way to tell him that I told Agate.

I want to make sure we are okay.

I figure we'll have time to talk. Basically we're done learning. Last week in English, we watched a movie (*The Outsiders*, because it's on our reading list). Last week in social studies we watched a movie (*Moana*, because it's about culture). Last week in math we watched a movie (*Cinderella II*, because the school owns a copy). I went to the bathroom during history class and I missed the Vietnam War. I figure that science will be the same. I figure we've learned everything there is to know about igneous versus metamorphic rock—something I hear comes up a lot in life—and I'll be able to grab some time with Kevin under the cover of whatever nonsense Ms. Maddox has scheduled.

It doesn't work out that way. I forgot, but the regional science fair is on Thursday, and the kids who are going are trying to get ready. When your town is half-full of astrophysicists, the science fair is a big deal. The school trophy case is *full* of science fair stuff.

Kevin's one of the kids going, obviously. And I'm not.

So the class is spent with the science fair kids buzzing

around near the lab benches—busy with their display boards and glue sticks and our teacher—while the rest of us are stuck erasing marks from textbooks.

Hercules susses out the situation instantly: He heaves a huge sigh and sprawls out flat on the linoleum, melting across it. He's bored. He's also hot. The Nebraska spring has slammed on its brakes and cornered, *Tokyo Drift*-style, straight into summer, with hot, sticky mornings and rumbling storms in the afternoon.

The Team Science kids are chattering but it's not easy to hear what they're saying, because there's a standing fan right behind me. When I look up, Kevin is listening to Juniper Higgins, who is leaning in close to him to say something, but he's looking at me. Our eyes catch but he looks away. So does Juniper, and she blushes.

The fan blows across the back of my neck, lifting sweat and riffling the pages of my textbook. I push my forearm down across the spread and get to work on the faces that someone has added to the planets of our solar system.

Pluto has Xs for eyes.

Now Juniper is talking to Mary Ellen and to Gavin. Their parents all work at the Big Ear, with Kevin's mom. They're talking and I can't hear them.

I brush the dark little worms of used eraser stuff off the page and onto the black soapstone of the lab table.

Maybe they're talking about the science fair.

I can't catch Kevin's eye.

He knows now. He knows I didn't tell him for months.

I'm out of stuff to erase, so I scratch doodles in the grime on the soapstone counters with a fingernail.

Kevin and me were pretty okay out in the rock-throwing field. I thought we would probably keep being okay.

But by the time science is over we're not okay.

Agate was right, way back the first day we met: Grin And Bear It is divided into sides, and Kevin is on Team Science. His mom has made sure of that. The other kids on Team Science, the ones who spent the whole class looking at me: Do they know? I want to ask but I can't, not at school. I think Kevin probably wants to talk to me about it, but he can't, not at school.

We sit together at lunch and we try to talk about Minecraft. We try to talk about the horror that is *Lady and the Tramp III*. We try to talk about Herc's latest skill, which is wearing the harness that puts a handle on his back like he's a rolling suitcase. Hercules is a little freaked out about it, and that makes me worry he'll be in the half of guide dog puppies that can't be guide dogs. We try to talk about that. We *try*. But it's like when you get a bad sore throat, and you chew over things a little too long because you know in a second you have to swallow and it's gonna hurt.

We stop talking and I get a swallow in. I was right: It hurts.

That night Kevin doesn't call.

Tuesday we don't even get to have lunch together. He gives me a bro-punch in the arm and ducks out to practice for the science fair.

158

Silence can build, you know. Like bricks.

It shouldn't be my job to break it but also I can't stand it, so on Wednesday after school I go over to the Hello Hello.

It's so hard to go, but I go anyway. I'm sure it will be like every Wednesday; I'm sure Kevin will be there.

He's not.

His sister, Zeny, is behind the cash register. She smiles at me. "Hey, Simon. Hey, Herc." No one else is in the store just then and her words seem to echo around. She calls over her shoulder. "Dad! Come say hi to Simon."

According to Kevin, about once a month one of the junior scientists decides they want to leave science and has this storm of guilt and second-guessing. They come to the Hello Hello, and Doc Matapang just lets them sit and babble. He feeds them and listens until the dam breaks, and he soaks it all up until they feel better.

I am afraid he's about to do that to me. I'm afraid he'll try and it won't work. I'm not like a dam. I'm like a glass. If I break I'm going to be broken forever. I don't want to say hi to him.

But I don't manage a getaway before Doc appears from the back room, wiping his big hands on his apron. "Hey, Simon," he says. "Kevin's not here. His mom took him to Ogallala for the regionals."

Herc whines. He's not used to the handle-harness, and definitely not used to the way I'm holding him twisted halfway through a turn toward the door.

"Oh." I get Herc straightened out, looking down at him

159

like that takes way more attention than it actually does. "I thought that was tomorrow . . . ?"

"His mom wants him to settle in. Be well rested."

"Sure," I say, even though that's ridiculous: Ogallala's not that far away, and how much rest do you have to get before a science fair, anyway? It would be easy to just drive there in the morning. Kevin probably thinks his mom is being ridiculous again. But he hasn't said so.

I don't know what Kevin's thinking.

Kevin's dad is looking at me. "Okay," I say. I lift my hand from Herc's harness, open and close my fist a couple of times. My fingers are numb. That's a sign of stress, which I know because I've been in therapy for, like, two hundred thousand hours. "Okay. Thanks."

"Simon— Kiddo, wait." I freeze up. I like Kevin's dad. I'm not afraid of Kevin's dad. But when I freeze it feels like fear. "Let me make you something."

He starts assembling halo halo: the sweet red beans and the coconut jelly at the bottom, the shaved ice in the middle, the coconut and crème caramel pieces on top. He makes a little production of cracking open a can of super sweet condensed milk and pouring it over the top. It's just how I like it, even though he doesn't stop to ask what I like. I guess he's been paying attention.

He puts in a long spoon and passes it to me, looking me in the eye. "Something terrible happened to you."

"Yeah." It's only one word but it cracks. "Yeah."

"I'm very sorry."

160

I look down. "Me too."

"'Halo' means *mix*," he tells me. "So 'halo halo' means *all mixed up*, more or less."

I kind of nod. I think he told me that once, or Kevin did. It isn't news, anyway.

"Well," he says. "You sit on down and eat that. Kevin will be back Saturday night, and you can both come here Sunday, after church."

"But you're closed on Sunday."

"We are, but it's also the day I cook through *The Great British Bake Off* technical challenge. We're having kransekake."

"What's that?"

"I have no idea," he says cheerfully. "But we can find out together."

"That sounds— Uh. Kranse-cakey."

"I'm a good baker, Simon," he says. "It will be good." He taps his fingers lightly together, pad to pad—it's an echo of how Kevin laces and twists his twiggy fingers together, but it's both stronger and softer. Doc Matapang is a big man, but he moves so delicately, like he's never hurt anyone in his life, and never could. "Come Sunday," he says. "Don't stop coming."

That's a nice thing for him to say, but it would be better if Kevin said it. It would be better if Kevin said it, but Kevin is gone.

seventeen

in which we don't die in the Mojave Desert but almost die in the school basement

Thursday.

I won't see Kevin before school's over—there are only two days left before summer.

They are not going to be fun days. Ms. Hafsaas, the turkey-raising gym teacher, has been doing this thing called Run Across America all year, where the seventh and eighth graders collectively . . . wait for it . . . run the distance across America by doing laps around the school. It was on pause for the winter when I got here, but we started up again when the snow melted. We're almost done, and Ms. Hafsaas is determined to see us reach the Pacific.

Apparently, she's so determined that she has wrangled extra periods from the other teachers, and we get to go transcontinental all Thursday afternoon. Both the seventh- and eighth-grade classes get sent out, which totals like twenty-five people because of all the kids on Team Science who qualified for the regional fair. The two grades take turns running, alternating laps around the school and parking lot with periods of hanging out in the shade of the silver maples or on the school steps. We've been at it for an hour and collectively we've reached the Mojave Desert.

And we are going to die there.

It's hot and humid, with clouds and a lot of wind. Wind should feel good when you're running, but this wind feels as hot as dog breath. It sucks. At least it's hard for people to gossip when we're all gasping for air.

I run with Agate. Everybody expects Agate to be bad at gym, because she's fat or whatever, but she's not, not really. She knows what her body can do and she just goes ahead and does it, even if she does turn flamingo pink under her cloud of carrot orange hair. Two weeks ago, one of the other girls called Agate a hippo. Agate told her that hippos can charge at thirty kilometers an hour, and that hippos, not tigers or anything, are the large animal that kills the most humans. Then she smiled so big her molars showed and went back to running across Utah.

Today, she turned up in a brand-new tank top featuring a hippo wearing four red running shoes.

We lap around the front of the school for like the hundred and tenth time. There's a table beside Ms. Hafsaas that has all our water bottles on it. I grab mine and suck some down. Ugh: The water is probably hotter than I am.

163

I squirt some into my hand and give it to Herc to lap up. The bottle is almost empty.

Football Brent comes shuffling by and Ms. Hafsaas claps her hands at him. "Pick it up, Fritsch, let's go, let's go." Brent shuffles a little faster. Little does Ms. Hafsaas know that he shortcuts across the back of the school instead of going around the parking lot.

Meanwhile, Agate has stopped for water, too. "You should refill these," she tells Ms. Hafsaas. "It would reduce the risk of heat injury."

"Keep your feet moving, VZ," Ms. Hafsaas scolds. (She's the kind of teacher who likes to call kids by their last names, though apparently Van der Zwaan is a little much.) "You don't want your muscles to cool down."

"I don't feel like that's going to be a problem," says Agate, but she stops toe-bouncing and starts to sort of jog-bobble in place. "Did you know that the risk of dehydration actually increases when it's humid?"

"Agate, I am your *health teacher*."

"That doesn't mean you know things," says Agate, bobbling away. "And this thing is interesting because it's counterintuitive."

Oh boy. I can see Ms. Hafsaas's knees lock and vibrate with what gym teachers call motivation and the rest of us call rage.

Joyce from the leadership team laps us, her ponytail swinging like a metronome and her eyes kind of crazy, like she's got the California foothills in sight.

164

I crouch down to give the last of the water to Herc. The light is weird all of a sudden, sort of green and tumbling, and when I look up past the table and Ms. Hafsaas's looming whistle and nose, the trees are weird, too. The leaves on the silver maples are turning downside up, like they're looking skyward and holding their breath.

Hercules barks once and for just a second the whole world falls still.

Sirens.

I slam into the sidewalk before I even know what the sound is—I'm just *down*. The sirens are loud like the end of the world.

Someone grabs my arm. I crab away, my chin scraping on concrete. I clamp my teeth together so I won't make any noise—no sounds to give me away. Someone is shaking me and shouting: "O'Keeffe!"

A lot of people are saying things, but it just sounds like background noise. I can feel the hard fingers on my arm being peeled away. Then there's something soft against my cheek, stuffed animal soft. Something wet licks my ear. I fling my hands up over my head and then realize I shouldn't move and I freeze again. My muscles are all locked up and I want to be completely still but I can't stop shaking.

"Simon?" The voice comes from inches away. The sirens are very loud but the voice is so close I can feel it in the little hairs on my skin. "Simon? It's a tornado. I want to say it's just a tornado but tornadoes are actually bad so it's a tornado but not *just* a tornado. Can you hear me?"

I can hear but it's like I can't figure words out. A warm hand closes around my wrist. Not like someone grabbing me—like someone ready to rescue me, to pull me out of a hole. A wet nose pushes against the pit of my elbow where it's folded against my ear, and I can hear the whimper and it's a puppy, it's Hercules.

It's Hercules, and Agate.

I open my eyes into the cave of my arms. I see flashes and spots and my body is gulping air.

Sirens. The town sirens are on top of the school. The town sirens mean—

Ms. Hafsaas is shouting at everyone to head inside, leave everything, head inside.

"What's up with O'Keeffe," says someone nearby. I close my eyes again. I can't breathe. My chin is scraped and my heart feels like it's got claws.

"Hey, Simon," says Agate. "So, you are having a panic attack."

The siren is incredibly loud. It's so loud that it could drown me. I can't breathe and the air feels green and weird.

"You are having a panic attack but also there is an actual tornado," says Agate. "Can you breathe? Keep breathing. I asked my sensory processing specialist to tell me about panic attacks so I could help you and I learned that telling you to breathe is the best thing. Please keep breathing. I would like that very much."

Okay. Breathing. In for five. I try but when I get to hold for six I can't hold my breath. I gasp and gasp. In for five.

Five things you can see. I am lying on the ground under the water-bottle table. I push myself up a little and try to get over on my side.

Agate is sitting beside me with her hand clasped around my wrist, and Hercules has squirmed into the tiny space between us. Mrs. Hafsaas is crouching to peer under the table. Behind her the sky is green-black and kind of . . . circling.

She says something that has my name in it.

Something wet and hard hits my ankle: a raindrop as big as a quarter. I jerk into a ball. A gust of wind comes straight down, hail-stone cold, and then is gone. Another raindrop, another one. My chest is tight like someone put straps around it. "Breathe, Simon," says Agate. "Breathe."

Then the table flips over and crashes down behind my head. I hear Agate shout before panic turns me inside out.

Oh God, oh God.

The next thing I know I'm throwing up and blacking out and Ms. Hafsaas is dragging me inside. Agate is shouting something at her and trying to get her arm off me. Hercules is ahead of us, backing up as we stumble forward, barking short, strong barks. He's like a sheepdog in front of a stampede, but he's small and it's not stopping the teacher.

Then somehow we're inside. We're inside and we're downstairs. It's dim and smells like cleaners and that weird rubber smell you get if you put your nose right up to a basketball. Everyone is down there, and some people are even doing that thing they teach you to do with tornadoes

167

in school when you're a kid—they're curled up on their knees with their heads on the floor by the wall and their hands folded over their hair. I don't know why they teach us that. I don't think tornadoes care. I don't think that's going to save anyone.

Now that I'm breathing I can't stop.

"I don't want to be in here," I say between gasps. I'm getting dizzy. "I don't want to be in here." There are flares and red throbs in my eyes. My mouth tastes like metal. Agate squeezes my wrist hard, and I grab onto my dog's harness handle and squeeze it, also hard. "I don't want to be—"

"You're not there," says Agate. "You're Simon from now. You're okay."

I'm not okay. We're all inside, hiding and waiting to die. "We've gotta—"

"Dude—the hell?" It's Football Brent, who was cheating on Run Across America but didn't get left outside to die, because that's not how it works. It's not that good people get to live. "O'Keeffe, are you *crying*?"

I can feel the entire school staring at me.

"Leave him alone, Brent Fritsch," says Agate. She tugs me down until we're both sitting against one of the walls. Miss Rose shows up with a cup of water for me. There's a crash of lightning that sounds like it hit the roof, and several people scream. The power goes out. The emergencies come on above the red exit signs. The whole space is dim and red.

Hercules climbs into my lap and pushes his head into my chest. Herc is trembling. I squeeze him tight.

168

Agate keeps holding on to me through the whole thing. She knows I'm stuck in a well, and she's ready to pull me up.

The sirens finally stop.

• • •

The power is still out, and when it doesn't come back on they decide to send us home.

"Sack Butt's got a girlfriend," singsongs Football Brent—who actually plays soccer and is not even very good at it—as he gets up to leave.

"Your assumptions are bad and your analysis is bad and I hope you *feel* bad," Agate snaps. Her grip hasn't shifted. For all I know she's never going to let go and that's *fine*. I feel like without her I might just float right out of the world.

We go up to The Pits and sit on the top of the tower of steps and watch everybody turn and look at us on their way out. I don't want to go out there. I have a confused idea that there will be police cars and media trucks. Like there were in *Contact*. Like there were that day in Eagle Crest. I know that's not true but I keep thinking it.

I also know my parents are probably on their way here at supersonic speeds.

Anyway I'm not going out there. Hercules is quiet, leaning on my leg. He's probably feeling worn out after the fuss. He's still pretty little.

"I guess the tornado missed the town," I try. My voice sounds hoarse, like I've been screaming. I hope I haven't been screaming.

169

"They can be very localized," says Agate, bouncing her heels off the carpeted side of the step. "Especially small ones. There might be damage we can't see from here."

I look down at her hand, clasping my wrist. She's two shades lighter than I am, and two sizes softer. Her fingernails are short and raggedy but also painted a weird color that catches the light and looks sometimes lavender, sometimes sea-foam green, like mermaid scales.

"I am sorry you had a panic attack," Agate says.

Panic attacks and trauma reactions are two different things and I feel like I should say that, but it's complicated.

"It is not the same, but I'm worried about my ducks," she says, still not letting go. "And my goats. And my bees. And Todd. And my little brothers and sister." She sounds like she's listed those in order of priority.

"Do you have to—?" I raise my hand so she can let it go if she needs to leave, but she doesn't.

"Jasper and Coral will come find me here," says Agate. "That's the family emergency plan."

Family emergency plans. You'd think my family would have one, except basically our plan is run to each other and hold on for dear life, and it's not working right now. My parents are *still* not here. The school is almost empty, and with the power out it's dim and quiet. There's no hum from the air conditioner, no chatter of voices. A fire truck goes by, a few streets away.

We listen to the siren fall, and Agate squeezes my wrist. "I'll stay," she says.

"Okay."

I put my other hand on Herc's head, squeezing him to make the skin between his ears tent up and relax. He whuffs because he likes that.

We sit for a while. It's quiet. I can hear the wall clock tick. In the basement, before, there were whispers. I could almost see the story about me rippling, one kid leaning into the next, passing along the truth about what happens when you google my name.

It's over.

a note about the patron saint of getting hit by lightning

Saint Barbara—the person, not the church where my dad works—is the kind of saint who is called a virgin martyr. The virgin martyrs were girls who were supposed to get married but didn't want to get married. Now, these days, if you don't want to get married you just do your thing, no big deal. But when the Romans were still in charge, refusing to get married was reason enough for someone to feed you to the lions or chop you up with a sword or something else awful.

A surprising number of girls chose option B. It kind of makes you wonder about how bad Roman boys were, to be honest.

Anyway, there are a bunch of these virgin martyrs, and Saint Barbara is one of them. She's got the usual story, except with the twist where, after she's martyred, the people who killed her got struck by lightning. So Barbara gets to be a saint, *and* she gets posthumous revenge, which you've got to admit is pretty sweet.

She used to be a super-popular saint because of this

Catholic get-out-of-jail-free card: If you die while calling on Saint Barbara you won't go to hell. She is the patron saint of firefighters, bomb makers, artillery men, and—because the Catholic Church is exactly this twisted—anyone and anything in danger of being struck by lightning.

There are churches named for her all over, including the big one in Grin And Bear It, Nebraska.

Which has just been hit by lightning.

eighteen

revenge of the Jesus Squirrel

I don't find that out right away, of course.

I sit there with Agate in The Pits while the school empties, and my first clue that anything is wrong—I mean anything besides my cover getting blown and my entire life falling apart—is when my mom comes bursting through the main door.

"Simon!" she shouts.

"Mom!" I tear away from Agate without hardly noticing. I even lose my grip on Hercules's new handle as I go staggering and running down the perching stairs of The Pits. My sneakers squeak loudly as they hit linoleum. The office door opens, but Mom doesn't stop to check in with Ms. Snodgrass.

"Simon! I'm so—" She's across The Pits. She grabs me and crushes me against her. "I was on a callout—halfway to Bessey—and Dad—" Her fingers dig into my back.

"Dad?"

"The church—" She stops and moves her hands to my shoulders. She's still holding on tight.

Fear dumps itself over me, cold like water. Something's wrong. "What happened to Dad?"

"He's fine!"

I don't believe her. Why would I believe her? She's gasping like she's just run through the Mojave, too.

"He's fine, Simon, but the church—"

"Mom, what happened?"

"The church. St. Barbara's. It's been hit by lightning."

"What?" I say. Because, come on, that's too much.

My mom doesn't elaborate; she just hauls me out to the hearse and takes off. I hope there's no dead body in the back because it would totally get carsick as she peels through the five-block trip to the church. We get there and the hearse hops the curb and skids to a stop nose to nose with the fire truck. Mom and me and Herc tumble out onto the sidewalk, which is easy because we're parked in the middle of it.

We've arrived at St. Barbara's, which is on fire.

But not very much. I mean, grading on a curve, it's hardly on fire at all. The fire truck is sitting unused, its roof lights spinning. There's the littlest thread of smoke rising up from the steeple. The only reason you can tell the church is on fire at all is that there is a crowd of onlookers. They're gathered on the sidewalk and on the big wide front steps that lead up toward the door. I hear someone shout "Simon!" and my dad pushes his way from the back of the crowd and comes rushing down the steps. "I heard the sirens—" He grabs me. "I . . . but I had—"

"Yeah," I say. "Yeah. What—?"

"The church—"

Neither of us is making sentences, but you get it. Dad was worried about me because of course my parents are traumatized, too, and they know about my trauma, and they worry about that—but obviously it's hard for the guy in charge of the church to leave the church when it's actually on fire, even if only a little bit.

When my mom grabs me hard, she's like an eagle who's going to carry me off. When my dad grabs me hard, he's like a bear who's never going to let me move again. I smush my face into his shoulder. I can smell brass polish—*eau de sackbut*—and Dad smell and smoke.

Mom peels me away and says: "Martin?" She jerks her chin to show that he should look behind him.

Of course, there are a lot of people around—it's not every day the town church catches fire. The people nearest us, on the sidewalk, have given us some space by politely forming a ring of spectators. The people on the steps part like an honor guard. The volunteer firefighters, Andy and Doug, all done up in their fireman outfits, are coming down. They are carrying a gurney.

My dad goes white and starts to cross himself.

But the firefighters step closer and we can see it isn't a body on the gurney.

Not exactly.

176

My father's Sign of the Cross stalls out between "Holy" and "Spirit."

"Well, Padre," says Doug. "This here's your problem."

On the gurney is a mass of sticks and twigs and insulation, all smoldering. In the middle of them, as if on a funeral pyre, there is a squirrel. A very dead squirrel. Its little arms and legs are flung wide, and its little tongue sticks out as if it died of surprise. It's a gray squirrel with black tips on its ears and tail.

It's the Jesus Squirrel. He's back.

Or he was.

"See, the deal is," says Doug, "you've got the lightning rod on top of the steeple, but it doesn't do you a lick of good unless it's attached to a cable that carries the lightning into the earth."

"And I'm guessing it wasn't?" says Mom.

Dad is looking at the Jesus Squirrel, goggle-eyed.

"Well," said Doug. "Maybe it *was*. It appears, like, that this fella here chewed through it."

Dad sputters and swallows, like he's going to break into tears. Herc yips. "He's—dead?"

Andy looks Dad up and down. Doug takes off his firefighting helmet and holds it over his heart. "'Fraid so. Gone to meet his maker."

"Was it a pet?" asks Andy, trying to make sense of what's very clearly an impending breakdown.

Dad looks at him, eyes wide and sincere. "It's the Jesus Squirrel."

"Martin . . ." murmurs my mom.

"It's the what now?" says Andy.

"It's the Jesus Squirrel, and this is Ascension."

Ascension is the day when Jesus, having risen from the dead, leaves Earth to go live in heaven. He always picks a Thursday to do this, so it's one of those holy days I lose track of. Dad knows, though.

"He's been called home," says Dad. "It's an act of God."

"Well, now," says firefighter Doug, scratching his ear. "That's a matter for the insurance company."

Dad boggles at him for an instant, then starts to giggle. Actually *giggle*. Like, the kind of giggle that makes the firefighters take a step back.

Mom touches Dad's shoulder and he just crumples— reaching out and hauling me in as he folds into her.

"I heard the sirens." My dad chokes, laughter threatening to topple over into tears. "Simon—" His arm across the back of my neck is shaking.

"It's okay, Martin," says my mom. "Simon's okay. It's going to be okay."

It's not okay. It won't be okay. Moving to Grin And Bear It was my chance to outrun Eagle Crest, but now—the Team Science rumors, and everybody seeing my big trauma thing today, and now Dad melting down . . . there's no way it will ever be okay again.

A few steps away, the Jesus Squirrel smolders gently.

His work here is done.

nineteen

in which there might be damage we can't see from here

Friday. The last day.

I wake up early like always to take Herc outside—just around the block, nothing fancy. He's doing better with his handle harness. There are branches down after the storm yesterday. There are dark puddles. The whole town seems empty, like there was a giant parade that went past and took everyone with it, leaving leaves and twigs scattered about like wet confetti.

Nothing seems quite real.

When I breathe in I can feel my ribs moving and then I get to thinking about breathing and then it's like I have to keep thinking about breathing or maybe I'll stop. That doesn't seem quite real either. Like, maybe it wouldn't be a bad thing.

I have to go to school now.

I just keep thinking that, through scooping poop and

fending off the peacock. *I have to go to school.* Through rattling kibble into Herc's dish. *I have to go to school.* Through getting dressed. Through pouring Frosted Flakes. I lift the dripping spoon to my mouth and think: *I have to go to school.* I do it again and think: *I have to go to school.*

The miracle is, I actually go to school.

And I almost get there.

The school is eight blocks away, and I do fine for seven of them. Then I turn the corner, and the back of the school is right there. So are all the students.

It's not quite time for the bell and everyone is outside, standing around in knots. It's the last day of school, but for me it's like the first day of school. As I go past the bike racks, the kids straddling their bikes stop talking. They turn and watch me go by. Just like that first day, back in February. Except back then they just looked. This time they look and then turn and pretend they're not looking. This time their voices fall to hushed. This time I know all their names.

This time they know mine.

I hear "Simon O'Keeffe" whispered, stirring. I hear "Eagle Crest."

I feel like something in a display case—like a bug with a pin stuck through me. Like the frozen kid in the photograph: the one who comes up if you google my name. It's the first day of school for that kid. The one who everyone knows.

The other Simon O'Keeffe, the one who only wanted people to think *Simon who? I didn't notice him really*—that kid didn't make it.

180

My hand tightens on the leather grip of Herc's harness, so hard it's like I can feel every stitch in the seam.

I walk past the bike racks. Along the side of the school, the row of silent windows. Even my dog is a little on edge. You can tell because he keeps sneezing, which is a dog's way of telling you to chill out and get it together. I try. Every time I pass another group of kids, there's silence and then whispers.

We go around the corner, cut across the little staff parking lot. It's got to be almost time for the bell. I feel like I'm braced for it. Like it's an arrow drawn back on a bow and pointed at me. I finally reach the front of the school.

I see it.

The front steps. There are orange ribbons tied to the step railings. There are some signs taped up. On the bottom step there are three teddy bears. Some flowers. Candles.

My heart rises up into my throat and I stop breathing. I stop walking, too—so suddenly it jerks Herc's harness. He sits right down like he's trained to, and then looks back over his shoulder, his tongue flopping out.

It's a shrine.

A shrine, like they had at Eagle Crest for . . . the other kids, the kids in my class, my friends. I still know all their names. It's a shrine for the dead.

Hercules yips, wondering why I stopped him. I don't look at him, so he turns back and sniffs at the sidewalk at his feet.

There's sidewalk chalk there. I stagger backward a step, and then I can read it. It says, "Stand with Simon."

181

My throat does a thing and I can taste barf in my mouth, just a little. I swallow and I have to close my eyes so it doesn't get worse. The world behind my eyes is red and pulsing, and I can hear the silence pointed at me, feel the staring, the targeting, and then I hear a cheerful call of: "Simon!"

Hercules barks an "Oh, hi there!" bark, and when I get my eyes open, it's to a blur of carrot-colored hair. It's Agate, bouncing on her toes.

"Agate," I croak. I take another step backward. She's standing way too close, and paying no attention to the ribbons and candles at all.

"Simon! You'll never believe what I found out about . . ." She drops her voice. "Our project."

"What?"

She shoots me a look around and slips close like she's going to whisper something. I take another step away.

"It's *next week*," she says. "Jade sent me a printout of the charts, and she said I could borrow her theodolite and I need to double-check the right ascension but it's *perfect*, Simon. Next week on Wednesday Vega will rise directly in line with—"

While she's babbling, I look down at her feet and see she's standing right on top of my name. *Simon* disappears beneath her sandals. She's so *close*. I drop the dog harness and bolt sideways three steps and throw up all over the orange day lilies.

Everyone is staring, *everyone*, and Joyce from the

leadership team is knocking on the office window, trying to get a teacher out here—her fists make sharp glass clacks.

I lean forward, my fingers clawing into my kneecaps. "Simon . . ." I hear tiptoes, and then Agate is rubbing a hand up and down between my shoulders. "What's wrong?"

I can't believe my ears. "What's wrong?!" I'm jerking upright, I'm spinning around. "What's wrong!" I shout. Agate takes a step back. Her big eyes are wide like craters. "They built a shrine like I'm dead, Agate, and you're talking about space aliens!"

"But, Simon, I— Is this about your trauma and anxiety?"

"Of course it's about my trauma and anxiety! All I wanted was to fly under the radar! Do you remember, I told you that? And you said there wasn't any radar!"

"But there isn't any radar," she says—and for the first time Agate has a small voice. I am screaming at her but her voice is small.

"Then why is everybody staring at me?" I spin around and throw my hands into the air. Hercules barks. "Hey, everybody! My name is Simon O'Keeffe! I survived the Eagle Crest school shooting and all I got was this lousy T-shirt!"

Agate slaps her fists against her thighs. It makes a sharp sound, over and over, and I wince, I wince, I wince. There's throw up all over the day lilies. There's slug holes in the hostas by the brick stairs. There's orange on the steps. There's my name smeared and trampled.

The bell rings, a real hammer hitting a real bell, sounding

like a real catastrophe. My body jerks again—like it has wanted to with every bell, thirteen times a day for four months—but this time I let it. This time I turn and run.

• • •

When I get home, the phone is already ringing.

My dad's on the landline that gets our calls and the ones for the parish. He's standing in the downstairs hallway with the cord stretched out around the kitchen door frame, the phone pressed to one ear, hand pressed to the other, because the party line is ringing, too.

He looks up when I come through the door and for just a second his face slips like he's hit an icy patch, and I see terror and joy and other huge things. Then he gulps air and says into the phone: "Never mind, Ms. Snodgrass, he's right here."

The phone says something.

The party line stops ringing.

"Yes, he's fine," says Dad, nodding at me like declaring me *fine* will make me fine. "No. We'll keep him home today, I think." The phone says something else. "Yes, I'm sure." I can hear that my principal is still talking, but Dad hangs up on her.

"Sy—" he starts.

I make a noise and throw myself at him. He wraps me in close. I can feel his kiss in my hair. He snuffles like he's been crying.

"They called to say you were missing."

Missing? I'd been standing right there, throwing up on the flowers. Joyce from the leadership team had been knocking on the glass. If Ms. Snodgrass cared about me, she could have come out the door. Or she could have, you know, kept people from putting ribbons and candles on the front steps. I'm sure it's a tripping hazard or something. "They should look out the window," I mutter.

"What?"

"They should have looked out the window, if they wanted to know where I was. They built me a shrine, Dad."

"A . . . ?"

"Shrine. With orange ribbons and signs and candles."

"And teddy bears," he mutters.

"Three of them," I say. "Like I was—"

"Like you were dead," he says. "Well." My dad, the pastor, coming up empty. The party line rings again, and we both jump. Dad stares at the ringing phone, then turns his back on it. We get about three more steps down the hall and sit on the stairs. Hercules does his thing where he bends into a U between my legs, so he can lean on both my knees at once. I scratch his ribs.

"The phone's been ringing all morning," Dad says. "About the fire, but also—"

"Eagle Crest," I say.

Dad leans past my shoulder and reaches in to stroke one of Herc's soft ears.

"There were some questions already this week," he says. "Word's been trickling out, but now the dam's broken."

185

But I'm not a dam. I'm glass. "Was it Kevin's mom?"

"Maybe." The party line has stopped ringing, but now the house phone rings. Dad ignores it. "Probably."

"I hate her."

"That's strong," he says mildly.

"I do, though. I hate all radio astronomers."

I think of Agate, looking up the declension of Vega. I think of how her strong voice went small.

"I miss podcasts," says Dad. "I miss Netflix. I miss the *Washington Post* online."

"Yeah," I say. "Your life is a tragedy."

Agate's voice went so soft.

I should—I want to tell Dad about it or maybe get up and run up the stairs, but at this point, Pretty Stabby starts screaming, and there's a shout answering him: "Don't even try it, you overdecorated dinosaur!"

Mom's home.

Dad and me get up from the steps as Mom comes sweeping in, the screen door banging behind her.

She's in one of her gray pantsuits, with her hair pulled back in a bun. This is not surprising: She left on a callout or something before Herc and me even finished circling the block at dawn. But there is mud smeared across her suit jacket, and her pants are wet to the knees. A scratch runs across one cheek. She looks like an undertaker pirate.

She also looks like she's about to run someone through with a sword.

My dad doesn't exactly pull me behind him or anything, but he's gentle and protective when he says, "Isobel . . . ?"

The phone rings again—the house line. Mom glares at it, and it actually falls silent.

"Curtis," she says, her voice clipped, "lost a body." She pushes her hands along the sides of her hair. "Simon, why are you home?"

I want to say: "Because my life just came to an end, Mom." What I actually say is: "Curtis what?"

"Curtis Grubsic," says Mom, chopping the air on each word. "Lost. A body."

"He—what?" says Dad.

"How?" I say. "Where? Who?" (When? Why? That unit from English class came in handy after all.)

"Frank Semple," says my mom. "Eighty-two. Heart failure. And I wish I knew. It was a simple pickup from the nursing home. All he had to do was pick the right person and then roll the gurney into the van."

"So, what—?" says my dad.

"He didn't latch the back door," she says. "And the gurney—"

"Oh *no*," I say.

"Rolled out," she says. "Somewhere. Probably on Highway 385."

I try not to know too much about the equipment Mom works with, but I can't help picturing the stainless steel gurney with the black body bag on it, sliding out the back doors of the van, rolling down the dotted yellow line in the middle of a rural highway, heading for freedom. A laugh bursts out of me. Both my parents look at me weird, but not too weird, because in my family we're all weird together.

"The railroad tracks maybe?" my dad guesses. "The ones by the truck stop where the 385 crosses the interstate—it's rough there, it could have jolted the doors. Or there's that place by Salt Creek where the water went out. . . ."

"Martin, I *looked*." Mom sinks onto the stairs.

I sit down beside her, and there isn't enough room but my dad kind of wedges himself in there, too. Hercules can't figure out who needs a good therapeutic lean the most. He cuts eyes from one to the other of us, looking stressed.

"Has Greenway called yet? Or the state police?"

My dad hesitates. "I've been on the other line."

Mom glances sideways at me, gears turning in her head. "Word's out?"

"Yeah," I say. "Really, thoroughly, definitely out."

"They put up orange ribbons outside the school," my dad explains. "And candles."

My mom is silent for a long moment, then says: "Well, heck."

She wraps her hand around the back of my neck. She smells like wildness: water and mud and leaves. "I suppose we could always change our name to Frankenfurter and move to Come By Chance, Newfoundland."

"Cut and Shoot, Texas; Spread Eagle, Wisconsin; and Tightwad, Missouri, are all real places," I tell them.

The phone rings.

188

The jolt is small, but it's a jolt: It's another electric shock on top of a day of electric shocks and my body is all wrung out and my brain just crumples up. I fold forward and lean my face on Herc's back. I can smell his sun-warm coat and his houndiness. He whines. My parents lean over me, arms around each other, and it feels like they're angels spreading their wings over me like in a picture.

But the phone just keeps ringing and ringing, and all we can do is hold on and hope that it will stop.

twenty

in which my dad goes Black Sabbath

It's the Solemnity of the Ascension, the seventh Sunday after Easter, and St. Barbara's Catholic Church of Grin And Bear It, Nebraska, smells of scorched squirrel.

My parents let me stay in my room all day Saturday, and even participated in some therapeutic Lego time. But by Sunday they've hit "Shake it off, Simon" mode. And anyway, like with Kevin's family and science fairs, in my family there's no skipping Mass. So here I am in church.

I'm by myself because Mom is meeting with Greenway about the missing body, and Dad is up front serving the Mass. (It's Father McGillicuddy's week at his other parish, Holy Martyrs in Gaylord.) Sometimes I sit with Kev these weeks, but this week he's an altar boy and I am definitely *not* sitting with his mom.

Honestly? It's a little throat-narrowing just to be looking at Kev. We haven't talked yet.

Anyway, I'm sitting by myself, in the fourth pew from

the front, mumbling along and feeling the eyes on the back of my head. And it's . . . fine. I mean, our life in this town is clearly ruined and I hear Newfoundland is cold and I can't even look at Kevin up there on the altar, high-tops sneaking out from under his white vestments, and I'm basically so stressed that my stomach is going to come out my throat—but it takes a lot to derail a Catholic Mass.

The Church has been doing things the same way for two-thousand-odd years and the Mass has got a lot of momentum. Usually people are barely awake. Of course, usually people didn't just find out that their deacon's son is the survivor of an infamous shooting and their deacon has been lying about/omitting that, this whole time.

Dad finishes the Gospel reading, and I swear the place is totally silent. You could hear a squirrel drop. In the pew in front of me, Dolores Pellnor is reading along in her missalette, running her fingers under the words to make sure Dad gets all his lines right. I look at the back of her head. I can feel other people staring at the back of mine.

" 'For behold,' " reads Dad. I glance up and he's looking right at me. " 'I am with you always, even to the ending of the world.' "

I duck my head and pretend to need to pay attention to Hercules. Dad adjusts the red ribbons in the big book, and closes it. The cover makes a slap. Dad takes a deep breath. I can hear it from here.

And then there's silence. It goes on. And on. And on. Like Dad actually ended the world when he said " 'end of the world.'" My hands grip the top of the pew in front of me.

You're supposed to sit down at the end of the Gospel reading, but there's a cue for that and Dad totally dropped it. People start to shuffle around. Herc makes a worried noise and Mrs. Pellnor glances around to glare at him, but then she catches sight of me and her face goes all-caps TRAGEDY, like the theater mask. "Oh, honey," she whispers. It's the kind of whisper that isn't actually quiet—I'm sure everyone in the church can hear it. "Oh, honey, what are you doing here all alone?"

I start backing up, but Mrs. P. moves fast. She covers my hand in her baby-powder soft ones, and starts patting me—first my hands and then my face as I kind of lean backward. "Oh, honey. It's just a *miracle* you were spared. If you were mine I'd never let you go."

Everyone is stuck standing but I sit down, out of her reach. That seems to break the spell that has a hold of Dad. I've got my eyes closed, but his voice rings out, loud and sure, a medieval brass instrument of a voice. "'You know neither the day nor the hour!'" he says.

Everyone whips around.

"That's what Jesus tells us in the first reading," Dad says. "He has been raised from the dead, and the apostles want to know when he's going to found the Kingdom of God on Earth. And he doesn't tell them. 'You know neither the day nor the hour,' he says."

Okay, this is the homily—the book report on the Bible

192

that the celebrant gives every week. You sit for the homily, so people start sitting down, the rustle of it half-covering Dad's words as he goes on. He's talking kind of fast. "And then Jesus leaves them. He is lifted into heaven. They ask him when God is coming and he doesn't tell them. He won't tell them. Maybe he *can't* tell them. But he definitely leaves."

I'm picturing Jesus rising into the clouds like a lost balloon when my mom slides into the pew beside me. Hercules wiggles all over when he sees her but doesn't bark or jump onto the pew, because he knows he's not supposed to, and he's going to make that guide dog cut, he's the best. She doesn't pet him, because he's working. She does put her hand on the back of *my* neck, giving me a couple of soft strokes. She gives Dad a Nebraska wave—lifting one hand and curling over the fingers.

From the pulpit, he gives one back.

Heads in the front three rows of the church pivot around to see who he's waving at. Mom waves at them, too.

Then Dad starts speaking again, and there's another wave of rustling as people turn back and at least pretend to pay attention.

"I have so many questions," he says. "For instance, what did the disciples mean when they asked Jesus to restore the kingdom? For instance, who are the men in white who tell the apostles they will see Jesus return, just as they saw him go? For instance, did the believers in the early church expect the world to end in their own lifetimes? There are whole branches of theology I could get into here," he says—and trust me, he could. The church is starting to settle in.

But Dad doesn't settle. He shifts. "Instead let us just imagine: We ask Jesus what will happen, and he doesn't tell us. He won't tell us. Maybe he can't tell us. And then he leaves.

"My brothers and sisters, we are on our own."

Dolores Pellnor sniffs into a hanky. It is not an approving sniff. My mom rubs the back of my neck again. The scratch on her face has gotten darker since it scabbed over. She still kind of looks like she might have a sword.

"God loves us," says Dad, who is probably too far away to see Mom's run-them-all-through-with-my-blade expression. "God loves us infinitely, we're told—even more than a parent loves a child. That's hard to imagine. But he sends us out into the world like a parent sending a child to school. We don't know why. Maybe it's because he wants us to be free to grow up. But he sends us out into the world, and anything can happen to us there. Anything!

"We pray but it happens anyway.

"We ask why and God doesn't tell us. He won't tell us. Maybe he can't tell us. We only know he doesn't stop it. He never—"

Dad's voice breaks. There's a ringing silence. I lean into Mom's armpit and look up at the vault of the ceiling. It's painted sky blue and still has patches from where the Critter Getters pulled out the squirrel nests from the rafters. But also it's just old, and showing it: Long cracks wind through the plaster, and the paint bubbles and lifts.

My dad is still silent. Dolores Pellnor isn't the only one sniffing now. Individual sniffs and coughs echo around the church. They seem loud. Behind Dad, Joyce from the leadership team (who is also an altar girl because of course she is) is sitting with her hands in her lap. Kevin is fidgeting. His fingers knot. He rolls his wrists with a snaky motion.

"My son, Simon," says my dad.

I straighten away from Mom and I look anywhere but at Dad. Over toward the side door there's a statue of the Virgin Mary with swords in her heart and a look on her face like she's trying not to fart. I feel Hercules leaning against my knee, working his wet nose under my hand.

"It's not a blessing that my son, Simon, was spared," says Dad. "It's not part of some plan. If I believed that, then I'd also have to believe there was a reason that the others were killed. That it was part of God's plan to take them. To take Lillian and Demarcus and Tyson and Siwa and Mason and Khalil and Keegan and Connor and Ximena and Isla and Mateo and Jayden and Brooklyn and Colton and Aliyah and Emma J and Emma O."

My dad stops, again. The silence is tight. Hercules whines, and I can feel him quiver. Then all of a sudden he jumps up onto the pew beside me. The scramble of his claws is loud, and for just a second I think that guide dogs can't care so much that they do what they're not supposed

195

to do—but I can't think about that right now. Instead I curl down to take care of Herc, helping him settle in my lap. With my head down I can't tell if everyone is looking at me or if everyone is trying not to, but it's one or the other and either way it feels like crosshairs.

"God didn't take them," says Dad. "God doesn't shoot kids. He didn't do that to them."

Mom's hand is between my shoulder blades. Herc turns and tries to work his head inside my sweatshirt, his muzzle into my armpit. I wrap my hand around the leather grip of his harness.

"There is no plan. Stop saying that."

I scoop Herc up like he's much littler, tuck him under my arm like a football, push past my mom, and bolt for the nearest door. Everyone seems as frozen as the Virgin Mary. Everyone watches me go.

The door slams closed behind me with a huge sound, like two thousand years of Mass coming off the rails.

• • •

I'm not crying.

I don't think I'm even sad. Angry, maybe? Shocked? I'm panting. I don't know where to go.

My mom shows up like a shark from the depths. She doesn't say anything. She puts an arm on my shoulder, steers me. I put Herc down and he comes and leans on my shin, his handle ready for my hand. My mom guides me around the back of the church—less traffic—and almost

196

like we're sleepwalking we start to head to Slaughter.

"Simon . . ." she begins.

But right then I hear footsteps pounding up behind me. My first response is terror, because of course it is, but I manage to stuff that down and get to my second response, which is to turn around.

Kevin is running down the street toward us. His altar boy white robes flap around him and his purple hair is flying everywhere. "Sy, wait up!" he calls.

I haven't told my parents all the gory details about how Team Science turned away from me and Kevin vanished, but I've told them enough that my mom slides in front of me and puts her hand on her hip, like she's gonna unsheathe that sword of hers. Right now she's mad at everybody: Curtis the body-loser; Saint Barbara asleep at her saint switch; whoever arranges tornadoes; all radio astronomers; Dad.

"Mom . . . Hey, Mom?" I tug on her arm. I don't know if I want to smack Kevin or hug him, but either way I don't want my mom there. "We'll just be in the park, okay?"

We're passing Lions' Lagoon, which is a little play park with a splash pad in it on Neihardt and Fifth. It's hot and the splash fountains and squirters are on; there are tiny little kids happy-screaming in their high voices.

"Are you sure, Simon?" Mom asks.

"Yeah . . ." I say. "Friend stuff, you know?"

My mom makes a clicking noise with her tongue like a hunting bat, but she backs off, walking toward home. After a minute, Kevin bounces to a halt in front of me. "Dude." Kev puts his knuckles to his mouth instead of swearing. "I mean: your dad— Dude!"

"I know."

"I mean, *holy*—" He puts a lot of theology in the one word. "That was the most metal sermon I've ever heard."

And . . . he's kind of right. I mean, the last thing I needed was a high-drama sermon on school shootings, but on the other hand, it was a giant *back off* to a town that really needed one.

But then, with the topic of my dad's breakdown/homily completely exhausted, silence drops on us. Kev and me stand there in the pause and it's as awful as putting on wet jeans. We both fidget.

All of a sudden Kev steps in and gives me a huge hug. His holy robes are scratchy and he's sweating in them. "Simon, I was a crap friend. I knew my mom was— That you didn't— But I didn't know what to say."

"It doesn't matter."

"It *does*, Sy."

"No, I mean, it doesn't matter what you say. But you've got to say *something*, bonehead." I smack the side of his head. "That was *not cool*, you skinny, stupid-haired, cowardly Cornhusker."

"Copy that," he says, pounding my back.

I hug him back, real hard.

Hercules barks because hugging makes him happy, at least when it isn't Mrs. Pellnor.

198

"Can I—?" says Kevin. He's pulled off his white robes and is looking at Herc, who is of course wearing his future-service-dog vest, complete with the sign on it that says *Do not pet.*

I look down at Herc, too. "Release," I tell him, letting him know he can stop guide-dogging.

"Herc-u-lees!" cries Kevin, because he also knows what "release" means. Kev shoves an armful of robe at me, and I let Herc go and he love-lunges toward Kevin. Kev rolls him into a little wrestle in the grass by the sidewalk. They must have mowed it yesterday: Herc and Kevin are getting covered in grass clippings. It smells like green.

Suddenly I'm like, *forget it.*

Forget flying under the radar. Forget hiding. Forget ordinary time.

It doesn't matter what you say, but you have to say something. All of a sudden, I know exactly what I want to do.

"So, Kevin," I say. "Me and Agate are going to fake a message from outer space."

Kevin sits up on the grass. "Umm. What?"

"Agate's got it all worked out." I unsnap Herc's harness so he can wiggle on his back. I feel weirdly calm. My fingers are robot steady. "She says this week Vega rises right behind her tree house. When it does, we're going to beam prime numbers right at the Big Ear."

Kevin looks at me with his eyes wide. "Beam with what?"

"Your microwave," I say. "I need you to help me steal it."

"Dude," he says, and breathes out real big, like someone hit him or he's gearing up to lift something heavy. He sits up, knees splayed and hands hanging between them. For a long time he doesn't say anything. Then: "Is this about my mom? What she did?"

"No." But Kevin's mom is, like, patient zero in the zombie rumor apocalypse that swept through Team Science, *and* she runs the Big Ear, so it's not like that hasn't crossed my mind. "Okay, maybe kind of. But Agate started in on this months ago—right after I moved to town. I didn't exactly say yes, but—"

"You forgot to actually tell her no?"

I plop down beside him, both of us with our knees bent up, facing in the same direction—off toward the church, and beyond that the school, and beyond that the Dismal River National Forest and the radio telescope dishes hazy on the tops of distant hills.

"I'm going to give people in this town something new to talk about. You in?"

Kevin pauses.

"Yeah," he says. "Okay. Avengers assemble. I'm in."

twenty-one

in which the Avengers assemble

So we steal Kevin's microwave.

It's not even hard, because he took it to the regional science fair and it's still in his mom's Prius. Kevin nabs the keys from her purse, pops the trunk, and hauls the microwave out before she even knows we're home from church. We load the microwave, plus its manual, plus all of Kev's science fair notes and the display posters rolled up in a shipping tube, into the trailer of my bike. Herc has to squish up against the mesh on the other side. Soft golden bits of his fur poke through the black nylon grid.

I tell my mom where we're going, obviously, because otherwise she'd hunt me down to make sure I was okay, and then kill me. By the time me and Kevin get to my house, my dad is back from church and on the phone. He's so on the phone that his head is bent over and his eyes are closed. He doesn't even look up at me. Mom tells me it's the chancery—the bishop's office—which is the Catholic

201

equivalent of being called in to see the principal. Plus, Mom is looking pirate daggers at him. He's going to catch it from her as soon as he's done catching it from the actual Imperial Majesty of the Roman Catholic Church, and she's scarier. But I can't say I feel bad.

Anyway. The smile Mom gives me is a little sharp, but she's glad I'm with Kevin, and glad we want to bike down and see Agate, glad we want to do normal things. She actually says "normal things," and somehow I fail to mention that the normal things we want to do include faking a message from space aliens.

She looks at Dad, who is still on the phone, then gives me some cash so we can hit up the Groceries and Go For It and load up on snacks.

So we do that. In the grocery store, we can tell that Dad's giant *back off* has backfired. I collect carrots and hummus, whispers and stares, crackers and cheese, Cool Ranch Doritos, plain chips, three expressions of sympathy, juice boxes, jelly beans, and an actual pat on the head. Spread Eagle, Wisconsin, is sounding good—but so is completely blowing the lid off everything people think they know about me.

I mean. If anything in the world can possibly get the town of Grin And Bear It off the subject of Simon O'Keeffe and his disaster family, it will be a message from aliens.

Then I think: The last time I saw Agate I shouted at her. She rubbed my back and I *screamed* at her. Her voice went so so small.

202

What if it's gone all the way to nothing?

That's what I think, the whole way through the Dismal River National Forest, listening to my bike wheels hiss across the mushroom-colored puddles that groove the gravel roads. What if my best friend has nothing to say?

• • •

I kinda forgot about this, but it's Kevin's first time on the Van der Zwaan farm.

He does not exactly get to ease into it.

As usual there's a lot going on. Agate's three-year-old brother, Onyx, is halfway up the crab apple tree, attaching a rope to the laundry-line pulley in an attempt to hoist Todd the dog like a bucket. The twin babies are in a playpen in the shade of the tree, banging on pots with wooden spoons. There are for some reason ducks everywhere. But the centerpiece of the action is the goats.

There's a pen, like for puppies, set up in the shade in front of the barn, and three of the goats are in it, with Agate's mom, and her teenage sibs, Jasper and Coral.

Agate is nowhere in sight, so Kev and me look at each other, and then walk our bikes over toward the pen, the gravel crunching under our tires. Agate's mom is on her knees, facing the back end of a goat, and she doesn't see us.

"Mrs.—uh, Pearl?" I call. She half-turns. This gives us a good view of what she's doing. What she's doing involves being elbow-deep in female goat anatomy.

The goats are having baby goats.

Kevin turns green.

"Oh," Pearl says. "Simon. And . . . ?"

"This is Kevin," I say, trying to look at her face and not her hands. "He's, uh—another friend of Agate's."

"I didn't know she had another friend."

"Sure," says Kevin. The goat that Emo-Twin Coral is standing beside abruptly makes a noise like a demon with indigestion. There's some sliding and slime and suddenly a baby goat.

"Sure," says Kevin again, swallowing hard. "Agate's a hoot."

"If you laugh at my sister, I'll cover your bike with animal birthing lubricant," says Emo-Twin Jasper.

Kevin nods, purple curls bouncing. "Specific warnings are important for everyone's safety."

At that point, Todd the dog stands up, shakes to shed the rope that Onyx draped on him, and ambles over to us. Hercules perks his ears in pure delight.

"Agate's in her tree house, Simon," says Pearl. "But to be honest, I'm not sure she'll be glad to see you."

My stomach knots up. "Yeah," I say. "But we'll just—"

"Go ahead," she says, and then *her* goat makes a noise, and she turns back to her work. Coral's baby goat is already tottering to its feet. Coral shoots us a look as we go by. It says both "I hate you" and "Rescue me."

We don't. Kev picks up the microwave and I get the snacks and the science fair stuff and my dog, and we head out down the side of the field. Kev is nearly as green as his old hair. "Glad you're on Team Science instead of Team Farm?" I ask him.

"Dunno, man. Biology is a science and that was *a lot* of biology." He shifts the microwave in his arms. I know from helping to steal it that it's not super heavy, but it does look awkward. "Did you and Agate have a fight?"

"Kind of. She was trying to tell me about the space alien messages and I was freaked out about something else. I sort of blew up at her." I pause. Todd the dog is keeping pace with us, like one of my grocery bags might have beer in it. "Actually, I totally blew up at her."

"Was this the tornado thing?"

"You heard about that?"

He tries to shrug but it doesn't work because his arms are full of microwave. "Small town, Sy-my-man."

Right.

"It wasn't really the tornado. But the next morning, everybody knew, and . . ."

"I heard about the ribbons and stuff, too."

Of hecking course he did. Small town.

"Trade?" I say, putting the snacks down. The path down to the tree house skirts behind the duck pen, dips into some trees, and then heads along the side of the goat meadow. We're about to do that part, and it doesn't seem fair that Kevin should carry the microwave the whole way. Kevin fills my arms with microwave. He takes Herc, the grocery bags, and the papers. We shuffle onward, up out of the tree dip, around the corner.

205

"What's everybody saying?" I ask.

"That you lost it. Like, just totally broke down."

"That's about how it—"

But at that point, midsentence, we run right into the space alien.

It's human-shaped and wearing a white space suit, but with a giant featureless head made out of copper mesh. I yelp and jump backward. Somehow I'm thinking about the angels in the Gospel this morning, how they started the way angels in the Bible always start: *Don't be afraid.*

The space alien in the goat meadow starts: "Is that a microwave?"

I blink.

"Uh," says Kevin. "No?"

The space alien lifts the hood of what I finally get is a beekeeper's suit. Underneath the hood is Agate's emu-farming neighbor, Mr. Bagshott. He's got a contraption like one of those metal detectors old guys take to the beach, and he's trying to wrangle it, plus a can of spray paint, plus a pair of dowsing rods, plus a clipboard. The hood is one thing too many for him—he bobbles and grabs at everything, but only the giant metal detector doesn't go crashing down.

"You can't have a microwave here!" he sputters. "It's— it's— Do you have any idea how much electromagnetic radiation a microwave like that can produce?"

"About four hundred thirty watts," says Kevin. He lets go of Herc and starts picking up Mr. Bagshott's stuff. "I mean, for this one, specifically."

I hug the big white box to my chest.

"I am *trying*," Mr. Bagshott spits, "to screen this property for concerning electromagnetic sources. And you brought a *microwave*?!"

"Not on purpose," I say. Though it's hard to imagine how we could have done it accidentally.

Todd the dog gives a huge sigh and lies down on the orange X that Mr. Bagshott has sprayed on the field. Hercules starts licking the old dog's nose.

"It's a prop," I say. "For Kevin's science fair project."

Kev piles the clipboard and spray paint and dowsing rods into Mr. Bagshott's arms. "Anyway. We were just going—" He gestures at the tree house in a way that's both wild and vague. "So we'll do that." He takes the microwave from me and we scoot off as fast as microwave-ily possible, sucking our cheeks in so we don't laugh.

"Rocky!" Mr. Bagshott's roar follows us. "Rocky!"

Agate's head appears at the railing of the tree house. "Hello, Mr. Bagshott!" she bellows politely. "Have you found any concerning electromagnetic sources?"

"Rocky! Call your dog!"

Todd is still lying directly over the spray-painted X. He rolls slowly onto his good hip and sighs. Really, all he needs is a drink with a little umbrella.

Agate cups her hands around her mouth so she can politely explain at top volume. "I'm sorry, Mr. Bagshott, but Todd is his own dog. I *could* call him but he doesn't have any drive to please me."

"Hey, Todd," calls Kevin, because he's a decent guy. "Come on, boy!"

But Todd doesn't have any desire to please Kevin either, and I've got nothing. So we leave Mr. Bagshott and his new service dog to their problems and trek on. It feels like a long way. Agate doesn't move, and she doesn't shout to us. She just watches us come.

When we finally get to the tree house, she's moved to sit at the top of the ladder, her feet dangling down into empty space. She looks at us between her knees. "Hello, Kevin Matapang," she says. "Hello, Simon."

"Hey, Agate," says Kev.

I say: "Hi."

I don't know what else to say. Kevin kind of gives it some space.

"I've been thinking," says Agate, drumming her heels against the top step of the ladder. "About Einstein's theory of time."

"Okay," I say. Hercules is wiggling because he's excited to see Agate. The plastic loops of the grocery bags are cutting dents into my fingers.

"Because you said you wanted to be Simon from Now, right," says Agate. "That's what's important. Simon from Now and not Simon from Then."

Hercules is wiggling harder. His excitement overcomes his guide-dog training and he barks just once.

"So I thought I should tell you," says Agate, "that there isn't any now."

"I kind of think there is, though," says Kev. He bobbles the microwave a little. Things are always heavier when you're stuck standing still with them.

"No, you're wrong. Einstein says that the past still exists and the future already exists. The whole thing's like a field and you're just standing somewhere in it. There's nothing special about where you're standing. And I'm standing someplace different, and sometimes we can talk to each other and sometimes we can't, but there is nothing special about where I'm standing either. There is nothing special about now."

"Wow," says Kevin, whose mom is an astrophysicist. "So, you're, like, super smart."

"Yes," says Agate. "But sometimes people don't like that."

"I like that," I say.

"Me too," says Kev. "And I'm gonna think about that time field thing for, like, three years, but right now this microwave is getting heavy."

Agate does what I'd hoped she do: She lights up like the moon. "You brought your microwave!"

"Simon recruited me to Team Space Aliens."

"Simon!" exclaims Agate. She pushes her hands over her mouth for a second, like she's trying to hold in a squeal of joy, then drops them and flaps them around.

"If I lift it, can you pull it?" says Kevin.

"Oh, yes," she says. "I'm also very strong."

So the two of them wrangle the microwave up the ladder

steps, and then we fire-brigade the snacks up. Finally I go up and pull Herc by his harness, while Kevin boosts him from the back end and he scrambles. It's amazing how much Hercules has grown: He's still a puppy, but he's a puppy with long legs and a let's-go attitude now, not a round little ball of fuzz and shyness.

Let's go, Hercules.

Let's go, Team Us.

Herc goes off exploring the tree house with his tail wagging, and I pause for a sec and lean my shoulder against Agate's. "Hey. So. I wanted to say."

She turns and blinks at me. "What?"

I can't quite get it out. "So you're super smart."

"*And s*uper strong."

"And I'm super sorry. For yelling at you. That's what I wanted to say."

She drops her chin for a sec. "It's okay," she says, her voice little again.

"It's not, though. I was . . . There was a lot going on. But I didn't mean to blow up at you."

She smiles a little and leans her shoulder against mine. Today she is wearing a shirt with some kind of graph on it. It says *Mean Is Just So Average.*

Kevin crests the ladder. "Oh man," he says, looking around at the tree house. *"Sweet."*

Agate's been busy up here. There's a star chart on one wall, a lot of star-shaped Post-it Notes in yellow and orange. They're covered with her neatly looping handwriting. She

210

has a list of the prime numbers, a chart with times on it, all kinds of stuff. It's both cool and a tiny bit serial killer.

"My sister Jade who's away at college sent me the charts so I can know when and where Vega rises here." She's talking to Kevin because this is the part she already told me. "And she said I could borrow her theodolite."

"Her what now?"

"Her theodolite," says Agate. "It's a surveying instrument with a rotating telescope for measuring horizontal and vertical angles. We can use it to line up the microwave with Vega and with the Large Radio Telescope."

"Why does your sister have a the-odd-. . . ?"

"Thee-ah-duh-lite."

"Right. Why does she have her own theodolite?"

"Because in high school she had a special interest in land surveying," says Agate. "And in my family we believe in supporting self-directed exploration. That's why Coral and Jasper are allowed to do that to their hair."

"The emo-twins have a special interest in looking morbid?"

"Yes, they do," says Agate. "They also have silk-screening equipment. Here, Simon." She reaches into an old blue milk crate full of tools and hands me a hammer.

"Uh." I swing the hammer a little so it feels more real. There's a lot going on and I'm not sure why I'm holding a hammer. "Why?"

"The first thing we need to do is build a platform for the microwave to sit on," Agate says. "Then we can use the microwave to generate the signal, like in Kevin's Australia story."

I remember the story Kevin told while we were watching *Contact*, about how a defective microwave accidentally tricked a team of radio astronomers.

"Then, really," says Kevin, folding his dark eyebrows together, "what we have to do first is figure out how to get the microwave to run with the door open. I mean, if you want to send a signal with microwave beams. This one doesn't leak much microwave radiation. I proved that with, you know—" He waves a hand at the tube of posters he brought with him. "Science."

"Oh," says Agate, crestfallen—her red curls literally seem to droop. "But can you?"

"Maybe," he says. "I brought the manual." He gets it out, grabs a juice box the way Todd grabs a beer, and flops into one of the beanbags. Agate flops into the other beanbag as if Kev just showed her how to do it.

"So I'll just go over here and do the grunt work, I guess?" I say, waving the hammer at the milk crate of tools and the little pile of scrap lumber.

Agate nods at me brightly. "Remember that triangles make very stable braces," she says.

"Yeah, I know. I got an A in toothpick bridge–building based on that one fact alone."

"His exploded," says Kev.

"Oh!" says Agate. "Congratulations, Simon!"

For the next hour or so, while Agate and Kevin pore over

manuals, I saw and bang and screw together two-by-fours to make triangle braces to attach to the railing, and find a bit of plywood to set on top of them. Clearly I'm not the brains of the outfit. I'm the snacks and repressed trauma of the outfit. But also I'm making this happen, and it feels kind of good to have tools in my hands, to make noise and cut and build things.

Hercules sleeps on his side in the sun, his long puppy body arched like a bow, his little poochy belly bare and pink. Sunshine catches in the pale hairs of his coat.

I've just about got the triangle braces ready and the top built when Kevin and Agate appear jubilant: It turns out that to make the microwave run while it's open you just trick it into thinking it's closed by jamming the little latch thing in the door with a paper clip and some duct tape.

They tell me all about this, bursting with their own brainpower, and then they admire my triangular braces. Mr. Dwyer, the eight-fingered shop teacher, would be proud of me.

The only question now is where to put the braces and shelf so that we can see both Vega rising up and the Big Ear. Apparently we have to be able to see both if this is going to work. Agate says this like it's obvious, and Kevin seems to think so, too, so I don't ask. We scout around, putting our ears down on the top railing, and finally pick a place at the back corner of the tree house balcony. The tree house is on the top of the wooded hill at the edge of the Van der Zwaan farm, backing onto Mr. Bagshott's emu pastures. In that direction there's mostly trees and emus grazing, like a scene out of *Jurassic Park*. In the other direction is the long slope of the goat meadow, then the duck barns and regular barns and Van der Zwaan farmhouse, looking small beneath the huge weird tower of the Big Ear.

Agate checks with her theodolite and declares it a good spot. She bounces around. Apparently tomorrow we'll have to figure out exactly where the braces should get screwed in, but for the moment we seem good to go.

So naturally right then I think of something. "Wait— where are we going to plug in the microwave?"

My two genius friends stare at each other, mouths open. Hey, the trauma of the outfit contributed.

We all turn around slowly and look down at Mr. Bagshott. And his extension cord, trailing him all the way back to his barn.

twenty-two

in which the Avengers steal an extension cord

Step two, steal an extension cord.

I mean, acquire.

No one wants to steal Mr. Bagshott's extension cord, because we watched him put it in his emu barn and we know that emus have five-inch talons and can kick with the force of a sledgehammer, and also because we know that stealing is wrong. Agate's family's extension cords are all tied up running goat-birthing equipment (I didn't ask), but Kevin figures that the Hello Hello will have some extras. So the next morning, Agate comes over and we go to meet Kevin there.

It's Monday, the first Monday of the summer. My dad is on the phone again, this time to the *National Catholic Reporter*, which is like the Catholic version of the *New York Times*—the biggest of newspaper big deals. From what I can get from his side of the convo, he's trying to explain his view on the divine plan—or the absence thereof—and how that relates to squirrel infestations. My mom is out meeting with the state police about Mr. Missing Body.

Their lives are falling apart right alongside mine.

I should probably care more.

Agate cares. We walk down Main Street, me with Herc and Agate pushing her cargo bike. (She has to stop in at the feed store for more animal birthing lubricant.) It's sunny and nice out—not hot like last week—with a little breeze. Our little town looks perfect as a movie set, all petunias and fluttering flags.

There are also orange ribbons all over. Swell.

As we walk down to the Hello Hello, Agate tries to explain the small-town interconnections of Mr. Missing Body to me. "Miss Semple and Ms. Snodgrass our principal are twin sisters," she says.

"Miss Semple?"

"She likes people to call her Connie, but my parents say I should use last names. She runs The Haute Goat." The Haute Goat is a shop on Main Street that sells goat soap, angora wool shawls, pillows with goat silhouettes on them, coat hooks shaped like goats, that sort of thing. I've been in there to socialize Hercules to perfumes. The woman who runs it is kind of watercolory—soft and drippy—and it's hard to imagine her being twins with our killer-owl principal.

Agate isn't finished. "Mister Missing Body Semple also had many nieces and nephews, including Doug Semple,

216

who is the firefighter, Kristen Semple from the insurance office, and several members of the farming community."

We're walking past the dentists' office, which is called Grin and Brush It. They've got a poster board version of an orange ribbon taped up in the front window between the miniblinds and the glass. I trail my fingers over the glass as we walk by. They make a high, thin squeak. Herc turns to look at the noise.

One way or another, the entire town is talking about me and my family.

But maybe, just maybe, the subject is about to change.

We head into the Hello Hello, where Kevin's dad is behind the counter. He smiles, all soft like the weather. "Ah, Simon: good. I saved you the kransekake."

Right. I was supposed to come over yesterday, before I got sidetracked by my dad's Death Metal Sermon routine. I worry for a minute Kevin's dad will be mad at me, but for some reason it's easy to just let that go.

"Hello, Dr. Matapang," says Agate. "We are meeting Kevin here. I cannot try halo halo because texture mixing is hard for me."

"Well, then, you can have some kransekake, too," he says, heading for the back room. "And you can call me Doc."

Agate, whose parents want her to use last names, looks puzzled; I don't know where she's going to land on this one.

Doc Matapang comes out carrying his creation: a giant tower of ring-shaped cookies. He looks proud when he puts it in front of us and I don't blame him. The thing looks like you could launch it into space. "No nut allergies?" he asks us, and when we say no, he plucks the top cookie off, snaps off its bottom, and passes it to Agate.

He hands me the broken part and the next layer down, and then helps himself to the third layer. The cookies are nutty and crunchy and mine is sticky on the outside—Doc used caramel for glue, which must be why he got rid of that bottom part for Agate's texture thing. In a minute there are crumbs all over the table. There's sun coming through the front window, lighting up the board games on a cube shelf and math on the chalkboard Doc keeps for the junior scientists. The whole thing is Team Science Maximum Cozy. I notice there aren't any orange ribbons in here, either.

We're starting on the next layer down when Kevin comes plunging through the door, elbows and purple hair swinging, ready to make progress on our mission. "Dad, can I borrow some extension cords?" he asks, before the bells have even stopped jangling.

Doc M just smiles. "Slow down, son, it's a kransekake day."

"Hello Kevin we're over here," says Agate, with that missing-commas way she has.

I settle for leaning out past the chalkboard and waving. Herc barks hello.

"Sit with your friends a minute," Kevin's dad tells him, and heads for the back room.

Kev swings around the corner of the chalkboard and

flumps onto the squishy couch beside me. I release Herc so he and Kevin can love each other up.

Agate smiles at him. "I forgot to ask you about the regional science fair competition, which I know is important to your family."

"Oh, yeah, Kev: How'd it go?"

"I got a bronze. I have to go to state."

Agate blinks. "Do you *want* to go to state?"

Kevin takes a beat. Just a beat, but it feels like a big one, like my dad dropping the "sit down" cue at Mass.

"Sure," he says. He twists a finger into his purple curls, like I do with the phone cord when I can't wait to hang up. "My mom, you know, she . . ."

"I know," I tell him, and put my hand on my hip in the Zeny-approved quoting style. "She wants you to have *choices*."

"But one of your choices is saying no," says Agate.

"You should talk!" I laugh. This is the person who just showed up with a puppy and recruited me to Team Fake Space Message as if no one had ever said no to her in her whole life.

"What?" Agate frowns. "Nos are important."

I remember that with both things—the puppy and the alien message—both times I did the Simon Says Special. I didn't say yes and I didn't say no; I tried not to stir anything up at all. I glance at Kevin. He looks thunderstruck, like his brain is Jesus-squirrel smoldering. I look back at Agate.

"Right," I say. "You're right. And—I don't know if I said, but, this message mission? That's a yes."

Kevin's dad shows up right then. He's so silent for a big guy—but for a change it's not me that gets startled. Kev half-leaps out of his seat. Doc Matapang passes him an orange coil of extension cord.

• • •

"You know," says Kevin. "They only send three people to state from the western region, so it's a big deal."

"I know," says Agate. "Also I read all your project notes and they were really good and interesting."

"So why are you—?"

"Guys," I say. "I think we still have a problem." We are walking up Cather from the river, Agate and Kev pushing their bikes and me walking Herc. Agate has scored the animal birthing lubricant from the feed store, and also bought the longest extension cord she could afford with the extension cord money she brought along. That turns out to be fifty feet. The one from the Hello Hello is thirty feet. Kevin has liberated the one from his garage for another thirty feet. "We're still going to be thirty or forty feet short."

"Twenty-eight," says Agate, who has measured the distance from the emu barn to the tree house with her borrowed surveying equipment, because of course she has. It's almost noon, and it's getting hotter: Squiggles of air are showing above the new asphalt patches. We *can't* get stuck at the extension-cord step of our secret plan. That would never happen to the Avengers.

We go past Lions' Lagoon, past the little kids tearing around and the moms buying water at the ice-cream cart, and the high-school kids lounging on the curb licking red, white, and blue Popsicles. The moms whisper and the high-school kids stare. One of them raises a power fist at me. Great. Sure. Power. I ignore him.

There's basically only one more place to check for extension cords: my place. I have spent way too much time in the Gardens of Peace and Memory with a rabid peacock and a plug-in weed whacker, so I know we have an extension cord, and I know it's long. I just haven't come up with a way to ask my parents if I can borrow it. They're still kind of fighting, and they will channel that into being very responsible and asking me a lot of questions.

But we luck out. No one's home in the home part of the funeral home: Dad's left a note saying he's gone to the church; Mom is nowhere to be found. I check the garages first, just in case I left the extension cord there. Agate trails me. Kevin keeps jumping up to get a glimpse through the callout van's back windows.

"It's completely boring in there," I tell him. "There's, like, a loading ramp and bolts to tie a gurney down."

Kevin scrunches his nose and tries one more jump, then knocks his hands against his knees. "Did you find it?"

"No, but that's okay: It will be in the big closet in the

basement." I lead my friends through the side garden, past the fountain, onto the front porch.

Kevin doesn't figure it out until I open the front door. "Wait," he says. "The big closet in the basement *by the morgue*?"

I turn around in the doorway. "Yeah, but—look, it's just a hallway—"

"No, but . . ." says Kevin.

"Oh!" Agate speaks on top of him. "Are there bodies in here?"

"Not unless Mom found Mr. Semple."

They look at each other, scared and thrilled. I hold the door open for them, and they practically tiptoe into the plush entryway.

The front of the house is like the back of the house, scrubbed clean and dressed up for—well, for a funeral. It's got the same dark wood on the staircase, the same roses in the plaster work, the same rippled glass in the old windows, but instead of being covered in Lego, dog hair, and sackbut parts, it's covered in potted ferns, guest books, and wooden racks full of hymn books. The big front rooms—the gathering room and the viewing room—are empty. We go past them. In the hallway beyond the sweeping staircase my mom's office door is shut. Bathrooms, a coat room. The kitchen that always smells like punch. The thick carpet soaks up sound, and it's quiet the way a haunted forest might be quiet. The door to the basement stairs is at the end of the hall, and when the floorboards there creak Kevin actually jumps.

"You guys seriously don't have to come." My hand's on the basement doorknob, which feels like the point of no return. "It's just a closet—but I could go by myself. Meet you on the porch?"

"I want to go!" whispers Agate, bouncing. As usual her whisper carries like high bells. She's not lying—she never does.

Kev looks around to see who might have heard her. Then he realizes I'm looking at him. "No, I mean, I do, too," he says, sounding like maybe he is lying, but we *just* had that thing about saying no, so I've got to figure he's not. I open the door.

The steps have the same vibe as the upstairs—hushed and plush—and there's a fake fern under a spotlight at the bottom of them so that if someone opens this door they don't freak out. There's also a big sign over the fern that says *Private*, so if somebody opens this door they don't go down.

We go down.

Around the corner, past the fern, is where things change. The basement has a linoleum floor and shiny beige paint like a hospital. There are lockers and a corkboard with chemical safety signs on it. There's one of those sinks where, if you get something in your eyes, you can squirt them clean. Against one wall there are racks full of chemicals: bleach, but lots of other stuff, too. Agate runs a finger along one shelf. "Does your mom's work make her queasy?" she asks, pointing to a row of a dozen white plastic bottles. The stuff that's in them is the exact same pink as Pepto-Bismol.

"It's embalming fluid," I say. "They take out all your blood and fill you up with this stuff. It's pink because it turns bodies more . . . you know, pink."

"I did not know that," says Agate, delighted.

Kev is not as enthused. "Dude, it kind of . . . smells in here." It does. Like bleach.

Mostly.

"Fun fact!" says Agate. "The chemical that makes the smell of dead bodies is called cadaverine."

"And I'm out," Kevin singsongs.

We edge past the chemical racks to the storage closet. Unfortunately, my dad's philosophy of "a little holy chaos" extends to home organization, so this is going to take a little rummaging.

"No, that's not the fun part of the fun fact yet," says Agate. "The fun part of the fun fact is that cadaverine is also used in perfumes."

"Oh gross, why?" says Kev, all in a breath. "Why?"

"Because it also smells like . . ." She drops her voice, looks up and down the hall, and whispers, "Sperm."

"Agate!" Kevin leaps into the storage room behind me and promptly gets tangled up in a coiled mess of fall leaf garlands. (My mom is not the kind of person who likes seasonal decorations, but in funeral homes it's kind of professionally required.)

"*Why*, Agate?" Kevin cries. "Pass me the bleach, I'm going to pour it directly into my brain."

224

"You will have to take your hands off your ears first," says Agate, reasonably. Fortunately I've finally spotted the banana-yellow loop of the extension cord sticking out from under a taped-up Christmas tree box labeled *Easter*. I tug the cord out, causing a minor holiday-themed avalanche. Kevin jumps. He's been jumpy since the kransekake and the thing about choices, and I'm not sure why. It seems like a good thing, almost: Jumpy is better than frozen.

I hold up the extension cord. "Mission accomplished!"

"Great," says Kev. "Send a quinjet and a class-five extraction team." He's still holding Herc for me. We all beat a fast track up the hallway.

But when we get to the bottom of the stairs, we hear voices.

The floor is creaking overhead. We hear a door—and see that we've left the one at the top of the stairs open.

"Guys—" Kevin hisses, just as one of the voices gets loud for a second and we all recognize it. It's our principal, Ms. Snodgrass. She has that tone like she wants us to *think about what we've done.*

Mom's office is right at the top of the stairs: They must be in there. We can hear every word. And with the door open—we stare at each other and start to creep backward down the hall.

"Miss Semple, Ms. Snodgrass," says my mom. "I— I don't know how to tell you this. We found your father's body."

"But that's good news," says Miss Semple, the watercolor lady from The Haute Goat. She sounds relieved, puzzled.

225

"At—" Mom hesitates again. "At a truck stop. In Iowa."

"*What?*" says Ms. Snodgrass.

Mom's totally getting detention.

Kevin and Agate and me are about halfway down the hall, between the stairway at one end and the big double swinging doors at the other. Only dead people and my mom go through the double doors, and we're not going to, so we're stuck next to the rack of Cavity King cavity fluid. Unless you're a seasonal decoration or a jug of embalming chemicals, there's nowhere to hide.

"It seems," says Mom, inching forward like she's on a tightrope, "that at the truck stop off the Bessey exit, the gurney, ummm, became entangled with a tractor trailer. And then was pulled along, you see. With the truck."

"To Iowa," says Ms. Snodgrass.

"Connie, June," my mom says, "I can only imagine what—"

"Dad always wanted to take a road trip!" Connie says.

Kevin chokes.

"He had it all planned!" says Connie. "He and Mom bought an RV. They were going to take the I-80 all the way to Teaneck, New Jersey."

"I'm sure that—" says my mom.

"They were going to see the Stonehenge built out of cars! And the future birthplace of Captain Kirk! And the original Dum-Dum lollipop factory!"

"Fun fact," whispers Agate. Kevin shushes her.

"But then Mom got sick right after he retired, and,

he—they—" She makes a kind of sea-lion barking noise. Herc perks up his ears.

"Where exactly did they find my father's body?" says Ms. Snodgrass.

I can actually hear my mom square her shoulders. "At the world's largest truck stop," says Mom. "In Walcott, Iowa."

"That was on his list!" cries Connie, and begins to howl like a beagle. Hercules tips back his head and joins in. His joyful voice bounces off the concrete walls. Kevin jumps and then—

"Oh no!" Kevin cries. "Oh no!"

Bottles of Cavity King cavity fluid, white like jugs of milk, thud down onto his knees and back, and go sliding across the smooth floor. "Help!" he squeaks.

"Kevin!" Agate exclaims, and we all start to catch the falling bottles and steady the remaining ones. Herc makes his alarm bark, and my mom (who had been saying something about "unusual circumstances" and "media interest") cuts herself off midsentence. Huddled together amid the toppled bottles of embalming fluid, we hear the footsteps on the stair. My mom appears, with our principal glaring behind Mom's shoulder and her sister peeping out from around the corner. "Simon?" Mom says.

"Ummm . . ." I lift the heavy yellow coil in my hand. "Can we borrow this extension cord?"

twenty-three

in which I get things all lined up

So that was morning and evening, the extension cord day.

Mom has some words for me about the extension cord and the basement and appropriate boundaries with my friends but her heart's not in it. Her heart—or at least the professional part of it—got hit by an eighteen-wheeler and dragged to a truck stop in Iowa. She wants to talk about her call with the state police and her fight with the insurance company and the fact that the Semples even before all this wanted to have "On the Road" on their father's gravestone. She laughs and she snaps.

Dad says that trauma is collective but we all process it differently.

Then Mom yells at him because *my* trauma is not *collective* trauma, and he apologizes to me for the metal sermon thing.

So it's a scene, and a close call, but I do not get grounded.

Good thing. It's Tuesday now. Wednesday is the day Vega is supposed to rise behind the tree house and we are not ready—there's still lots of theodoliting to do. After lunch, Kev and I cross our fingers that goat-birthing season is over and bike down to the Van der Zwaan farm.

Goat birthing season is *not over*, but we escape it and head to the tree house. We've got angles to calculate and sight lines to check and star maps to read and reread.

When I say "we," well . . . if we're the Avengers, then Agate and Kevin are Tony Stark and Bruce Banner with ten doctorates between them and I'm like . . . maybe Ant-Man. I leave the astrophysics up to them. But I *did* have the genius idea of bringing over one of my dad's metronomes, and so I get to practice opening and closing the microwave door to steady beats. It stays open one click, then shut pause one. Then open two clicks, shut pause one. Then three clicks, shut pause one. Then five clicks, pause. Then seven, pause. Eleven, pause. Repeat. Prime numbers.

The sound ticks through the tree house. The air is still. It's awfully hot. It reminds me of visiting my grandmother in her old farmhouse. I always stayed in the attic. The stairs were ladder-steep and the ceiling was all low angles and little nooks for the windows. Every corner was full of everything my grandmother never threw away: bins of quilting fabric and empty tin cans inside other empty tin cans. It was freezing at Christmas and roasting on summer break, but it was also kind of a pirate cave, a pioneer cabin, a treasure vault. In the summer, the heat pulled little beads of sap out of the bare pine planks of the ceiling, like pinpricks of amber.

In Agate's tree house I close my eyes and I can smell that. The metronome goes *click tick click tick* and I count two, pause, three, pause, five, pause, seven. I think about nothing. Or everything. I think about attics and tree houses and supply cupboards. I think about my old dead friends and my new alive friends and my dog.

Agate said there was nothing special about now, but it kind of feels like there's something special about now.

• • •

On the other hand, however long you think it's going to take three twelve-year-olds to use a surveyor's theodolite to line up a microwave between a star with a radio telescope, it takes longer than that.

Plus, it's not even a star—it's where a star is going to be *tomorrow,* which is kind of a hard thing to align with. Kevin and Agate try to work it out with their charts and pencils and angles, and I help by sorting the snacks into cupcake cups.

"Fun fact," I say. "Jelly beans are coated with shellac to make them shiny." Agate looks up from her chart. Her dimples are trembling, ready for the *and.*

"And," I say, "shellac is made from insect secretions. Jelly beans are covered with bug juice."

Agate and me both look at Kevin, who has frozen with his hand dipping into the jelly beans like one of those claw

230

games. His fingers fly open. "Gross!" He shakes his hand to get the stickier jelly beans loose. "Dude, where do you even *get* this stuff?

I just grin at Kevin. "A magician never tells."

"It's a really good one, though," says Agate.

"Freaks," mutters Kevin. He frowns down at his chart and then up at the sky. "This is hard. This has, like, got trigonometry in it."

"I know some trigonometry," says Agate. "I could get a book and learn more."

"Yeah . . ." he says. Silence stretches out. Kevin plucks up a couple of jelly beans because the bug juice has slipped his mind.

There's no way I am going to help with trigonometry, so I lie down beside Hercules on the sun-soaked planks of the tree house deck. I can see the twisting tree branches that make the railing, and the actual trees behind them, the top of Mr. Bagshott's emu barn, and the blue, blue sky.

Birds go by. Hercules sighs in his sleep. Emus honk in the distance. Agate and Kevin struggle with math. It must be intense because Agate is doing that thing where she pokes herself in the wrist with her pen.

I roll onto my side to scratch Herc's rib cage. The Big Ear is behind me, the railing is in front of me, the blue sky beyond it, and—and then, by the blessed Saint Barbara, I am struck by an actual idea. "Hey, guys?" I say, rising up onto one elbow. "What if we do this backward?"

"Huh?" says Kevin.

"What if instead of your calculations, we put the microwave up, line it up with the Big Ear, put up the telescope thing—"

"Theodolite," says Agate.

"And wait for Vega to, like, rise into the crosshairs."

"Oh!" says Agate, leaping up. "That's so smart! Simon!"

"Hey! Try to be a *little* less surprised."

"But it's *really* smart! Simon!"

"That'll *work*," says Kevin.

"The radio astronomers will be so excited!" says Agate, bouncing up and down on her toes. "Tomorrow!"

Tomorrow.

It's all perfect. We put up the microwave—I mean, we accidentally knock out a section of the railing in the process, but we put up the microwave. My triangle braces, attached to the remaining railing, are super strong, and my platform is level, and my metronome prime number game is perfect.

Kevin and me bike back to town and we're ready, we're going to make it work.

But when I get back to Slaughter, there's a news van parked in front of my house.

a note about news vans

By the time the police walked me out of Eagle Crest Elementary that day, it had already been forty-seven minutes.

I know this exact number because the *Omaha World Herald* published a big time line and I memorized it. Every bit of it, from the school secretary phoning 911 at 9:56 to when the police got the whole place swept and finished taking the kids out at 10:43.

So, when me and two of the officers scuttled out the back door with somebody's body-armor heavy and flapping around me, the media was already there.

The news vans were scattered about like someone had dumped a box of Matchbox cars onto the playground. I remember their lights and the camera people shouting. The swing of police flashers, sirens, the blart of bullhorns.

I don't like news vans.

I don't like how the news vans didn't go away. They started parking better, but they didn't go away. There were hundreds of them, from all over the country, and they stayed for weeks and weeks. They went to all the funerals. They bothered my mom at the funeral home, and they bothered her even more when they figured out that she was not just the funeral director, but also my mom, *the mom*—the one who had the kid who didn't die.

My dad, of course, who was helping to plan the funerals for my friends who were Catholic, because that was his job—he became *the dad*.

And I was *the kid*. The one in the picture.

We were the story.

There was this one reporter, Kathy Catchpole from KNUB (Nebraska's News Source!) who kept filming at the front door of the funeral home, until Mom got so angry that she put on her best Professional Face and granted Kathy an exclusive and hauled her away from her camera and into the basement to show her what *exactly* was involved in an open-casket prep following an incident with a high-powered rifle.

Kathy Catchpole from KNUB threw up a couple of times and didn't run that story.

That was two years ago. But now, Kathy Catchpole from KNUB is standing in front of my house.

twenty-four

in which I am promoted to teenager

I see her and freeze. I freeze like a rabbit. I freeze like that kid who will die if he's seen.

Then I realize, she won't know me. Eagle Crest was two years ago. I'm four inches taller and I have a much better haircut and an awesome guide dog puppy. She's not going to know me.

But I know her. She's so out of place she looks weird, like she's an animation lost in the real world. Her eyes are impossibly green-blue, her shirt is impossibly green-blue; she is lipsticked and perfect.

Hercules presses his nose against my knee and whines.

Right.

I walk right behind the news van, turn the corner from Cather to Third Street, and walk along the side garden, pretending like news vans have never shown up in my nightmares. On the other side of the wrought iron, Pretty

Stabby keeps pace with Hercules and me, high-stepping along all bad-tempered and showy, like the tuba player in a marching band. It's getting toward the end of Pretty Stabby's interested-in-girl-peacocks season, and he's desperate. When we get to the corner, he snaps his tail open.

Just as he does it, some sleazy brass music slides under the scene, and it's like the real world has developed a sound track. Specifically, someone is playing "The Stripper" on a trombone. Possibly a medieval trombone. Pretty Stabby sways and gives Herc and me the old *bump bump shaky.*

"Not if you were the last bird on earth," I tell him.

We clear the corner of our garage and there's Dad standing on top of our picnic table blowing into his sackbut. He's not exactly playing Gregorian chants.

There's nothing like a common enemy to help people bond after a fight. Kathy Catchpole from KNUB (Nebraska's News Source!) is the enemy. Dad's on my team.

I get one glimpse of him standing on the picnic table and I totally forgive him.

"Hey, Dad!" I shout at him.

"Hey, Simon," he says, sliding his sackbut closed. "How was your playdate?"

"Yeah, playdates are what six-year-olds have? And the media's here."

"I know," Dad runs through a quick—and loud—scale. "I'm pretending it's not happening."

"How's that going?'

"I'm considering going around front and pretending a

236

little louder." He slides the sackbut closed and heads for the back door. "Grilled cheese?"

I've been eating Cool Ranch Doritos and jelly beans dipped in bug juice for hours, but that's no reason to turn down Dad's grilled cheese.

We go into the kitchen. Dad bangs around in a cupboard, puts a skillet on the stove, and starts buttering the outside of the bread. Once the cheese is in, he pops the whole thing into the skillet with yet more sizzling butter and starts pushing it around. My mom can barely be bothered to toast her Pop-Tarts, but my dad is a pretty decent cook. His back is turned, which gives me the chance to lick the last of the red and green Cool Ranch Doritos flavor specks from my fingers.

A few minutes later, as Dad is putting the grilled cheese on the cutting board, the news van drives by. I guess Kathy Catchpole is done now. My dad watches me watching and shakes his head. "She'll be back. And KNUB aren't the only ones who've called." The knife crunches through the grilled cheese.

"Is Mom in trouble?"

"Unless she throws Curtis under the bus."

"How about throwing him under an eighteen-wheeler?"

Dad snorts, then sets the cutting board full of grilled cheese fingers at the table. He gets both pickles and jam out of the fridge, and sets them out with a couple of saucers. "Isobel's not going to try to lay this on Curtis—"

"Even though it's totally his fault."

"Even though it's totally his fault. You know how big your mom is on taking responsibility. Facing up to things."

"Unlike me."

"Not what I said, Sy. Be fair."

"Yeah, okay." I put some jam in my saucer and dip a grilled cheese finger into it. Then I line it up with a finger of pickle and take a bite that's got everything at once. Dad does the same. Don't knock it till you try it.

Out in the garden, the peacock bu-girks like he's out for blood. Which makes me wonder: "Where *is* Mom?"

"She's gone to meet with the Semple family. Offer to handle all the media, etc."

"And, like, avoid getting sued?"

"Oh, I doubt it," says Dad, making a cheese-jam-and-pickle finger. "They're having the meeting at an attorney's office."

"Oh."

"Don't worry. She carries insurance for exactly this— well, not *exactly* this, but for this kind of thing. We're not going to lose the business or our home—whatever your catastrophizing brain is doing, Simon, tell it to stop."

Yeah, not going to happen.

Because, yes, all of a sudden there is a catastrophe unrolling in my head. I mean, I get why Kathy Catchpole is here. I get that *Mr. Semple Goes to Iowa* is one of those Florida Man kind of stories, where someone hides their drugs in an alligator and then loses an arm. I know it's going to get picked up places and make money or ratings or views or however people like Kathy Catchpole keep score.

I told myself that Kathy Catchpole wouldn't know me, and she won't. But she will know Mom—Mom is very memorable, especially to Kathy Catchpole. If Mom has to get in front of a camera . . . even if no one else makes the connection to Eagle Crest, Kathy Catchpole will.

I stop chewing. The grilled cheese and jam and pickle get all weird and tangled and sweet-sour-mushy in my mouth.

"She'll put it together," I manage.

Dad taps his fist into the cup of his other hand. "I know, Simon," he says. "I know."

• • •

Okay, family huddle.

By which I mean, Lego build.

The first year after Eagle Crest was pretty rough, but I discovered that what I liked about Lego before, I still liked about Lego after, only more. The pieces laid out in their trays, rustling through them to find exactly what I need, the plastic *click-clack* of the pieces moving against each other, the keen edges and slick sides of the bricks under my fingers, the press and click of setting the right piece in the right place.

So we started doing Lego as a family if we needed to talk about something. It's great because you don't have to look at each other. Plus, long silences aren't as hard if you're also looking for the gray bow piece to finish the edge of a wing.

Yep: Family Lego Huddles are officially trauma specialist approved.

The last time we had one of these, I found out we were moving to Grin And Bear It. When Mom gets home and Dad calls this one, I can't help wondering if there's another earthquake like that in store.

Mom has changed out of her pantsuit and is wearing an old Nirvana T-shirt, which is like a security blanket for her. Mom's forgiven Dad—our common-enemy thing worked on her, too—but her brain is thoroughly stuck on Mr. Missing Body. "Connie and June want to go ahead with the visitation on Thursday. They've got family coming in from Colorado."

"Well," says Dad, flipping backward through the build instructions with a little line creased between his eyes. "Isn't that good?"

"That's fine—except that the locusts will be in full swarm by then."

"There are locusts now?" I mean, hey, with my luck it doesn't seem impossible.

"The media," Mom says.

Dad is looking back and forth between the Lego instructions and the actual Lego. "Something's gone wrong here somewhere, Simon."

"Understatement of the century, Dad."

I like Lego because it's hard but it's step-by-step doable. On the other hand, if you miss a step, then you hit a problem you can't solve without going backward. I'm in the middle of a giant model of the Saturn V rocket, which

Agate will be impressed with, if I can get the two sections to join together, which they won't do. There must be some mistake somewhere, something out of place, where I just can't move on.

"I don't think they'll leave until we give them some kind of statement," says Mom.

"We?" says Dad.

"Me," says Mom.

"Dare you to wear that formaldehyde shirt," I mutter.

Mom smacks the side of my hand.

"It doesn't have to be a long statement." She tucks her hair behind her ears, assuming the persona. *"Slaughter and Sons regrets this terrible incident and asks for privacy for the bereaved family."*

"That's good," says Dad.

"Except that Connie Semple has ordered a banner that reads *Gone Trucking*. She wants to hang it on the porch."

Dad's mouth drops open.

"Yes, really," says Mom.

"And Ms. Snodgrass—?" I ask.

"Is *very disappointed* that her sister would even *consider*, et cetera, et cetera. She has this *look*—I would not want to have that woman for my sister."

"Or principal," I say.

"So probably the best thing is to get the interviews done tomorrow," says Mom. "Before that circus starts."

"Will the reporters leave after that?" asks Dad.

"We can dream."

"The thing is, Mom, it's Kathy Catchpole from KNUB. When I got home she was filming in front of—"

Mom gently lifts the half-rocket from my grip, sets it down, and folds a hand around one of mine. "Simon. She already called about you."

"*What? How?* How did she put it—?"

"Breathe," Dad murmurs, taking my other hand.

"From the Semple family?" Mom answers. "From the name on the Slaughter incorporation papers? From the pamphlet she lifted from the crematorium? It wouldn't be hard. KNUB has already officially requested a family interview with us."

"Oh no," says Dad, squeezing my fingers. "Absolutely not."

Mom wraps her hand around the back of my neck and strokes it up against the roots of my hair. "Simon, please know: No matter what happens, we're not letting Kathy Catchpole from KNUB put you on TV."

"Oh, look," says Dad, standing up from the folding table and looking out the window. "Speak of the devil . . ."

"What?" I ask.

Mom and I stand up, too. We don't go to the window, because we don't want to be seen, but we can see down into the big side garden, the one with the crushed gravel path that runs past the fountain, and under the crab apple trees. Wandering up the path right now is Kathy Catchpole herself. She's scanning the house, clearly looking for the family entrance, ready to bang down our door like she did in Omaha. My family draws together—Dad in the middle, me and Mom on either side—and we watch.

Kathy Catchpole is so busy looking for the door that she is not looking at the garden. She is specifically not looking at the fountain, where Pretty Stabby is lurking picturesquely on the edge of the bowl.

"Her blouse . . ." whispers Mom.

I realize that Kathy Catchpole's blue shirt is in fact peacock blue. Pretty Stabby slowly extends his neck.

"We should warn—" begins my dad.

"Oh no." Mom slips an arm through Dad's elbow. "I think our media statements will have to wait until tomorrow. I need this time to prepare."

Kathy Catchpole is scanning for a door. The peacock is scanning her. His tail begins to rise. Kathy Catchpole starts to turn around and Pretty Stabby snaps his tail open. Kathy Catchpole freezes. Dad is humming something that it takes me a second to recognize as the fight music from *Star Wars*.

Mom leans her head on Dad's shoulder. "I love a Boss Battle," she says. "So cathartic."

On cue, Pretty Stabby bu-girks like all the bu-girking demons have risen from the pits of hell to turn the rivers to blood and eat bones of the earth. Kathy Catchpole puts her hands up, which is not going to help.

My dad stops humming—not like he can be heard anymore. He has an arm wrapped around me and after a minute I can feel him start to shake. "We're not letting anyone put you on TV," he says. "I'm sorry this is happening to you. I'm so sorry." He's *crying*.

Mom leans closer to him, speaking softly. "*Martin*. It's okay. We'll get through this. We'll keep Simon out of it. It's okay."

Dad speaks over her. "*Simon*," he says, "I'm sorry this is happening again."

"But no matter what happens," says Mom, "Kathy Catchpole is not putting you on TV."

Pretty Stabby launches himself from the rim of the fountain; Kathy Catchpole stumbles backward, out of sight.

• • •

We wake up Wednesday to news. Literally.

My dad—the one whose great tragedy is missing the *Washington Post* online—pays a fortune to get newspapers delivered to our house. We get the *New York Times*, the *Omaha World Herald*, and on Wednesdays the weekly edition of the Greater Grin And Bear It *Plain Talk*.

I'd blame this on radio telescopes, but the truth is we got newspapers in Omaha, too. My dad never met a dying industry he didn't want to support. My dad uses a fountain pen. My dad buys artisanal cheese.

Anyway. By the time I get Herc back from his morning business, our kitchen table is deep in newsprint, with the *Plain Talk* on top.

While I'm pouring breakfast for Hercules, I do what I shouldn't do and glance at the front page.

The thing you've got to understand about the *Plain Talk* is that it's about halfway between an actual newspaper and a thing to wrap around the grocery store flyers. The most-read sections are the sports write-ups—which feature every Little League home run and under-eight soccer score in the tri-county area—and the classifieds. So basically it's small-town gossip, but official. Today it features three headlines:

"Local Body Lost, Located"

"The Squirrels of St. Barbara's"

"Tragedy Dogs Local Teen." That one's about me.

"Before you say anything," says Mom, who is standing by the downstairs espresso machine, trying to brew coffee with the power of her mind, "I've already filed a complaint."

"Yeah?"

"You're not a teen yet. Makes me feel old."

"Right," I say. I unclip Herc's future-service-dog vest and hang it on the rooster hook beside the party line—which is off the hook. "Phone calls start early?"

Mom makes this sound that's all vowels. Mom is not a morning person.

"Did you want me to make you something?" Obviously I know how to work Mom's espresso machines: It's a survival skill. Besides, Mom is standing there with the plastic thing the water goes in, like she got lost on the way to the sink. She holds it out to me.

"Double espresso, please, baby boy."

I take the water thing and fill it up at the sink.

"I hope Mandy is proud," Mom mutters.

"Who's Mandy?"

"Kevin's mother."

"Mandy Matapang?" I say, marveling at how bad that sounds. "Jeez. Now we're even." I pop the water thing onto the back of the coffee machine and flip the switch to grind for a double. For a minute the kitchen is full of noise. "Should I read any of those?"

"Probably," says Mom. "There might be a test later."

I make a mom-type grunt as I use the thingy to push down the ground coffee.

"Kevin made the paper, too," says Mom.

"Really? Where?" But then I spot the little box in the bottom corner that teases a story about the kid who made the state science fair. The box tosses to an actual story buried on page three, where it will be next to the Farmers' Swap-n-Shop.

"And," says Mom, more slowly, "Mr. Semple's afterlife adventure made the front page."

"I saw—"

"Of the *World Herald*."

"Oh."

"And the *New York Times*."

"*Oh.*"

"Which way did you go with Herc this morning?"

I blink at her. Hercules looks up at his name, water dripping off the little bald patch on his little golden chin. "We went down Cather. Toward the river."

"I'd steer clear of downtown," says Mom. "There are

three news vans parked in front of the Hello Hello. This Semple thing is officially news. I expect to see it in tomorrow's *Le Monde*."

The coffee machine sighs, and I pass Mom her tiny cup of magic morning elixir.

"You are my favorite child," she says, taking it. "Anyway. I'll be delivering a statement at three. Along with June Snodgrass and Connie Semple and the lawyer for their family."

"Okay," I say warily.

"And tomorrow, we're all driving to North Platte. Your father and I will be doing a small 'Where are they now?' piece with a PBS crew out of Denver."

"On camera?" I have to stop for a second so I can keep my voice steady. "About me?"

She takes my arm. "You can stay in the hotel, okay?"

"Mom—"

"I'm sorry, Simon. I'm really sorry. But they'll just keep— I don't think this is avoidable."

"That's okay," I say. "I mean. We tried vanishing. I mean." I'm repeating myself and my voice is cracking and yet I kind of mean it. I kinda am okay. "Maybe people will want to hear that I lived. That we all lived. Maybe—you know, they'll have this other thing to talk about, too."

I know she'll just think I mean the missing body.

She does: "Mr. Semple is glad to be of service."

I should feel worse for her, but to be honest my head is full of warm air and metronome ticking.

Mom finishes her coffee and makes a face because it's gone. "You're not going to have to get on camera, Simon. Okay? Your dad and I have got this. And it's PBS. It will be so tasteful that no one will watch it."

Somewhere in here my dad has shuffled into the kitchen in his dad-est jeans and a pair of slippers. Mom pushes the papers across the table toward him.

"Look," she says. "Trifecta."

"Well, isn't that perfect," he says, scrubbing at his face. "The stars have aligned."

Speaking of.

"Hey—I wanted to tell you—Kevin and me want to go over to Agate's tonight."

"For a sleepover?" says my mom.

Yeah, that makes it sound like I'm eight, but now is not the time. "She has some astronomy thing she wants to do. She has her sister's telescope thing set up and everything." It comes out practiced and smooth. In my time in Grin And Bear It, I have become very good at telling the truth in a way that's super close to lying. I could swear I'm pulling this off. Yet my parents exchange a look.

"Simon," says Dad. "You know we think it's great you have friends here, but—"

"Come on, Dad, no 'but.'"

"But with things so stirred up around here—I'm not sure I want you out of reach overnight."

Here's the part where I lose practiced and smooth. To be real, I never thought I'd have trouble getting permission

248

for a sleepover. That doesn't happen to the Avengers. "It's not out of reach—it's two miles from here. I go there all the time."

"Simon, less than a week ago, the school called to declare you missing."

"I was missing for, like, two minutes! Plus, the only reason I went missing was because they also declared me *dead.*"

My dad starts to say something but swallows it. He pushes his lips together, his chin wobbling. "Not helping, Sy."

"Look," I say—and I finally get a trump card. "I don't want to be here if the media is here."

Mom puts her hand on Dad's arm.

"Of course, Simon," she says. "Whatever you need."

twenty-five

in which I pull the trigger

So Wednesday after supper—T minus two hours to Project Little Green Preteens—my dad drops Kevin and me and Hercules off at Agate's house to get ready for what we tell everybody is an epic campout start-of-summer slumber party in the tree house. Mom and Dad are going to pick me up at ten tomorrow so we can go to North Platte and they can be on TV.

Agate's mom takes a break from goat birthing to talk with my dad and compare parent notes, and me and Kevin and Agate and Herc trek down to the Van der Zwaan basement for camping gear. (Yep, the Van der Zwaans own camping gear. Color me surprised.) Hercules has a good time sniffing around the jars of tomato sauce and peach preserves and the tubs of extra duck feed. No one is caught in an avalanche of embalming fluid, but I do have to pull my puppy away from a partially disassembled vintage tractor.

We gather our stuff: an air mattress and some sleeping

bags, a lantern, and three of those LED lamps that you strap to your head like you're heading to the coal mines.

"I saw you in the paper," says Agate, as we drag the stuff up to the lawn. "I saved a copy. Do you want it for your scrapbook?"

"Definitely no." We've borrowed Onyx's wagon to haul stuff down to the tree house. I start trying to fold the blue air mattress so that I can fit it in the bottom. It's somehow both stiff and blubbery, and it's like it's got a mind of its own. "Hard pass. Help me with this thing?"

Kevin puts the sleeping bags over the propane tank so he can help me, and Agate frees up her hands by putting all three headlamps on. The elastic bands push segments into her cloud of curls. She looks like she's wearing a bad clown wig. "I kept the article about you, too, Kevin," says Agate as we wrestle with the mattress. "Do you want it?"

"Sure, whatever," he says. "My mom might even put it on the fridge."

"Beside your homework chart?" I say. Then backtrack. "Sorry."

"No, you're right. Except it's my report card." He shrugs. "So, I guess you're officially famous? I mean, again."

"I guess." We finally get the air mattress in.

Agate looks at her watch, and then at the sky. "Ninety minutes."

"Maybe I should put *your* article on the fridge," says Kevin, loading up the sleeping bags, releasing a cloud of musty sleeping-bag smell. "Give my mom a chance to,

251

what does Ms. Snodgrass always say? 'Think about what she's done'?"

"The Mr. Semple news is drowning it out anyway," I say. "It was in the Omaha paper—did you see? And the *New York* flipping *Times*."

"Whoa!" Kevin grins at me like the devil in one of those stories where the devil has good hair. "Let's hear it for competing headlines."

"It will be a new most disgusting thing for so many people!" says Agate. She takes the handle of the wagon and goes bouncing off across the goat meadow. Kevin and me have to scramble after her with our backpacks and bags of snacks. The sun is low, and the light is kind of stretched out and warm.

The whole time—from the basement rummage to the mattress wrestling to the newspaper news—the whole time, there's this feeling in me. Like I'm a bottle of soda and someone gave me a big shake, like I'm just going to bubble over or maybe explode.

Its uncomfortable, but it's not the same kind of uncomfortable I've been feeling since Eagle Crest. I mean: It doesn't feel like something terrible is going to happen. Just like something's going to happen. I'm jittery. When we finally get up in the tree house, I bounce on my toes like Agate does. I make fists and open them, over and over.

Agate checks her watch again. "T minus seventy minutes."

Kevin starts trying to blow up the air mattress with the

252

foot pump while Agate checks the alignment of the theo-dolite. I don't have a job. I need a job.

"Did you ever do that thing with the Diet Coke and Mentos?" I ask them.

"Oh, my dudes, that's so much fun," says Kevin.

"In my family we're not allowed anything with dyes or aspartame," says Agate. She pauses. "What thing with the Diet Coke and Mentos?"

"You are missing out!" says Kevin. "See, you drop a Mentos candy into a two-liter bottle of Diet Coke, and it makes this fountain of foam. Like, with any kind of nozzle you can clear twenty feet."

"Really?" says Agate.

"Pro tip, though—do *not* do it for the science fair. There is so much stuff you have to read and it is. All. So. Boring."

"Oh, I don't do science-fair kinds of things," says Agate, who is literally in the middle of double-checking the sights on a theodolite so we can beam prime numbers at a radio telescope.

"Yeah?" says Kevin, instead of pointing this out.

"Science fairs box natural curiosity and exploration into an artificial rubric," says Agate. "Also, they are competitive. My family does not do competitive. Jasper and Coral are barely allowed to be in 4-H."

"The emo-twins do 4-H?"

"Last year. They showed calves. Why are we talking about Diet Coke fountains?"

"I don't know," I say. "I just feel—" I find myself pushing

253

a hand against my breastbone, like I'm trying to keep the bubbles in.

"Like you're going to throw up?" Agate guesses.

I shake my head.

"Excited?" she says. *She's* excited. She's almost glowing.

"Mattress," says Kevin, dusting his hands, "inflated." He pulls the pump away and seals up the little inflation nub with its plastic thing. Then he flops onto his back in the middle of the mattress. The bounce of air sends the clamshell of jelly beans flying off the foot of the bed.

Agate rescues them and flops next to Kevin.

I look at them for a sec, then slowly lower myself to sit with my legs dangling out the gap we accidentally knocked into the railing beside the microwave.

I've got my back to them but I know they're there, my two friends. The long June evening is settling in. Even the smells seem to get thicker this time of day. I can smell goats, and something different from goats that's probably emus, and the sweet green smell from somebody nearby cutting hay.

Jelly beans rattle in their plastic case as Agate refills her cupcake cup. "You know, I'm pretty sure there's dye and fake sugar in these," Kevin says.

"If I eat them in the tree house they don't count," Agate says, solemnly. "The tree house is outside the world." I turn around. Agate's letting her head tilt backward off the edge of the mattress. "I really like it here," she upside-down says.

"Yeah." So do I.

The sun is almost down. Agate's watch beeps and lights

up, round and yellow. "T minus one hour," she says. "About. Watching Vega with the theodolite will get it to the exact right second."

We wait for a few minutes, not saying much, but all comfortable about that.

"Can I do it?" I ask. "Push the button? On the microwave."

But I almost don't say "push the button." I almost say "pull the trigger."

• • •

For the first part of the last hour, not much happens.

Agate and Kevin agree that I can be the one on microwave duty. It starts to get dark, and then darker—that kind of blue dark, where you can still see everything, but the green of the trees and the red of Mr. Bagshott's emu barn both look black. At T minus thirty minutes it's time to plug ourselves in.

Microwave plugging is the most dangerous part of our plan. Or not dangerous, really, because even if he catches us, Mr. Bagshott's not exactly going to throw us to the emus. But it's definitely the sneakiest, heistiest part of our plan, which is why we waited for it to be almost dark.

It turns out to be so easy it's almost disappointing. We plug our fire-hazard chain of extension cords into the outdoor plug on the side of the barn, thread it through the tall grass and short scrubs under the trees, and haul the other end up into the tree house. It's even long enough.

We get back up the ladder with seven minutes to spare. We wait. We're so antsy that even Hercules gets antsy, pacing back and forth on the tree house balcony, his toenails clicking. He tries to gnaw his harness, which he hardly ever does anymore. I stop him.

Agate looks at her watch and then leans on the rail. There are fireflies blinking on and off in the long grass by the fence. One blinks and then one blinks back, like they're looking for each other. She looks at her watch again, and then up at the sky, toward where Vega is starting to clear the trees.

Three days ago, I couldn't have picked Vega out of a lineup. Now I know all about it. A blue star, a bright star—the brightest in the northeastern sky—and one point of the Summer Triangle.

I love the Summer Triangle, and I have two friends.

"They'll be so excited," Agate whispers.

"Who?" I whisper back. I don't know why we're whispering.

"The scientists." She beams at me and takes a breath so big she shudders, and bends to fiddle with the theodolite.

I go to stand beside the microwave—off to one side, so I can reach the button but won't get cooked like a Hot Pocket, which Kevin says wouldn't happen, but still.

Kevin looks at his watch. (Before I moved to Grin And Bear It, I never saw kids wearing watches.) Agate peers into the theodolite. She shakes her head. Waits a minute. Looks again. Waits a minute. Looks again.

256

I think I'm going to burst.

Agate looks up, wide-eyed. "Start the metronome," she whispers.

Kevin and I stare at each other, panicked, because we forgot this part, and I'm already in position, and Kevin whirls around and goes scrambling through the sleeping bags and backpacks and snacks until he emerges with the dark pyramid shape that's my dad's second-best metronome. The rhythm we picked is already set. He winds it and fumbles with it until he can get the arm released. The tempo is all over the place until he gets it set down, but then it starts tick-tick-ticking just like we practiced.

It's working.

Everything is working.

Agate is kneeling with her eye pressed to the theodolite, tapping her hand against her leg with hummingbird speed. "Almost," she says. "Almost." Kevin has his fingers folded tight together, his thumbs pressing into his nose. He looks like he wants to whoop aloud.

"Start it up," says Agate, and I put five minutes on the microwave and press start. A light comes on inside it, and it whirs to life.

"Allllmost—" says Agate. And then: "Now!"

I close my eyes, and I pull the trigger.

Concentrate. *Tick*, close. *Tick*, open. *Tick tick*, close. *Tick*, open. *Tick tick tick*, close. *Tick*, open.

My heart is throbbing in my ears so loud it's hard to concentrate, but I practiced this. I practiced this so long, and I've got it. I beam the primes. Five. Pause. Seven. Pause. Eleven. Pause. Repeat.

We send it three times.

"Stop!" shouts Agate, even though there's nothing to stop. Door shut now, the microwave continues to whir, glass plate spinning inside it. Agate clamps a hand over her mouth. Kevin squeals, flops back onto the mattress, and begins to roll around like an otter. "We did it!" he whisper-shouts. "We're aliens!"

Hercules whuffles in joy and dives in to be an otter with Kevin.

"The tree house," I say, "is officially not part of this world!"

Something big. Something big has happened. It's happened inside me, like . . . like something getting born, stretching out, like I just hatched and have wings. I feel light and heavy and super weird and like I could be a tornado and like I could run across America forever.

The microwave beeps three times and clicks off.

I very on purpose do not start crying.

This time it was me. This time I pushed the button.

For a long long long long minute, we don't say anything.

"Next time we should put a cup of water in the microwave," Kevin says finally. "So it doesn't cook itself to death."

"Important safety tip." My voice is all weird and gulpy. "Thank you, Kevin."

"Dude," says Kevin, getting up from the air mattress. "Look." He gets up and comes over to the railing.

258

We see what he's looking at.

We come and stand next to him.

Across the goat meadow, beyond the barn, in the shadow of the radio telescope is the trailer park of science—all the little rinky-dink buildings where the radio astronomers do their radio astronomer thing. And lights are coming on over there. One by one by one.

There's not a lot to see, but we watch it like fireworks— really slow fireworks. We watch the lights coming on. Distant figures dashing. After a while cars start pulling up—their headlights bumping down the dirt road to the telescope, their engines just barely audible over the night boom of emus and the crickets.

"Oh," says Agate. She reaches out and grabs my hand. "We did it."

We did it.

We really did it.

And no one is going to care about Eagle Crest, or orange ribbons—no one is going to care about the Jesus Squirrel or Mr. Missing Body—not anymore.

Not when there are aliens.

Agate's hand is warm in mine. Kev slings an arm around both of us, then leans in and bangs his head against my shoulder. "Hey, guys," he whispers, like he's got a secret. "Guess what?"

"What?" I whisper.

"I brought microwave popcorn."

twenty-six

in which I google alpacas

The radio astronomers are still scurrying when we finally fall asleep, sometime in the middle of the night. I have this long adventure dream about secret agents and chase scenes and aliens—and I wake to someone whispering "Kids?"

I sit up, making the air mattress wobble and sending Kevin rolling off the other side. He props himself up onto his elbows, blinking. The whisperer is Pearl Van der Zwaan. She's standing a few rungs down on the ladder, eye-level with us, even though we're lying down. For a second I can't figure this out, why her face is rising out of the floor, her red hair like the sun.

"Sorry, Simon," she says. "Sorry, boys."

It's dawn. There's dew on the floorboards of the tree house. The birds are making a radio-astronomer-like ruckus.

"Up you get, Agate," says Pearl. "It's we-live-on-a-farm o'clock."

I would have expected Agate to be one of those people who just switches on in the morning, but she rolls over and says all in one breathy mumble, "Sorry, Mom, I am getting the eggs right now." Then she makes a tiny half-snore.

"Sorry to wake you, boys," Pearl Van der Zwaan says. "It really is morning for us. Simon, your parents will be along in a couple hours. And, Kevin, your mom called. She was hoping you'd be okay spending the day with us. Apparently something came up at work."

Kevin's eyes widen as he tries not to grin from ear to ear. "Sure," he says. "That's fine."

"Oh, good," says Pearl. "We could really use an extra hand with the goats today."

Kevin's not-grinning face cracks a little. "What . . . ?"

"Birthing season's peaking!" Agate's mom says, like she's telling us the bouncy castle's ready. She vanishes down the ladder.

Kevin's face changes: He looks like he stayed up all night watching zombie movies. Agate laughs her way all-the-way awake.

A couple hours later, all the eggs are gathered and washed, the ducks are fed, the bedding for the pregnant goats (who are in the barn, collectively moaning) is all changed, and I am beginning to hate farming. But not as much as Kevin, who has been given an oversize emo-twins T-shirt to wear, featuring a scuba diver playing a tuba. It hangs off his scarecrow body, flapping around his elbows and knees. I'm actually relieved when my parents pull up.

261

It's time for our television adventure.

Agate sees the car pull through the gate, shouts "Oh!" and goes running into the house. When she comes back she's got a package: something about the size of a folded pillowcase, wrapped in brown grocery-bag paper. "For you," she says, thrusting it into my hands. "Because of how we fought but aren't fighting anymore."

"Should I . . . ?"

"Open it!"

I do. It's a homemade shirt, black with white and orange letters. They say: *I survived the Eagle Crest school shooting and all I got was this lousy T-shirt.*

Me and Agate and Kevin stand there looking at the T-shirt. Kevin's jaw drops. Agate beams. My mom pauses from her parent chat with Mrs. VZ and looks over at the shirt in my hands as though it's Miss Semple's *Gone Trucking* sign. Her mouth makes a perfect O.

And me? The thing that was bubbling in me starts to bubble out. I don't even know what it's going to be, but it turns out to be laughter. I giggle like a preschooler, and I throw my arms around Agate. She's shorter than me so I end up with a nose full of frizz. "Thank you, Agate," I tell the hair. "It's perfect and I am never, ever going to wear it."

"Simon?" says my mom. I look up and she's smiling, too. "We've got to head out, kiddo."

Kevin slings an arm around me, last minute, and leans in to whisper: "I will give you my Latham Commemorative Cornhusker jersey if you take me with you."

"To the Best Western Hotel in North Platte?"

"To *anywhere but here*," he hisses. "For the love of God, Simon. They want me to help the goats have babies."

"Now we'll both have a trauma," I tell him. "Get them to make you a shirt!"

"Dude," he says softly. "Good luck."

• • •

For the trip to North Platte, Mom has rented a Honda Civic—the most normal car ever to normal. There are no suspicious smells. No tiny peacock feathers still hiding in the folds of the upholstery. No doors sized for dead people.

It feels so weird to be this normal. We drive the normal car. We check into the normal hotel room in the normal way. There's a desk clerk and a couple of people in the lobby—checking out or risking the hotel coffee. Herc gets a glance or two, but no one asks for his service-dog papers, and no one looks twice at us humans, not even when Mom gives the clerk our name.

We go to the room. The carpet is gray and cream; the walls are cream and gray. The beds are white. The TV is black. The room is like a box of average, and it's like it could average us out until we vanish.

I mean. My mom is in trouble for losing a body. My dad is in trouble for starting a death-metal squirrel cult. Last night me and two friends impersonated an alien civilization using a microwave, a metronome, and an air mattress. Plus, in two hours, my parents have to drive across town and sit

263

down in a TV studio for a tasteful but heartfelt interview about how the famous family of Eagle Crest survivors is getting on, two years later.

But in the hotel, we're average.

I take Herc out of his vest and he goes zooming around the room, mapping with his nose. Dad heaves our suitcase onto one of the beds, unzips it, and flips it open. "I packed our bathing suits," he says.

"There's a pool?" Mom is setting up her laptop at the room's one desk. "Oh, internet, I missed you."

"What do you think, Simon?" says Dad. "A swim when we get back?" He has hung up their interview clothes and is unfolding the ironing board. It makes a rusty screech.

"Ummm . . ." I say. When I was little, hotel pools were the best part of going places. But thinking about swimming today feels just completely nonsensical, like an invitation to hang upside down from the flagpole. Not bad, just . . . "Ummm . . ." I say again. I can't get an actual thought together.

Mom has logged into the hotel Wi-Fi and is googling "espresso near me." She pauses and looks up at me. "You okay, kiddo?"

My head shakes no, but what I say is: "Just tired." Faking an alien message takes a lot out of you.

"This will all be over in a couple of hours," says Mom. "Will you be okay here?"

"Are you kidding? There's internet! And TV."

"Simon—" says Dad.

264

"Plus, Mom clearly loves coffee more than me." Mom already has directions to the TV studio plotted, complete with an espresso café en route.

"Absolutely true," she says. "I would sell you to the fairies for magic coffee beans."

Then Mom hugs me like an eagle, and Dad hugs me like a bear. I think I'm going to be okay.

• • •

My parents—ironed and starched, with a level of makeup that my mom usually reserves for corpses—leave in a bustle.

I turn on the TV. It takes me a minute to remember how to use the remote, how to call up the menu of what's on where. The best thing I find is *Mythbusters*. It's one I've seen before, so I settle onto the bed and kind of let it be background noise, the way I haven't done since January. It's a weird feeling, having TV again. It's like eating from a bottomless bag of potato chips or something—it's great in theory but actually it makes me feel a little sick.

I don't want to be on TV, not even on PBS. They'll probably use the picture from fifth grade—not the body-cam one that the internet likes, but the school picture-day picture that they ran everywhere like I was a kid on a milk carton. I don't like that picture either, not anymore. Maybe my parents will give them a new picture. Some family shot of me rolling around with my puppy, or fighting off a peacock with a broken umbrella.

That would be better.

265

Mythbusters ends, and my level of interest goes down from 25 percent to, like, 10.

Mom has left her laptop.

I grab it and set up a bed nest: all the pillows, the remote, Doritos, and Wi-Fi. I spread out a towel so we don't get busted and pat the bed until Hercules scrambles up beside me. He looks around the room from this new angle, his back stiff and his eyes big. At home he's not allowed on the beds, and since he's a guide-dog-in-training, we've been super consistent about the rules. He's not so sure about the change.

"I feel you, boy," I say. Herc looks at me. Then he sighs and drops down onto his belly—still not relaxing exactly. He's sitting like the Sphinx with his paws stretched out and his head held high. I roll my head off the pillows so that it rests by his paws. His puppy beans smell exactly like Frito chips. He lowers his head and rests his chin on my ear.

We stay there for, like, five minutes, and then I sit up. I let Herc drape his chin on one of my knees, balance the laptop on the other, and log in.

I look up Mr. Semple first. It takes me a little to remember my Google-fu and how to just get results from the last day or so, but when I do, I find him everywhere: For an ex-human, he attracts a lot of human-interest kinds of stories. Finally I find clips from the news conference. Miss Semple looks like she's been crying. Ms. Snodgrass looks like she's just eaten Mr. Tuna. I skip forward and unpause just in time to see Ms. Snodgrass going full principal. "When he was my student, Curtis Grubsic once showed up for a marching band performance so impaired that he somehow made his trombone explode. I cannot say I am much surprised."

Whoa. Mom might not have been willing to throw Curtis under the bus, but Ms. Snodgrass is. She's willing to find the bus, send it into reverse, and back it up a few times.

Small towns. In small towns, the permanent record principals are always threatening you with is a real thing.

Behind Ms. Snodgrass a banner flaps. It does indeed say *Gone Trucking.*

I scruffle Herc's ears.

I want to google myself.

I don't.

I google Dad instead.

I get a few hits off medieval-music blogs, some things from the Grin And Bear It *Plain Talk,* and finally the article from the *National Catholic Reporter*—the big deal newspaper he was talking to after the Full Metal Church Disaster.

The article is called "Pastoring Without Platitudes." It starts with the Jesus Squirrel, absolves Dad of starting a squirrel cult, drives by "the role of deacons in the rural church," and then—it's basically my dad's view about the downsides of things like miracles and providence. He comes down hard against them, and he sounds like a world-leading theologian when he does it. The article kind of paints him as a holy-chaos hero.

"*You dog!*" I say out loud with a smile, making Herc

look up, convinced he's in trouble. "Not you, boy. It's okay." I drop a hand onto his back.

I thought Dad was getting busted when I heard he was on the phone with the *National Catholic Reporter*. But now I wonder if he called them, and not the other way around. I wonder if I'm not the only one who wants to be known for something other than Eagle Crest. I wonder if I'm not the only one who's going to get his wish.

I grin for a while.

Finally, I take a deep breath. I open a new search box. I type in "Very Large Radio Telescope" and "Aliens."

Google explodes.

There aren't any newspaper articles or videos from the news, but there are blog posts and tweets and a thread on the r/SETI subreddit with so many upvotes that it could run for president.

The subject line of the top post reads "Is this it?" It describes a microwave frequency series of simple primes coming from Vega. It must be from a scientist: It's all skeptical and technical and this and that, but the replies under it are endless and ALL CAPS and are getting added by the second.

It's exactly what we hoped was going to happen.

It's way more than I was ready for.

My breath comes faster and faster and faster as I scan them until finally I slam the laptop closed.

"Holy cow, Herc," I whisper. "I think we're going to space jail."

268

He barks once and starts licking my hand.

I glance at the clock. My parents should be back pretty soon. I start closing tabs, still breathing hard. I put a hand on Herc's back and do square breathing for a little bit. TV is just launching into something called *Mummies Unwrapped* and is promising to tell me all about bog burials. I could channel-surf, just to calm myself down more, but I start watching instead. I mean: What are the odds that I won't come out of *Mummies Unwrapped* with a new disgusting thing?

I catch myself thinking that, and I realize I can't wait to get home.

Back to Kevin, and Agate—who will be in the tree house again tonight, covered in goat gunk and pranking a radio telescope without me.

Back to Grin And Bear It, Nebraska. Somehow, somewhere along the way, it got to be home.

Before I close the laptop, I fire up YouTube and find the remix of the Alpaca Incident where it looks like the alpacas are dropping a trap single.

Kevin was right. It kind of slaps.

twenty-seven

release the emus!

The first thing I notice when I get back to Agate's is the news vans.

They are parked on the side of the road where the tourists pull off to take pictures of the Big Ear. Mom said there were three downtown the other day, but now there are five vans, including one out of Omaha and one out of Denver. By GNB standards it's practically international news.

I'm going to take a wild guess and say they aren't covering the goat birthing season.

One of the camera people is set up to film and is being chewed out by none other than Dr. Mandy Matapang.

All the news vans have torn up the road something awful: It's so full of ruts and things it looks like someone blasted it. The local farmers are going to be so cheesed. I have to get off my bike and push it, which is how I make eavesdropping look natural.

"Absolutely cannot broadcast from here," Kevin's mom is saying. "There are bylaws, to protect the—"

"Ma'am, I understand that." It's a scruffy-looking guy in a vest with a lot of pockets. "We're writing it all to tape—"

"Writing all what to tape?" Dr. Matapang's exasperation overflows for a second, but then she starts mopping it up. "*If* we have a finding, we will confirm it with teams at other telescopes; we will go through peer review—"

"Ma'am—"

"This is not how science works!" she snaps.

But it is how Grin And Bear It works, Kevin's mom. *So there.*

I push my bike through the Van der Zwaan gate, lean it out of sight behind the big barn, get Herc out of the trailer, and walk down toward the tree house. It feels like I've been gone a million years, not one day. In the meadow, several dozen teeny baby goats are pronking around, and they look like members of a different species, like the Van der Zwaans have moved out and some different farmers with different animals have moved in.

But when I put my foot on the bottom of the ladder, two familiar faces appear above me, Kevin and Agate, both shouting: "Simon!"

"Help me boost Hercules?" I ask. Kevin springs up, and we get Herc hauled back up into the Team Little Green Preteens clubhouse.

"Dude," Kevin says, when I make it up. "I am so glad

you're back." He leans close. "I've seen things, Simon," he whispers. "Things no human eye should see."

"Goat things," Agate chimes in. She is wearing a purple tank top on which an otter is doing dumbbell curls. It proclaims her to be seeking an *Otter Body Experience.*

"I live here now," says Kev, collapsing dramatically onto the sleeping bag. The air mattress, I notice, is completely de-aired. "I cannot go back to the world of men."

"Simon," says Agate. "Was the television thing okay?"

Kevin sits up. "Oh, yeah, Sy—sorry—was the television thing okay?"

"It was fine," I say. "I mean. I stayed in a hotel. They had internet. We ordered Chinese."

"Did you watch your parents' interview?" asks Agate.

"I couldn't. I mean, actually couldn't—it hasn't been on yet. They taped it for later."

"Do you want to watch it?"

"Nah, it's all right. I've heard my parents tell that story before."

"Oh," she says. Then: "Simon, I'm not sure the radio astronomers are happy."

Kevin makes a goat-birthing noise.

"They were happy yesterday," says Agate, sounding heartbroken herself. She slaps her hands into her legs. "But today they're not as happy. Look!"

She points over the railing, in the direction of Vega. For a second I look up, expecting to see something in the sky, but then I spot them. Beyond the trees, the sloping meadow of

Mr. Bagshott's emu farm is swarming with junior scientists. They have some kind of detectors; they are taking some kind of readings. Mr. Bagshott is running from one scientist to another, waving his arms around, almost as upset as the day the emus broke loose.

Actually it's kind of the same scene—all he needs is the hat. He's too far away to hear but every once in a while a couple of syllables will carry. He sounds like a barking seal.

"What are they doing?" I ask.

"Looking for this thing." Kevin waves to where the microwave is covered with one of the sleeping bags. "Or anything else that might be messing with their signals."

"Mr. Bagshott is upset," says Agate. "He's very worried about electromagnetic sources."

"But why are they looking here? Did you do the thing where you moved the signal four minutes so they think it's coming from the stars?"

"Yes!" says Agate. "Four minutes less four seconds! Exactly! With the theodolite and my watch! The radio astronomers were very excited at first. We went into town yesterday and there were many rumors. But now Kevin's mom seems very testy."

"Yeah," says Kevin. "But it's not like *that* means anything."

Agate pauses to watch the men and women in their jeans and T-shirts and flux capacitors mapping an emu meadow.

"I don't know how we're going to plug it in today," says Agate. "There are so many people! Do you think they'll go away before Vega rises?"

273

When we unplugged the microwave from Mr. Bagshott's emu barn, we coiled up the part that crossed the open space between the barn and the little woods where the tree house is. The rest of the cord is still stretched out, but in the tall grass and scrubby little bushes, we decided it was pretty unspottable.

Of course, we weren't counting on a search party.

"Look, Agate," says Kevin, "Maybe we *shouldn't* plug it in again?"

"But we have to!" says Agate. "Three times is the charm."

"Science doesn't work like that," says Kevin, sounding for a second just like his mom.

"Yes, it does," says Agate. "Two times is a coincidence but three times is a pattern. It's called *data*."

"It's called *getting busted*, Agate!"

"Data is a plural word in Latin, Kevin!"

I think about the messages unscrolling on the laptop screen. I think about how that felt, how I told Herc we were going to space jail.

"Look, Agate," I start.

All of a sudden her face folds and her chin dimples wobble like she's going to cry. "I just wanted to give them hope. SETI is all about optimism! And seeking connection! And meeting other people like you and not being alone!"

"Hey!" I wrap my hand around her wrist. "I know, Agate, I know. Breathe, okay?"

274

Agate tucks her chin. "I'm not having a panic attack," she says. "I'm differently upset."

"Breathe, though." I sit and—since I'm still holding her wrist—she sits, too. "Herc, come," I command. Hercules comes over, tucks his head down, and leans the top of his skull hard into Agate's knee. "Good boy," I whisper.

"I'm sorry," says Agate.

"Why?" says Kevin. He's bent double, leaning his hands on his knees.

She sniffs in hard. "I just didn't want the scientists to be alone."

"They're not," he says. "They're all together, over there by the emus."

Just then we hear the barking seal voice that is Mr. Bagshott. He must be closer now—like near the barn?— because we can make out words. The words are: "That's it! I warned you!"

There's a grinding noise of something big moving.

Kevin turns. He stares. He puts one fist to his mouth.

"What?" From the floor, I can't see.

Kevin looks back at us, wide-eyed. "Mr. Bagshott has released the emus."

Agate and me jump to our feet.

The emus are coming out of the barn pretty calmly, just high-stepping along, but even so some of the astronomers are already backing away. Then, like someone flipped a switch and dubbed in some do-wonky chase music, the emus go collectively nuts. They rear back their emu heads, which wobble on their emu necks. They skitter and hop on their long dino legs. They jump up and do weird kicks. They do all this at speeds approaching the speeds of racehorses.

The radio astronomers drop their things and scatter.

This only makes the emus try weirder. They boom like engines turning over. One leaps so far into the air that it face-plants into grass.

"Wow," says Kevin. "They're like giant demented attack chickens."

They kind of are, if chickens were corpse black and six feet tall, with brains made of chihuahuas and bones made of springs.

"They're not attacking," says Agate. "That's their happy dance." She pauses. "Should I shout that to the astronomers?"

The astronomers are in fact running down the hill toward us. Some of the emus have taken off after them, and are running in loops around them, like they think the astronomers might throw them sticks. There are a handful of screams.

Kevin abruptly falls to the floor, yanking on our hands. We sit beside him. "What?" says Agate.

"They're coming this way," he says, huddling now and whispering. He's right. The scientists are stampeding for the gate between the emu farm and the Van der Zwaan meadow, which is only twenty feet away. "They'll spot us."

"Umm," says Agate. "The railing you're hiding behind has many spaces in it, though?"

Kevin pales, and then very carefully lifts a corner of the unzipped sleeping bag that's draped over the microwave. He hooks the drawstring onto one of the broken-off bits where the railing got knocked out. Now we have a bit of drooping, musty gray fabric to hide behind. We push close together.

Hercules wanders over and sniffs at the zipper. Kevin reaches out and reels him back in by his harness.

"Hey," I object.

"Dude, if Mom busts me doing this, I'll be grounded until *graduate school*."

"That does not sound likely," says Agate. She's whispering because Kevin is whispering, but her way of whispering feels like it's going to carry all the way across the field. "I hope they don't leave the gate open. The emus will escape, and they are very difficult to recapture."

We listen. It's a total zombie movie sound: rushing feet, people panting and shouting, the snap of stepped-on branches.

Kevin presses his shoulder against mine. We're huddled. We're hiding. And people are running.

It's. I try to breathe out. It's a little—

Hercules puts a paw on my leg—and then wiggles into my lap.

Right. It's fine. I'm fine. I wrap my arms around my dog. "They're going past," I say. "I don't think—"

"What's that?" Kevin hisses.

There's another sound now. It's slower. And stranger.

And closer. A heavy rustling. A snap. It sounds big—like a bear creeping up on us. A stick cracks right under us, like a gunshot. Agate grabs my wrist. We fold close together. Our breath almost stops.

Then, right above our heads, the microwave moves. Kevin yips in fear, the microwave slides on the plywood, catches, bumps, hisses as it moves—and suddenly falls. The sleeping bag goes down, too—a rush of movement and air and we're exposed and screaming, hearing the huge crash, throwing ourselves onto the floor in a heap.

Hercules goes squirting out.

We're in a heap.

I'm on the bottom.

There's angry shouting. Words are in it, but my brain isn't doing words.

The whole tree house shakes. I can feel someone coming up the stairs—I mean, the ladder. Hercules steps in front of us and barks, sharp and loud, and—

No.

I'm pushing away from the floor, getting to my feet, my friends falling off my back. I'm not going to be on the bottom of the pile. I'm going to be standing. I'm going to be screaming. I'm going to be—

A face comes into view at the top of the ladder. Then shoulders. A hand with something in it. A man.

I shout at the top of my lungs, spin to the gap in the railing, and throw myself into the sky.

a note about falling

They say that when you're falling, you're weightless.

They say that when you're falling, time slows down.

They say that when you're falling, your life flashes in front of your eyes.

Only the first two things are true.

Falling from a tree house doesn't actually take very long. Kevin works out the numbers later, because of course he does. Later he will tell me that the man was Mr. Bagshott, with an extension cord in his hand. Later he will tell me our fall took less than a second.

But if it is just one second, it's a second that stretches out shiny like a penny left on a railroad track. There's an endless moment where I don't need to breathe, and I don't need to catch myself, and I can't even feel the weight of my own bones. It's like I'm made of air, and I don't have any memories. I'm not afraid.

And I'm not alone. Agate is there. She's with me, and we're both floating. I see everything: the green of the trees going slowly by, the perfect blue of the sky, the way the hem of Agate's purple otter shirt lifts away from her tummy.

But nothing flashes, or flashes back.

Both twisting in the air, we catch each other like skydivers, wrist to wrist, hand in hand.

Then we hit the ground.

twenty-eight

in which we are driven out of Grin And Bear It

I hit the ground feetfirst and for a second I just keep going, my whole body buckling up like a Slinky. My ankles flare and my knees fold and one of them bangs into my nose and Agate crashes down beside me. She's on her back.

I look at her and there's blood.

"Agate!" I roll toward her. My ankles and my nose are doing that stubbed-toe thing where first there is impact, and then the pain starts ramping up like it's on a separate dial. But still I scramble to my knees. "Agate!"

She turns her head and blinks at me. The blood is coming from her—there's a cut that goes from her eyebrow, past her ear, into her hair, and it's bleeding a lot. A lot, a lot. There's a broken branch under her. I think that cut her. It's not even a cut, it's like a tear, like she's torn open.

"Hi, Simon," she says.

"Oh my God!" Kevin shouts, leaning over the rail. I

look up and Hercules barks and leaps down toward me.

I shout "No!" but Herc is already falling. It doesn't take him nearly as long to fall as it took us. I am still reaching out to catch him when he slams into my chest. The puppy knocks me flat and for a second I can't breathe, I can't see— red pulses fill up my eyes and I think I might throw up. There is shouting everywhere and feet running toward me. Kevin is there, and Mr. Bagshott's old sneakers. Mr. Bagshott is saying, "I didn't— I didn't mean—" The emu-fleeing scientists are there, like ten of them, a crowd. "Agate," I say, and try to find her. Hercules scrambles off me and starts whining and head-butting my hands and licking me.

Suddenly Pearl Van der Zwaan is looming over us. There's one instant where she's blocking the sun and even though her face is in shadow I see her go white. Then, like a switch has flipped, she's totally in charge. "Everybody back up!" she shouts, and it's like she's blown a magic whistle: Everybody does. She goes to her knees beside Agate and me. "You fell?"

"We jumped," says Agate. "Mr. Bagshott came up the ladder all angry and he triggered Simon's trauma but Simon decided not to shelter in place this time, so he jumped. He's my best friend."

"Okay," says Pearl. "How did you land? Simon?"

I can't remember—it's not important. I'm sitting up and Agate is lying flat and she's bleeding. I can see it running, pooling in the seashell places of her ear.

"Simon!" snaps Pearl. "How did you land?"

"Feet—" I say. "Feetfirst."

She nods and I understand from her face that she's going to get to that in a second.

"I hit my head," says Agate cheerfully. "But you should know that head wounds bleed a lot and that doesn't have to mean that they are serious."

"Where did you hit it? What did you hit it on? Which part did you hit?"

A cloud passes over Agate's smile. "I don't remember. . . ." She squints her eyes. "It hurts in the back."

Pearl smiles gently and slips a hand under Agate's head. "You've got quite a goose egg starting back here, middle miss," she says.

"Oh, but I promised I'd get all the eggs." Agate frowns. "I thought I got all the eggs."

It takes me a minute to realize she's not joking.

Pearl straightens up. "Right. We're going to the hospital." She stands up and starts pointing. "You, and you, carry my daughter. Simon, did you break anything? Can you walk?"

A scientist I didn't even notice looks up from taking off my shoes. "His ankles are really swelling."

"You, and you, carry my daughter's best friend."

She selects another scientist. "You, go to the barn, get a feed trough."

"A what?" says the pointed-to scientist.

"Metal thing, round," Pearl Van der Zwaan mimes a

283

laundry-bin-size with her arms. "Size of a beer cooler." She picks a sixth bystander. "You, go into the house and get some ice."

"The beer is in the fridge," says Agate. "But it belongs to our dog, Todd."

"Actually," says Pearl. "Get all the frozen corn kernels and all the peas out of the chest freezer in the mudroom. And some towels. They're wherever you think towels are. Agate's other friend, go find my purse—it's in the house somewhere. Get the twins to help. Call Simon's parents. Tell them to meet us at the hospital in North Platte. Got it?"

"Got it!" says Kevin, and runs.

Before I know it, I'm being carried up the field by radio astronomers. They walk sideways, making a bucket chair out of their arms. Hercules helps by circling us and darting underfoot to lick their hands. The whole thing is awkward, but we make decent time.

Still, it probably takes ten minutes to get up to the farmyard, and by that time, there's a crowd. The emu-charting scientists are all there, and some of the other scientists, and Mr. Bagshott, and Coral, and Jasper, who is holding a baby on each hip, and a couple of people from the media, and three stray emus hanging on the edge of the group like playground monitors.

Kevin is there—and Kevin's mom, too. Even through the crosstalk of the scientists trying to decide if they should put Agate and me down until someone can get a car, I can hear her lecturing Kevin: "—hard enough to get people to take SETI seriously without—"

I try to spot Agate, but I can mostly just see the T-shirts of the people holding me.

"Some children with a microwave—" Dr. Matapang's voice is rising.

Kevin is holding the purse that Pearl Van der Zwaan asked him to get. Like my eyes have focus knobs I zoom in on his fingers knotting around the handle—think about the way his fingers knotted and snaked when we were throwing rocks, when he said he couldn't stop his mom from telling everyone about me.

Yeah, I might be in shock.

"Honestly, Kevin, I thought you were more responsible than this. What were you thinking?"

"What was I thinking?" Kevin's voice is kind of flat and stiff, like he's rehearsing his science fair presentation. "Okay, what was I thinking? At the start I was thinking about Simon. Did you?"

"What?" she says.

The junior scientists holding me shift awkwardly. One of the media people has started to lift a microphone. One of the emus makes a weird honking noise.

"Did you think about Simon when you told everyone about what happened to him?"

"I—" she stutters. "I just wanted to be sure he had all the support—"

Kevin interrupts, talking faster. "Are you thinking about him now? Because he's hurt, Mom, Simon and Agate got hurt, and you're still talking about science." He's almost shouting.

"I just can't believe you'd choose—"

And Kevin bellows: "If you want me to have choices, sometimes you're not going to like them!"

There's a sudden, ringing silence.

An emu honks.

Before anything else can happen an old blue station wagon comes shooting around the house and arcs to a stop in front of us in a spray of dust. Agate's mom sticks her head out of the driver's window. "Put Agate in the front—" she calls, and as the scientists carrying her shift I can finally see her, my best friend: She's leaning back into their arms dreamily like she's stargazing.

My stomach goes *urk*.

Everyone starts moving.

The draftee scientists slide me into the backseat and stick my feet into a feed trough full of frozen vegetables. They put Agate in the front seat. Her sister Coral lifts her head and slides towels under it to hold it steady. "Be okay, you idiot," Coral murmurs, fumbling for a lever. The seat reclines. Agate's head drops nearly into my lap. The other half of the backseat is piled with car seats and board books and rain boots and ziplock bags full of Cheerios, all hastily shoved aside.

Kevin is there, with his mom right behind him, her eyes wide and wet now. Kev boosts Herc onto my lap. I grab his hand for just a second, because I'm scared, because we

286

got hurt, because I like his choices. Herc scrambles across me and tries to wedge himself between me and the pile of stuff.

Kevin's mom pulls him back gently by the shoulders and turns him around. He looks stiff for a second, and then he throws himself at her. Herc is still wiggling when the doors click closed.

Pearl Van der Zwaan guns the engine, then calls out the window again. "Jasper, you're in charge of the little ones. Coral, you're in charge of the goat births."

"Wait!" says Kevin, reaching after us. "Where are you—are they okay?"

"They're going to be fine," she says. She twists around and offers me an Agate-bright grin that looks a little stiff around the edges. "Okay, Simon? It's just a precaution."

It doesn't feel like a precaution.

It feels like a catastrophe.

• • •

We drive fast. The trees make the light flash. Gravel pings against the bottom of the car.

Agate tips her head back to peer at me—upside down, like off the edge of the air mattress, when she said the tree house wasn't a part of the world. "Did you get hurt?" she asks.

"Ummm." I look down. My feet are wrapped in towels and buried in frozen vegetables, along with some straw and goat feed and farm things I am choosing not to think about.

My nose hurts but not very much. "No. I just—I think maybe I jammed my ankles?"

"I did that once," says Agate. "Jumping out of the crab apple. I had them both x-rayed and the doctor said I had perfect arches. I'm in a textbook!"

The torn part that runs from her temple back into the hair above her ear is still bleeding, but only a little, like it's tired. "I'm really sorry, Agate. I just freaked out."

"Oh no," she says. "I'm glad we jumped. I'm just sorry about gravity."

"I've told you before, Agate Grace," says Pearl Van der Zwaan. "Gravity is a cruel mistress."

Agate sighs and closes her eyes.

"Don't go to sleep, okay?" I poke her in the middle of the forehead.

"That's mostly a myth," she says.

"Humor your friend," says her mom. "Don't go to sleep."

Agate's eyes are still closed. I lift a corner of the towel cradle and push a bit of towel against her cut. Her face squinches into dimples and her eyes open.

"I'm glad we did all of it," says Agate. Something happens to her dimples and they turn into the shining ones. "I'm really glad."

"Me too," I say. "I'm glad, Agate." Something cracks, as I realize I mean it—I mean every word of it.

Something cracks and I start to cry.

a note about saints

One of the best and hardest things about being Catholic is saints. We really believe in saints. We believe that Saint Barbara can wield lightning and Saint Anthony can find things and Saint Joseph can sell houses. For us, that stuff is real.

I know that sounds good. Maybe a little weird, but good, right? That there are holy people in the world and some of them get magic post-death powers?

Except, when you think about it, it's a little messed up that we make saints of girls who didn't want to get married and got killed, and boys who didn't want to make public sacrifices and got killed, and— Well, there are a lot of different saints, and they didn't all die in awful ways but a lot of them did.

It's like, somehow, they're holy because awful stuff happened to them.

And that's the only part we know about them. Maybe one of them was super good at soccer, or really liked stargazing, but we don't know. We only know the one part of their life, and it's the most awful part.

After Eagle Crest, a few people asked what saint I called

on. The idea was maybe my miraculous survival could be used as one of the two required miracles for someone new to join the saint club. But I didn't think of any saints. I didn't even pray.

So why would I get a miracle?

There were seventeen other kids in Mrs. Donaldson's fifth-grade class. There had to be somebody praying. Why didn't they get saved, instead of me?

I wonder: Is there a patron saint of radio telescopes?

Is there a patron saint of falling?

Is there a patron saint of best friends?

I suddenly want to know.

twenty-nine

the special now

I'm all cried out by the time we screech up to the doors of the emergency room. People in blue uniforms unload Agate and whisk her away. Her mom goes with her and the blue uniforms help me into a wheelchair and wheel me in. Then all of a sudden I'm alone in a hospital.

It's not a huge hospital, and it's not super busy, but it's got that hospital fug-green color and that hospital smell that's sharp and sour and makes you feel sick. I take a big, slow breath in and wait for the flashbacks.

They don't come. It's almost weird.

The blue uniform guy wheels me up to the triage nurse, a woman with lavender scrubs and things hanging on cords around her neck: her hospital badges, her glasses, a little rubber dachshund wedged between halves of a rubber hot-dog bun. "Are you alone, sweetheart?" the hot-dog nurse asks.

I look around but Pearl Van der Zwaan is nowhere

in sight. "I guess," I say. "But my parents will come. So I'm okay."

The surprising thing is, it's kind of true. If Agate is okay—*if*. If she is, then I am, too. Even though I'm in a hospital.

The nurse looks down at Hercules. "I'm afraid we don't allow—"

"He's a service-dog-in-training," I say.

Hot dog nurse lights up. "Oh, good. I love dogs." Based on her reactions here, I am going to say I'm not dying. I'm not even frightened. I feel a little drifty.

"Look," she says, lifting the dachshund-in-a-bun. She squeezes it and clear gel comes out its butt. "Hand sanitizer," she explains, rubbing it between her palms. "Want some?"

This lady is not helping with the drifty feeling.

"It combines three of my favorite things," she says, squirting cold dog-butt gel onto my hands. "Weiner dogs, hot dogs, and hand sanitizer." She puts on her glasses and clacks through a few screens on her keyboard. "So," she says. "Name?"

"Simon O'Keeffe," I tell her.

"O apostrophe K—"

"E, e, f, f, e." She doesn't know who I am.

"And what happened to you, Simon?"

"Um," I say. "It's kind of a long story."

• • •

292

Time is weird in hospitals: It gets all sticky and hard to see through.

I get triaged and checked in. I sit for some sticky, foggy time in the waiting room. Then they move me to one of those cubicles with curtains instead of walls. A nurse brings cold packs for my feet. I'm worried about Agate, and I'm even worried about Kevin. He didn't get hurt, but he did get left alone to explain about the stolen microwave and the prime numbers and how Agate didn't want to be lonely and I didn't want to be hidden anymore.

I wait some more. The curtains have a pattern of blobs and lines in sea green and goldenrod and lavender. Medical people come and go. They take my temperature for I have no idea what reason, and then wheel me off for X-rays.

Then more sitting. It's all taking forever.

After about two thousand years my parents show up. Okay, it's only actually been an hour and fifteen minutes. Whatever—it's plenty of time for them to work themselves into a panic.

When my family fights about who the traumatized one is, I always say it's me, and Mom's on my side, but Dad always says yes it is me, but also it is all of us. When I hear my parents' shoes come through the sliding door into treatment, I know it's them. I know it even before I hear Dad's voice asking, "Which way which way." I hear him, and know he's kind of right. It is all of us.

My parents are always going to remember the day the police called them. They're always going to remember the hour they spent with the other parents at the fire station, where they were promised news, and news didn't come, and didn't come, and then did come. They'll always remember hearing it was my school, and my class. But not me. They are always going to remember running into a hospital to find me alone in a cubicle, just like this one, just like now.

And me . . . I'm always going to be the kid in the cubicle. The kid in the pile. The kid in the picture with my hands over my head.

But also, I'm always going to be the kid in the red hoodie in the background of that one church-alpaca video, the kid who brings the puppy to school, the kid with the bodies in the basement and the Lego in the turret. The kid with the two weird friends who stole a microwave and subtracted four minutes from the universe.

I'm Simon from Now, but it's like Agate said: Now doesn't mean what you think it means.

Agate.

• • •

When my parents burst through the curtain, their faces are gray like wet newspaper. They look like they are about to come apart. There is grabbing and patting and questions.

What happened to you?

Agate and me fell out of her tree house.

How?

Actually I kind of jumped.

Why?

Because Mr. Bagshott was coming up the ladder and we were hiding and he was angry and I kind of freaked out.

Why was he there?

Because he found our microwave.

Why did we have a microwave?

Yeah, um, so . . .

My mom, who knows more about anatomy than the average person, listens to my stumbling story while pressing her fingers here and there on my feet and ankles.

My dad just stares at me like I'm very puzzling sheet music. "You and Agate and Kevin," he says slowly, "faked a message from outer space."

"Yeah."

"*Why?*"

"Agate told me once there didn't have to be a reason."

"In cases like this, Simon," says my mom, looking up from my ankles to flash Dad a "don't-start-with-your-theology-Martin" look, "there *absolutely* has to be a reason."

I become silent like silence is something that falls on me. I get silent the way you get wet in the rain.

My mom tucks the cold packs back around my ankles and taps me on the knee instead. "Baby boy, I am prepared to ground you until you graduate from high school, but I'd like to give you a chance here. *What were you thinking?*"

But the wordlessness has just soaked into me. It's my dad who finally asks: "Simon: Is Agate okay?"

"She fell—she jumped with me." I swallow. "She hit her head."

295

My mom goes pale. "Oh, honey," she says. "Oh, Simon. I'm sure—" But she's a funeral director. She doesn't lie to people. And she's not sure. She can't be sure.

Dad is a pastor, and he doesn't lie to people either. He scoops Hercules off the floor and tucks him into the gurney beside me. Herc goes straight into comfort mode, burrowing into my armpit. I wrap my elbow around him and pull him close. He starts licking my neck with his slippery tongue.

Just then, the curtain parts and a doctor comes in. He's young and tidy, like he's playing a doctor on TV. He's got the doctor white coat on, and he's carrying a chart.

He looks at my dog.

"He's a registered service dog," says Mom, who might not lie but can definitely tilt the truth. "My son has PTSD."

"Well," says the doctor, "then you'll be pleased to hear he also has perfect arches."

Just like Agate, I think, while the doctor shows my parents an X-ray, and how the bottom of my foot is as round as the top of a tennis ball. I don't tune in again until he pats my dog-free arm, saying something.

"Um? What?"

"I said, the good news is you didn't break anything. I want you to keep ice on it—twenty minutes on, twenty minutes off—for the rest of the day, or whenever it hurts. Keep your feet elevated, and lay off the basketball or however you did this."

"He jumped out of a tree house after pranking a radio telescope," says my mom.

296

"So don't do that again," says the doctor. "Have a quiet couple of weeks. You should heal up fine."

"What about Agate?" my dad asks.

"Who?" says the doctor.

It seems incredible to me that anyone doesn't know Agate.

"Agate Van der Zwaan," says my mom. "The other child in the accident. They were brought in together."

"Oh, I'm afraid patient privacy—"

"I've got a concussion!" It's Agate's voice, coming from behind the curtain. My mom turns, the curtain is whipped aside, and there's Agate, sitting in a wheelchair and wearing giant sunglasses. "Also three stitches. I am more seriously injured than you but I was triaged much faster." There's a Viking-looking guy pushing her wheelchair: this seriously huge dude with little braids in his strawberry blond beard.

"She's fine," says the doctor. "Concussion protocols, right, Dad?"

The Viking raises a red folder with a sticker of a brain on the front of it. "Got them right here. Though keeping this one down and quiet for a week is gonna be—"

"No screen time, no reading," says the doctor. "No sports."

"No problem," says the Viking. "We don't believe in competition."

"We can do Lego together," I say. "Lego would be okay, right?"

"Sure," says the doctor. "We'll start your discharge papers, young man, and you'll be on your way."

• • •

The Viking with the braided beard turns out to be Agate's dad, of course. "Stan Van der Zwaan," he says, offering his huge hand to my parents.

"Isobel O'Keeffe." Mom goes in for the handshake. "Simon's mom. And his dad, Martin. Is Agate all right?"

"Right like a rainbow," says Stan Van der Zwaan. "That's my girl."

My parents glance at each other like they don't know how to bring up prime numbers or radio telescopes or school shootings or any of the other things that need to come next in this conversation.

Stan Van der Zwaan rescues them. "Agate told me she had a new friend," he says. And to my parents: "I'm a long-haul trucker, but I call home every night to talk to the brood. Agate's been all about Simon for months."

"Simon likes Agate, too," says my dad, though fortunately not in a kissing-book way.

Stan Van der Zwaan grins. "I also heard about their little project. I've just been on the horn with the sheriff's office: turns out that you can get a ticket for pointing a microwave at a radio telescope—Agate's going to have her egg money docked until doomsday. But, it's not a crime."

Mom's looking up at him, and I can see her professional mask melt off and her face warm up like she's falling in love. I get it. Agate did that to me, the very first time we met. Mom grins. "They might add a law to the books, after this."

"Well," says Stan Van der Zwaan. "My Agate, you know—she was always going to make history."

Very softly, Dad says: "Our Simon already did."

"I heard." Stan Van der Zwaan looks at me. He is jolly as Santa Claus, but his eyes are very smart. It's a weird combo, but neither thing looks fake. "Hope that's okay?"

"It's fine," I say. And it is. It really is.

"I feel like you're going to want to know . . ." Agate's dad tugs at the braids in his beard, and bounces on his toes—just like Agate does, but also like the Norse god of earthquakes. "There's a couple of camera crews camped out by the front doors."

"Oh—" says my mom, looking at me, her funeral director face coming back.

"So if you want," says Stan, "I can scout a back way out of here. I mean, I've got an eighteen-wheeler across the street—worse comes to worst, I can bust us out a loading dock."

"I can top that: I've got a van and access to the morgue."

"Wait," I say. "Just—"

Everybody turns to look at me.

"Wait." I wrap my arm tight around Hercules, who wiggles his way around so that he's facing everyone, his puppy face loose and happy with his tongue hanging out.

I don't feel happy, exactly. But I do feel . . . looser.

Lighter. Like I did when I was falling. I didn't shelter in place this time. I saved myself. I was an idiot, but I saved myself. I hear myself saying, "I want to talk to them. I mean. I want to go out the real doors."

"Simon!" Agate has the same tone of happy wonder she had when I showed up with a microwave.

"Honey." Mom perches on the edge of the bed beside me. "Are you sure? It won't just be about the radio telescope. They'll ask—"

"Everything," says my dad. He sits on the other side of the gurney. They look at me, then at each other, and join hands across my body. There's a big, long pause. Light-years long. And then all at once the signal arrives.

"How about I go wrangle them," says Mom. "So they don't rush you once you're out the doors. Get them to set up someplace with a little dignity."

Dignity is one of her professional words, but maybe that's what I need. A dose of soft, sad, firm, stand-over-here.

"There's a little walking garden, across from the main doors," says Dad.

"Does it have a peacock?" I ask.

"Not yet, but we're going to donate one."

"Perfect," I say.

"Dad," says Agate. He looks down at her; she looks up at him; they communicate telepathically.

"I'll be your muscle, Isobel, if that's all right. In case any of them prove stubborn."

Just then the hospital people show up again. They've brought paperwork and a second wheelchair. Hospitals have this thing where they wheelchair you out to the curb, whether you need it or not, and then take the wheelchair back, whether you need it or not. It's like: You're not hurting yourself in here where you could still sue us, but get six inches past the giant revolving doors and you're on your own.

Anyway, I find out when I get down from the gurney and into the wheelchair, my ankles really do hurt. Mom manages to make the volunteer wheelchair pushers go away. The volunteers are already giving me soft, tearful looks. They know who I am. Dad lifts Hercules down from the gurney, and my puppy comes and stands by one wheel like he's been doing it all his life.

Stan Van der Zwaan crouches down. "One of Todd's?"

Agate beams. "His name is Hercules."

"Todd makes beautiful puppies," rumbles the Viking. "But we might have to stop breeding from such a strong-willed sire."

"Herc's perfect," I say, indignant for my pup.

"But Agate says he jumped out of the tree house after you?"

"So did she!" I object.

"And she would also make a terrible guide dog," says Stan, rumbling like a giant Viking oracle. "This one—you'll probably have to keep him."

I think about how Herc came under the bed with me

301

back on 5/15—how he came up on the pew with me during the death metal sermon, all the times he did the things I needed that he wasn't supposed to do. Keep him? I think I was always going to.

Stan Van der Zwaan ruffles my hair—is it a universal dad instinct or something?—and bounces back up to his toes. "Director O'Keeffe, shall we?"

"You sure, Sy?" says Dad. "Your mother is perfectly willing to smuggle you out under a sheet, you know."

"Yeah, I know. I'm sure."

Mom loops a hand through Agate's dad's elbow. Mom's tall, but he absolutely towers. He's the perfect muscle. "Oh, hey," I say. "Can you get rid of Kathy Catchpole?"

Agate's dad, who can't possibly know who Kathy Catchpole is or what I want done with her, smiles unnervingly and says, "Sure."

"Why, Stan," Mom says, "I think this is the beginning of a beautiful friendship." She reaches out and squeezes my knee one last time. Then she's gone.

Dad looks at me and Agate, sitting next to each other in our wheelchairs. "I'll go . . . let you kids talk?"

"Yeah," I say. "Just for a minute, okay? Until they're ready?"

He starts to pull the curtain closed around us and I call: "Dad, wait! Is there a patron saint of falling?"

"I don't know. Probably." He tilts his head and glances at Agate. "There's one called Christina the Astonishing. She could fly."

I laugh. I don't know why. "Okay," I manage. "Okay."

"We'll be right there, Simon," he says. "We'll be right behind you. No matter what happens."

"I know."

"And then you're grounded for six weeks."

"I know."

Then he's gone.

"Are you really okay?" I ask Agate.

"I barfed four times," she says. "Now I have to sit quietly in the dark for a week, which is going to be very boring."

"You can sit with me."

"And do Lego."

"I'm building a Saturn V rocket," I say.

"I love Saturn V rockets!"

Yeah, called it.

"I accidentally built a mistake into it. We'll have to backtrack a ways."

"That's okay."

She reaches out and grabs my wrist. We're quiet for a minute.

I mean. The little cubicle isn't quiet: There are beeps and blips coming from all around, voices, the lights buzzing. But we're quiet.

"Can I show you something?" Agate asks.

"Sure."

She reaches into her fanny pack—because of course she's still wearing her fanny pack—and pulls out a pen. It's a rollerball, the kind where you can see the ink through a little window in the side. Agate uncaps it and touches the tip, delicately, to the back of her hand. She holds it there a second. "Look," she says.

I bend over to look at her hand, resting on the crackled black plastic of the wheelchair arm. The ink isn't a dot—it's a tiny, tiny starburst. She has pressed the tip into one of the pinprick spots where fine hair would grow if we had hair on our hands. Instead of just spreading out, the ink is creeping into the tiny wrinkles that connect one dimple to the next.

The cubicle curtains stir a little, like seaweed under water.

"Can I?" She holds up the pen.

"Yeah." I put my hand on the arm of her wheelchair. Agate's pen just barely touches me and the ink—which is purple—spreads out across my skin.

"They look like lace agate," says Agate. "That's why I like them."

"I think they look like stars."

"Simon! You know that stars are spherical."

I remember telling her that I wanted to be Simon from Now—meaning not Simon Says Simon, the kid on Google, the frozen kid in the photo. We'd been talking about the message from space. Later, way later, after I yelled at her, the day we brought the microwave . . .

"What was that thing you said, about there not being anything special about now?"

"Oh, that. That's not me, it's Einstein."

304

"Nah. It was mostly you." Our hands are next to each other, so I bump her thumb with my thumb. "Tell me again?"

"Okay." I can tell she's smiling even though she has her head tucked down. It makes the back of her neck turn pink. "The 'special now' is the idea that the past is super different from the future, and we can't touch either of them from here," she says. "But it's not true. The past still exists, and the future already exists. They're just here, all around us, all the time."

I still don't get it, really. I mean, it's Einstein—what are the odds I'm going to get it? But I can feel it. It feels like falling: weightless, timeless, and free. If I were a saint, I'd be patron of both school shootings and radio telescopes. I'd be Simon the Astonishing, who could fly. Simon from Now, with a whole past, and a whole future.

"So, there is no special now," says Agate. She puts the pen tip in another one of my dimples. "There's only now." She moves the pen. "And now." She moves the pen. "And now. And now. And now."

Slowly, slowly, Agate Van der Zwaan covers me in stars.

acknowledgments

in which the author avoids the question "where do you get your ideas?"

When my older kid, Wayfinder, was in grade school, they came home one day and perched themselves on the edge of my cozy writing chair. We were in the garden shed, where I work on my books. Way was quiet and kind of glowing, with their eyes on the floor and the most secretive look on their face.

After an hour or so, Way told me that they had just spent four hours hiding in a supply closet. They wanted to ask where, in my tiny shed, I could possibly hide from the gunman who had apparently been loose in our neighborhood. Where I would hide next time. They took it for granted that there would be a next time.

And there was. Way was on a field trip, and when the bus returned, it was to find the school in lockdown. The school trip chaperones improvised a strategy: They would send the kids running out one by one from the bus door to the school door, ducking and weaving as they went.

"Like skeet shooting," Way proclaimed—they'd gotten a little older and a little sharper, or maybe they were just less scared. They mimed target practice. "Pull!"

I burst into laughter instead of bursting into tears. I mean, what can you do? Well. I can write.

in which the author says thank you

Writing this book took me years, because it always does. Along the way, so many people helped me, and this note is my chance to thank them.

From the dedication on down, I am grateful to the survivors of school shootings who have shared their stories. I have read so many of your essays and poems, watched your videos, and followed your activism. Thank you for raising your voices.

From the first spark of the story on down, I am grateful to my own kids, who have read sentences and scenes and several complete manuscripts. They've stood in for my readers and helped with my characters. My younger kiddo, who is the same age as Simon and Kevin and Agate (and who didn't want her name listed here), let me pick her brain about all kinds of things, particularly her own experience with autism. You kids lift me. I promise we'll do the dragons next.

My husband, James, read along, too, and so did my mom. My dad read a late draft. There's nothing better for one's craft than marrying another novelist, except maybe being raised by the kind of people who think Evelyn Waugh's *The Loved One* is a good present for a thirteen-year-old bookworm. You shape me.

My other early readers include my beloved in-person writing group, who have been with me for six novels now: Susan Fish, Pamela Mulloy, Kristen Mathies, and Nan Forler for tea and sympathy. R. J. Anderson, Ishta Mercutio, and E. K. Johnston are my local kidlit friends whom I call when the going gets tough. Seánan Forbes is always the first person I want to see my words. You, my fellow writers, keep me from going down like that horse in *The NeverEnding Story* when the word marshes grow muddy.

I had both a Canada Council for the Arts grant and an Ontario Arts Council grant during the years when this book was in draft—thank you to both agencies, for this and for everything. Thank you to my employer, the Perimeter Institute for Theoretical Physics, for being flexible about my weird word passions and for giving me the chance to meet Jocelyn Bell Burnell. You guys feed me.

Finally and foremost: Jane Putch, my agent, and Rachel Stark, my editor. Thank you for taking a chance on my most unlikely book—my "you're-writing-a-comedy-about-*what*?" book—and then making it better. So much better. It wouldn't be half the book it is without you.

a note about what's real

Because I collect stories the way crows collect tinfoil, some of the shiniest things in this book are real. Some of the realest are fake, though, so here's what's what.

There is a real National Radio Quiet Zone, protecting real radio telescopes, but it's in West Virginia, and it doesn't work like the one here. For instance, they do have internet—just not Wi-Fi. Grin And Bear It, Nebraska, is fictional. The Dismal River, though, is totally real. I've canoed on it. It's dismal canoeing.

Eagle Crest, the Omaha suburb where Simon is from, is fictional. It bears some superficial resemblance to Elk Horn, Nebraska, and to Millard, Nebraska, which is where I moved to when I was Simon's age. The school shooting is also fictional, but not fictional enough.

Box breathing, counted breathing, and the "five things you can see" techniques that Simon uses to cope with his PTSD are real, and useful whether you have PTSD or just have to attend junior high.

Jocelyn Bell Burnell, discoverer of pulsars, is real. The Little Green Men #1 signal is real. *Contact,* by Carl Sagan, is a real book, and a real movie. The story of the defective microwave that flummoxed radio astronomers is real. Most of the other SETI facts are fudged, though.

The alpacas are real. This story was told to me by Seánan Forbes, who is a docent at St. John the Divine in New York City. As far as I know, no one got fired.

Pretty Stabby is real—he lived in the garden outside the apartment I rented in Meyrin, Switzerland, and he was *awful*. A different peacock once fell in love with my daughter, who was wearing a green shirt.

The washed-out guide dog that doesn't want to please you and the squirrel (or sometimes another critter) that eats the communion Host may be urban legends, but both have made the rounds on Tumblr.

"Mom, someone's dead!" is a small-town-funeral-home story told to me by E. K. Johnston. The story about family discount cremations was told to me by a teacher somewhere near Moose Jaw, Saskatchewan. I can't find her name now.

The "corpses fart" fact and the "duct tape" fact are both from anonymous essays published in the collection *Mortuary Confidential*.

It's officially a bad idea to jam your microwave open while it runs, kids, and it probably won't work as shown here—there's an extra safety system inside microwaves that I didn't tell you about. But mapping the standing waves inside a microwave with damp cash-register paper should work and would make a good science fair project. Have at it. Go, Team Science.

in which the author's publisher is covered in stars

Before I sold my first novel, I had no idea how many people it takes to get a book in the hands of a reader. There are people who work on my books whom I have never met, a fact that always shakes me and makes me tear up with gratitude.

The publisher and the editorial director of Disney Hyperion, Tonya Agurto and Kieran Viola, have been cheerleaders for *Simon* from acquisitions on. Associate publisher Carol Roeder and executive editor Jocelyn Davies were early fans too, and helped see *Simon* through contracts. Dina Sherman of the school and library team read an early draft and had great feedback.

Authenticity readers did the vital work of helping me get things real and right without sliding into harmful stereotypes. Lyn Miller-Lachmann kept an eye out for Agate and autism representation. BT Friedenberg kept an eye out for the Matapangs and mixed-race Filipinx/white identity. Sue Knowles, an expert in supporting kids with trauma and anxiety, kept an eye out for us all.

If you're in love with books as physical objects—and who isn't—these are your people. The jacket illustrator is Celia Krampen. The designer is Phil Buchanan, and the design department coordinator is Andie Olivares. The creative director is Joann Hill.

These are some of the people who have worked hard to get this book into your hands. In marketing: Matt Schweitzer, Holly Nagel, Danielle DiMartino, Andrew Sansone, Maureen Graham, Kelly Clair, and Ian Byrne. The school and library team: Dina Sherman, Bekka Mills, and Maddie Hughes. In publicity: Crystal McCoy, Ann Day, Allison Citino, and Christine Saunders. The content packaging team, aka the people who think this would make a good movie: Augusta Harris and Lauren Burniac. In subrights, helping Simon and his family travel all over the world: Linda Kaplan, Christina Faubert, Sara Boncha, Lia Murphy, and Mili Nguyen. The mighty Disney sales team: Nicole Elmes, Monique Diman, Jess Brigman, Kim Knueppel, Michael Freeman, Loren Godfrey, Vicki Korlishin, Meredith Lisbin, Amanda Marie Schlesier, Vanessa Vazquez, Samantha Voorhees, and Erica Magrin.

These are the folks who keep the ship on the rails, and also point out that ships don't run on rails. The managing editor, Sara Liebling. The copy chief, Guy Cunningham. The copy editor, Sharon Krinsky, slayer of stray Canadianisms. The proofreader, Mark Long. The production director, Marybeth Tregarthen.

And the person who might actually run Disney Hyperion as far as I can tell? My editor's assistant, Elanna Heda.

The author lives and writes on unceded lands that are the traditional home of the Anishinaabe, Haudenosaunee, and Neutral peoples.

trauma is common. help is available.

The term isn't used in this book, but Simon has Post-Traumatic Stress Disorder, or PTSD.

PTSD is common in kids: the National Center for PTSD in the United States estimates that about one in twenty children and teens will develop PTSD. Like Simon, some people develop PTSD after witnessing or experiencing violence, but PTSD can follow illness, injury, abuse, neglect, loss—any kind of trauma.

If you have or think you might have PTSD, here are some places to learn more and get help:

National Child Traumatic Stress Network
www.NCTSN.org
Resources for parents and kids dealing with trauma

KidsHealth: Post-Traumatic Stress Disorder (PTSD)
KidsHealth.org/en/parents/ptsd.html
Resources for understanding and dealing with PTSD

Kids Help Phone (Canada)
KidsHelpPhone.ca
24/7 hotline kids can call, text, or chat
to get support for any mental health issue

Teen Line (US)
www.TeenLine.org/youth
Volunteer-run hotline kids can anonymously call
or chat for support on a variety of topics

Reaching out is an enormous step, especially if you're grappling with shame or secrets. It might take a lot of courage. I salute your courage.

Finally, if you have been through trauma and you have PTSD, please know that it's only a part of who you are. What you've survived might have shaped you, but it doesn't define you. You are a whole human being, and you are valuable. You are covered in stars.